The Money That Never Was

THE MONEY THAT NEVER WAS

BY

DAVID LUDDINGTON

Belvedere Publishing
www.belvederepublishing.com

First Published in Great Britain 2011
by Belvedere Publishing

Copyright © 2011 by David Luddington

All rights reserved. No part of this publication may be reproduced or transmitted, in any form or by any means, without permission of the publishers or author. Excepting brief quotes used in reviews.

First edition: 2011

Any reference to real names and places are purely fictional and are constructs of the author. Any offence the references produce is unintentional and in no way reflects the reality of any locations or people involved.

A copy of this work is available through the British Library.

ISBN : 978-1-908200-44-0

Belvedere Publishing
Mirador
Wearne Lane
Langport
Somerset
TA10 9HB

To Sarah, my wife and guide to all that's really important in this funny old world.

Chapter 1

The robbery should have gone like clockwork. The planning was meticulous, and each participant had rehearsed his part a dozen times. In fact, it would have gone like clockwork, had it not been for Tommy Penwrith's new bicycle.

Tommy was particularly proud of his bicycle. It had been his birthday present of the day before. He was especially pleased with the loud horn his grandfather had attached to the handlebars. A series of different buttons gave a variety of sounds. His favourite was the one that sounded like a police car. Tommy's grandfather was a tinkerer, or at least, that's what Gran always called him. In true form, he'd tinkered with Tommy's horn before attaching it to the bike. The volume level had now been increased tenfold making it sound like a whole squad of police cars.

***

Mr Green of course, knew nothing of Tommy's new bicycle or its enhanced warning system. So when he heard the approaching sirens he and his colleagues decided to abandon their project of relieving 'Shifter's Road Transport' of the contents of one of their vans. Had he known the true nature of the crates, he might have been a little more determined in his endeavours. But as his employer had not seen fit to enlighten him, Mr Green was not inclined to hang around.

***

When Tommy Penwrith cycled around the corner of the narrow Cornish country lane, the first thing he saw was Old Mr Trevellick's tractor. It was parked across the lane, completely blocking it. He pushed his bicycle onto the grass verge and squeezed his way past, expecting to see Old Mr Trevellick digging ditches or something on the other side.

But no, Old Mr Trevellick was not there. But there was a big van. It had 'Shifter's Road Transport Services' painted along the side. The cab doors were open, but there was nobody around. Tommy made his way round to the back of the van. The rear doors were also open. One of them was hanging from its hinges. He peeped inside. Piles of wooden crates filled the interior. They had the words 'Books for Pulping' printed on each one. This was all very strange, thought Tommy. He decided to go home and tell Dad. Dad knew about books. He had lots of books hidden in his shed.

***

Charles Tremayne stood on the touchline of the muddy rugby pitch. He watched as a dark haired lad pulled himself free of the scrum and headed for the goal mouth. The boy clutched the ball tightly to his chest and ran furiously for a few seconds before he was viciously pulled to the ground by three opposing team members. A loud thud seemed to reverberate through the ground as they landed in a heap.

"A thug's game played by gentlemen, yes?" A tall man in a dark immaculately tailored Italian suit moved alongside Tremayne. "Is that not how it is you English say?"

"Hello, Victor," Tremayne said, not taking his eyes from the boys on the field. "I thought you weren't due back until tomorrow?"

"Business is good. We reach conclusion quickly." Victor Tereshchenko smiled and clapped his hands as his son noticed him and came running to the touch line. "Alex! You play well today I think."

"Are you home now, father?" the boy asked.

"Yes, my son. Now go finish your game. We talk later."

The boy ran back onto the pitch.

"He's a good lad, Victor," Tremayne said. "I'm not sure how you managed that."

"It is not I, my friend. It is his mother. She is princess, far too good for me."

Tremayne turned to Tereshchenko. "Am I finished here now?"

"You have done well, Charles. You are the only one I

would trust to watch my son you know. We have understanding, you and I."

Tremayne surveyed the man in front of him. Victor Tereshchenko, former high ranking KGB officer and now probably high ranking Russian Mafia. Although nobody would dare investigate too hard. He had far too much money invested in British institutions to risk disturbing him. Tremayne had tangled with him on many occasions over the years but now he was acting as bodyguard to his son. The world has gone mad.

"We're both part of a world gone by, Victor. So I guess that makes us the same in some ways."

"But you still have your world, my friend. Your MI6 office and your secretaries and your cars. My world changed the day they took the wall down. I had to find new ways. I had to start with only these hands again." He held his hands up for emphasis.

Tremayne had a grudging respect for Tereshchenko. He'd managed to escape just before the Kremlin erupted into chaos and somehow emerged a few years later as highly respected figure in the business world.

"It's certainly a funny world, Victor. By all that's right you should be banged up somewhere and I should be living the high life."

"You come work for me, Charles. I look after you." Tereshchenko smiled and patted Tremayne on the shoulder. "Have good position, lots of secretaries!"

"Tempting, Victor. Very tempting. I might just call you on that one day."

***

Tremayne hailed a taxi and slid into the comfortable seat in the back.

"Where to, Guv?" the driver asked.

"Hyde Park." He felt like a stroll before returning to his flat for supper.

He pulled out his phone and keyed in the speed dial for the office. It was answered at the first ring.

"Hello, Charles. Problem?" Elaine asked.

"No, Tereshchenko came back early so the job's finished."

"That's good. Gemini wants you in here straight away then."

"What's that about?"

"He won't tell me. Just asked me to get you back here soon as."

"Okay, I'll be there in about twenty minutes. He disconnected the call and tapped on the driver's window in front. "Change of plan."

***

Charles Tremayne gazed out the office window and across the Thames. He'd seen way too much of this view lately. Although he liked London as a place to which to come home, he preferred to be on the move. But the end of the cold war and a series of budget cuts had meant that most of his work was now carried out closer to home.

The intercom on Elaine's desk buzzed, and Gemini's familiar voice said, "Send him in."

What appeared to be a conventional oak panelled door hissed as it slid to one side. It always reminded Charles of one of those doors in Star Trek. The familiar smell of old leather and cigar smoke drifted out as the door opened. Gemini reasoned that as this office didn't officially exist it therefore did not constitute a 'Place of Work' within the meaning of the smoking ban legislation.

Charles took his last breath of fresh air for a while and stepped inside the office. The pile of the carpet was so deep it seemed to lap around his ankles as he walked across it to the leather sofa. The leather squeaked when he sat down.

"So," he said. "You have something new for me?"

"Ah, indeed, something quite interesting," Gemini said. He pushed a pink folder across the over-polished mahogany desk.

"You said that about the Chinese diplomat's wife I was sent to guard."

"Yes, sorry about that one, Charles. But how was I to know she was a kleptomaniac?" "Well, you might have spotted something was wrong when she stole your ash tray. Have the police let her go yet?"

"Yes, the manager of the sex shop is still trying to press charges, but diplomatic immunity prevails. Whisky?" Gemini poured two glasses without waiting for a response from Tremayne.

"So, what's this then?" Charles picked up the file. "Some Arab diplomat looking to us to bail him out again after a night of debauchery?"

"No, this is altogether more interesting. It seems that the Foreign Office has lost some money."

"I would have thought that was a job for the Foreign Office themselves, or the police. Not MI6."

"Ordinarily, yes, that would be the case." Gemini poured the tiniest drop of water into his Scotch. The ice cubes clinked inside the glass as he swirled the mixture. "But there's something rather special about this money. It's not supposed to actually exist."

"Go on." Charles opened the file and leafed through the papers.

Gemini leaned back in his leather swivel chair and tucked his podgy thumbs into the pockets of his waistcoat, a sure sign of a lengthy explanation about to follow.

"For some time now, Her Majesty's Government have been supporting the government of... erm... well let's just say some small African nation."

"You mean we've been propping up another sorry little dictator?"

"I'm not quite sure that's how the Foreign Office would put it. Anyway, it seems that the president of this... erm... nation invited bids from various interested countries for permission to build... let's say various engineering works. Call them hydroelectric dams, power stations and so on. Our bid was successful. Partly due, I might add, in no small way to the sterling work carried out by this very department."

"So," Charles sat forward. "I assume the usual buttons were pressed on some Swiss banker's desk and the money whisked through the internet to land in this guy's bank. Where's the problem?"

"Ah, not quite. You see, this transaction was...how shall we say… somewhat unusual in its execution."

"You mean this grubby little dictator wanted the folding stuff? Cold, hard currency."

"Yes, anyway, we arranged to meet his plane and let him fly the money out from a small airfield near a place called St. Norwent Major in Cornwall."

"Why there?"

"Discreet, Charles. Very discreet. We can't very well let him jet out £250 million in a suitcase from Heathrow now can we? Bound to cause some consternation."

"£250 million?"

"Not an unusually large amount, as these things go."

"No? So what form did this £250 million take." Tremayne was slightly more interested. Of course, while not approaching the glamour of a mission to lift somebody out of the Kremlin and whisk them across the Berlin wall, this was still somewhat more interesting than baby-sitting sexually deviant politicians. Which is what he'd been doing most of for the last ten years.

Gemini continued, "Now, this is where things start to get tricky. You see President... um... the president of this... nation wanted the money in small denomination English currency."

"And nobody heard warning bells at this point?"

Gemini pulled a small silver gun from his pocket, pointed it at Charles, and pulled the trigger. A flame flickered into life from the end of the barrel with which he lit his cigar. It was his latest toy, Elaine had already warned Charles that Gemini been doing that to everybody for the last week.

As the smoke drifted in a blue toxic cloud towards him

Charles stiffened in his chair before giving a forced smile and settling back down again.

"I believe," Gemini continued. "That the Foreign Office were of the opinion that it didn't matter what El Presidente decided to do with his brown paper bag full of money as long as we got our military base... erm... hydroelectric dam. And if he and his wife wanted to pack up their shoe collection, move to Spain and open a bar then that was entirely up to them."

"So, what happened to the money?"

"It sort of, disappeared en-route to the airport."

"How, exactly?" Tremayne waved a hand casually destroying three perfectly formed smoke rings drifting in his direction.

"We were using a haulage firm called 'Shifters'. Couldn't very well send this by any recognised security firm. Sure to attract unnecessary attention. So we bundled the money into crates marked,' Books for Pulping', then sent it off. Sort of in disguise you see."

"How far did it get?"

"The lorry was hijacked some four miles from the airfield, near a small town called Little Didney on the South Cornish coast. We've got most of the chappies who did the hijacking. Most unlikely group you ever did see! They call themselves Mr Green, Mr Blue and Mr Brown. We guess there was a fourth who drove the other vehicle. We can get nothing else out of the others. Except, they claim that halfway through the hijacking they heard the police coming and made a dash for it across the fields. That's where our helicopter found them later. However, when we arrived the van and the crates were gone."

"And now you want me to find the money?"

"Precisely."

"Do you mind if I have a word with the gang?"

"Be my guest. But I don't think you'll get very far. They seem to know nothing at all about the money. They claim they were hired by a voice on the end of a telephone offering them £500 each to steal some old books. They thought it was probably pornography."

"Do you believe them, about the police turning up?"

"We don't know what to believe. But we do know that the only police car in the area was attending to a road traffic accident at the time."

***

Barry Penwrith slid behind the wheel of his new Ford Capri. He'd promised himself a Ford Capri since he was eighteen. The fact that Ford no longer made these things, and they hadn't since 1987 had never dampened his ambitions. And now it was his. At £4,000, he had a feeling he'd paid a bit over the odds. But he could afford to be a little bit extravagant today. Maybe tomorrow as well. If he was careful with the money, it might last several years. He wasn't quite sure how much there was; he'd stopped counting at £16,000, so he knew there was more than that. In fact, he'd hardly even started on the first crate. But it still wouldn't do to be too extravagant. You never knew when the odd little emergency would arise. A broken washing machine, slates falling off the roof, life was always full of surprises.

Barry was sure he'd seen a smile on Jerry Richards' face when he'd handed over the cash. He'd never trusted Jerry. He was a Londoner, a foreigner to these parts. But then, anybody who didn't have five generations in the graveyard was a foreigner to Barry.

As soon as he hit a reasonably straight patch of road, Barry pressed his foot to the floor and felt the 2.8 litre, fuel-injected engine push the seat into his back.
"Cor, bloody hell!"

The wide wheels made light work of the straight piece of road and within seconds, Barry was heading for a ninety-degree bend with high banks on each side. He pressed his foot hard onto the brake. The car shook and pulled violently to the left but showed little sign of slowing. He clipped the bank on the left side wing and bounced back into the centre of the road. He was just congratulating himself on his masterly control of the vehicle when the shape of Mrs. Pomfrey loomed in front of him. She was pushing her bicycle up the slight incline. In fact, she seemed to push her bicycle everywhere. He couldn't remember the last time that he'd seen her actually ride it.

He caught a brief glimpse of the look of horror on her face just before she dived for the hedge, remarkably quickly for a woman of sixty-plus. She had moved so quickly in fact, that the bike remained upright for the brief moment before the car struck it.

He heard a crunch, and the breaking of glass then felt the scrape of tangled metal rattling along underneath his new Ford Capri. He pumped his foot up and down on the brake, and finally managed to bring the runaway vehicle to a standstill.

Barry jumped out of the car and ran back to find her. She was just pulling herself out of the hedge. Twigs and leaves adorned her like decorations on a Christmas tree.
"Oh, it's you, Mr Penwrith. I thought it was one of these joy-riders you keep hearing talk about." She pulled a large twig from her hair.
"Sorry, Mrs Pomfrey. Brakes didn't work." His eyes darted between the woman and his car.
"Fair gave a woman a start, you did. Now look what you've done to my poor bicycle."
For the first time, Barry noticed the mangled heap lying by the side of the road. Her trademark wicker-basket that used to be attached to the handlebars now lay in shreds across the tarmac.
"I am sorry, Mrs Pomfrey." He picked up the bike, and the front wheel fell off.
"I have a good mind to box your ears, I have."
"I could pay to get it fixed, look!" Barry reached into his hip pocket and pulled out a pile of fity-pound notes.
Mrs Pomfrey's eyebrows disappeared up under her hairline. "Where'd you get money like that then, Young Penwrith?"

"I found it."

"Oh?"

"How much is it going to cost to get that fixed?" He nodded at her bike.

She glanced at the pile of money in his hand. "Five hundred pounds," she said.

Barry hesitated briefly. Then the iron gaze of Mrs Pomfrey weakened his resistance, and he counted out five hundred pounds. She opened her handbag in front of him, and he dropped the money inside. It snapped shut like the jaws of a hungry crocodile. He was relieved he hadn't been any slower, or he would have probably lost a finger.

Barry dropped Mrs Pomfrey at her cottage then headed off in search of Bob Farmer's motor repair workshop. It only took Bob five minutes to diagnose the problem, and another thirty for him to fit new brake pads all round. At a cost of a thousand pounds.

Barry hadn't realised quite how expensive Ford Capris were to service. But Bob assured him that was the going rate for Capri brake pads. Specialist parts, he explained. If Barry wanted to drive a performance vehicle, he was going to have to expect repair bills like that.

Barry drove away from the garage wondering if he should trade in his beloved Capri for something slightly more economical.

***

Charles Tremayne's footsteps echoed along the corridor. A series of iron doors on either side were the only relief in the cold stone walls. This section of the MI6 building had been built to house German spies during World War II and had changed little since.

He turned the oversized key in the lock to cell number twenty-one then pushed it open with his foot. As the door swung open, a wooden chair crashed to the ground just in front of it. Tremayne waited for a moment. A figure finally emerged to pick up the chair.

"Sorry," he said. "Worth a go, wasn't it?"

"Only if you want to lose your teeth," Tremayne answered. He studied the man. Mr Green was about six foot two and almost as wide. He had a shaven head and a goatee beard. He wore an ill-fitting dark blue suit and a white open-necked shirt that had once probably sported a tie before his arrest. Tremayne guessed that he had as much muscle between his ears as he did across his shoulders.

Tremayne stepped inside but remained close to the door.

"Now why don't you tell me about the man on the phone. "

"I don't know nothing. Like I told the other man, I just got this phone call see, asking if me and my mates wanted to earn a monkey apiece."

"A monkey?"

"Five hundred quid."

"Oh, I see." Tremayne spoke several East European languages fluently, but London slang always mystified him.

"Seemed like an easy little job."

"What did this voice sound like?"

"All posh like. He spoke proper English. Like he'd been to a real school or something."

"What were you supposed to do with these crates, once you'd lifted them?"

"We were told to bring the van back to London, where we'd be contacted."

"You weren't curious about what was in the crates?"

"No, five hundred quid's good money. Thought if we did a good job this time round, we might get some more work."

Tremayne continued with his questioning for several minutes longer, but it soon became clear that Mr Green knew nothing and was merely hired muscle. What puzzled Tremayne was whether the disappearing money had been a double cross. Or was there a third party involved? He headed back to Elaine's office.

***

"I need a car please, Elaine, and a hotel booking in a place called… Little Didney?"

"We've got a nice new Mercedes SLR just converted. Providing you promise not to trash it. When do you need it, Charles?"

"Tomorrow's early enough. The money's not going to go any further in the next twenty-four hours. Have you any idea where this place is anyway?"

"Little Didney? It's down on the south Cornish coast. A small fishing village. Hardly changed in the last hundred years. You still can't drive through the village; the streets are too narrow. Film companies use it from time to time when they want genuine eighteenth century back-drops."

"Well, book me in at the local Travel Inn."

"I've already checked that for you, Charles. There are no Travel Inns within fifty miles. Best I can do is the local pub. The Smuggler's Arms, they rent rooms."

"That will have to do, I suppose. Fancy making it a double room?" He leaned forward across her desk.

"No thank you, Charles. My husband might object." Elaine smiled her best fake coy.

"Can't you send him on a mission somewhere?"

"You keep forgetting, he's not in our line of work. He's a plumber. He might think it a bit odd if he got a call-out to Moscow."

***

Barry Penwrith was feeling pleased with himself. He had just arrived home with his latest purchase. A huge corner bath, which he felt would go perfectly in his cottage. Maisie would be delighted. He just hoped she wouldn't notice the scratches on its side where it had fallen from the roof of his car on the way home. Once he had installed it though, he could fill that in with a bit of Polly-Filla.

He dragged it across to the front door and propped it up against the wall. Maisie came out to see what the noise was.

"What's that?" she asked.

"It's one of them corner baths you always wanted."

"Well, you'd better take it right back. You'll never get that in our bathroom, you daft sod! You could do lengths in that thing."

Barry stood back to re-examine his purchase. She might have a point, now he came to think about it. It hadn't looked quite as big in the shop. In fact, at this point, he wasn't even sure how he was going to get it through the door. Then an idea came to mind.

"I could cut it into the wall a bit. That should do it."

"Where'd you get the money for something like that, anyway? I hope you haven't spent my housekeeping money again?"

"No, I found some. Look!" He pulled a handful of notes from his pocket and thrust them into Maisie's hands. "Go buy yourself a new frock, and an ice-cream for the boy. Then I'll take you all out for a chicken dinner tonight."

***

Mrs Pomfrey stopped off at the Smuggler's Arms for her morning sherry. She sat at her usual table by the fireplace. Although the August sun blazed outside, a small log fire still flickered in the hearth. It was a tradition; the fire hadn't been extinguished since Henry V stopped here one night and complained the place was, "Bloody cold!"

She slipped off her black brogues and wriggled her toes towards the flames. This time in the morning she normally had the place to herself, so she was somewhat disconcerted to hear raucous laughter coming from a nearby table. She turned, expecting to see a bunch of tourists. But it was Jerry Richards and Bob Farmer. Now, what would bring them in on a morning like this?

She tilted her head in their direction, her ears straining for scandal or gossip.

"£4,000, I don't believe it?" Bob Farmer said. "And I felt

guilty taking him for a thousand pounds for his brakes. You are a master, sir. I take my hat off to you."

Mrs Pomfrey didn't take long to work out they were discussing Barry Penwrith's new-found wealth. And although she herself had just taken Barry for five hundred pounds, she felt annoyed at the way these two were discussing their coup. Especially as they were both foreigners, neither of them having been born within the boundaries of the Duchy.

She cut short her usual hour-long stopover and went in search of Oliver Featherstone, the local vicar. Oliver Featherstone was more than just a vicar, he was a true Sage, a master of all things moral or ethical.

***

Charles Tremayne spent the rest of the morning in the reference library. It seemed that the village of Little Didney had gone largely unnoticed by MI6 as the only information on file pertained to population - 1,128. Mean elevation above sea level - 69 feet. And primary industry - home-made fudge.

He checked on the link to the Police National Computer to see what was known of the various inhabitants. The entire crime history of the village could have been written on the back of an envelope, and consisted mainly of minor motoring offences, the odd case of drunk and disorderly from a character called Imelda Pomfrey and one count of chicken stealing by somebody named Barry Penwrith.

The file gave the local Policeman's name as P.C. Albert Muchmore, and he had been in situo for thirty years. Tremayne guessed he was hardly over-stretched. One name however, did show a bit more promise. Jerry Richards, the local car dealer. Although nothing showed on the records of Little Didney, Charles was able to trace him back to his previous residence in the East End of London, where he had collected a string of minor convictions, most of which were concerned with the handling of stolen property. Cars and laptops seemed to feature heavily.

Well, it was a start, thought Charles. Although not promising. The jump from hooky laptops to £250 million was a large one.

Tremayne's next stop was the armourer, where he requisitioned himself a Heckler & Koch mark 23 pistol. He wasn't sure he needed that in Little Didney. But he felt naked without a gun of some description.

He stopped off for lunch at his favourite Japanese restaurant. Takimoto welcomed him like an old family friend and prepared sushi in front of him. Flashing knives and wafered slices of fish flew through the air with balletic grace to land on his plate in a poetry of colours. His savoured each mouthful then relaxed over tea before heading back to the office.

Elaine was still at her post. "How long do you think you'll be there, Charles?"
"Oh, one, maybe two days tops. I don't really expect to find anything. My guess is that the money was on its way out of the country within half an hour of the hijacking. Perhaps you'd better book me on a flight to Bermuda for the weekend."
"Why Bermuda?"
"Well, that's probably where the money will turn up. I could be there ready for it."
"I don't think Gemini will buy that one, Charles!" She gave him a big, knowing smile.
"Never mind. It was worth a try though. I'm fairly sure this whole thing has been a double set-up. My only question is how many layers are there? I take it the Foreign Office are still investigating things from their end? "
"Yes, I believe so."
"Well, perhaps they'll turn up something. What's the public line?"

"There isn't one. The Foreign Office are already denying the money ever existed, Shifters Transport have been paid off and reimbursed handsomely for their lost truck and the drivers have been bribed... err... recompensed for their trauma.

"Okay then, tomorrow I'll have a look at Little Didney."

***

Barry Penwrith stepped back to admire his handiwork. The bath fitted better than he'd thought it would, although six inches of it was still hanging out of his bathroom wall. But that was only the foot end. The only problem was, that in its present configuration, the bath taps were on the outside the house, and he'd need to go outside with a ladder to turn them on. But not to be deterred, he'd worked out that if he could divert the pipes feeding the taps, he might be able to set up a master control valve near the door. To do that however, would necessitate cutting the mains water pipe. A task which he was just about to commence when he heard a loud, "Cooeee!" from the front door.

Reluctantly, he set his hacksaw aside and headed downstairs to see who was cooeeeing him.

Mrs Pomfrey was standing in the open doorway. "I would have knocked," she said. "But you don't appear to have a door any more."

"Yes, I know. I'm putting in a new bath, you see." As if that explained everything. "What do you want?" He felt slightly concerned as he could see the Reverend Featherstone's balding head peeping from behind her hat. "What's going on? What do you both want?"

"Let me handle this, Mrs Pomfrey," said the Vicar as he pushed his way to the front.

"Certainly, vicar." Then just as the vicar was about to speak she continued, "Where did you get all that money from, young Penwrith?"

"Mrs Pomfrey, please!" said the Vicar.

"I haven't got any money. It's a lie. And anyway, if I *had* found some, which I haven't, it would be mine. And nothing to do with anybody else."

"We were just concerned, Barry. That's all," said the Vicar. "Maybe you should let somebody look after it for you. Or open a Post Office savings account or something."

Barry held out against the combined might of Mrs Pomfrey and the Reverend Featherstone for all of three minutes before succumbing and taking them to his hiding place in the woods. Mrs Pomfrey complained for the whole of the twenty-minute walk along the wooded track. Eventually, they came to Barry's hide out, a corrugated iron shed held together by bailing twine. So many rust patches littered the surface that it wouldn't be long before they all joined to create one large hole.

He removed the wooden peg that held the doors together and dragged them open. The vehicle took up the entire interior so all that could be seen were two more large doors bearing the inscription, 'Shifters Road Transport Services'.

"There, just like I told you," said Barry. He swung open the truck doors to reveal the pile of wooden crates.

"Heavens above!" said the Reverend Featherstone. "You say each one of these is filled with fifty pound notes?"

"Yeah, reckon so. Haven't opened them all. Thought I'd wait till I'd used up the first one."

"If what you say is true, there must be hundreds of thousands of pounds here. We should really report this to the authorities. You can't keep all of this, Barry."

"Well, perhaps they don't want it back."

"Whatever gives you that idea?"

"Well, I'd have thought if they'd wanted it back, they'd have come looking for it before now."

"He's got a point there, Vicar," said Mrs Pomfrey.

"Perhaps we should look after it for a while then. Wait to see if somebody comes to claim it."

"I think it should be counted first, Vicar," said Mrs Pomfrey. "I mean, if somebody comes looking for it, we need to make sure it's all there for them, don't we?"

"Hmm, I see what you mean. Right you are then! But

there's an awful lot here. I think we'll need some help counting this."

"I'll arrange for my ladies from the fudge-making group to come and help. They can be very discreet, and they're used to counting money from when we had the fudge stall at the market."

"I'll leave that in your hands then, Mrs Pomfrey."

***

Barry Penwrith had a horrible feeling he was losing control of this situation. But he didn't say anything. He just waited until they'd both gone then dragged ten of the crates deeper into the woods and covered them with a pile of branches and leaves. After all, he'd discovered how expensive it was keeping a nice car on the road. He'd need to put a little back. He went back to the truck to spread the remaining crates around, neither Mrs Pomfrey nor the vicar had particularly good eyesight nor had they attempted to count the crates. He ran to catch up with the others.

Barry's Capri and the vicar's VW Beetle were pressed into action ferrying the crates to the church hall.

***

Barry dispersed the crates around the room, hoping neither the Reverend Featherstone or Mrs Pomfrey would notice one was missing. As soon as the first crate was up-ended on one of the wooden trestles table in the church hall Mrs Pomfrey realised this was going to be a much bigger job than she had first anticipated

The eight ladies from the fudge-making circle valiantly set about their task. But by teatime, they had made very little progress. One of the ladies suggested commandeering the help of Mr Babcock, the local butcher. He had a large set of scales. All they would need to do would be to count one large pile of money, then weigh it, and a simple multiplication would tell them how much there was.

Mr Babcock insisted on accompanying his scales. Thereby adding both to the growing numbers in the church hall and to Barry's concerns that should the money come to be divided up, he would only get a pittance

By six o'clock that evening, Mrs Pomfrey's ladies had finished weighing the money. Mr Babcock sat at a corner table and repeated his calculations three times before announcing to the stunned group that, even at a conservative estimate, there was in excess of 200 million pounds piled up around them. Never before in the whole history of Little Didney had such a large group remained so silent. Barry calculated that meant there was over twenty million in the crates he had hidden in the woods. His legs stopped working and he sat down on the floor with a thump. Several people turned to look in his direction, and he tried to make out he was just sitting down normally.

Mr Babcock suggested that the validity of the currency be checked before everybody got too excited. After all, it might be forged. Although, to his untrained eye, it looked good.

Nods of agreement bounced around the room and much heated discussion followed. Eventually, it was clear there was only one person qualified to examine the notes, Mr Cobbledick, the local manager of the sub-branch of the Western Counties Bank. At this time of day, he would almost certainly be occupying his usual table in the Smuggler's Arms and nursing his early evening half-pint of shandy. Mrs Pomfrey dispatched a posse to collect him.

They returned with Mr Cobbledick after twenty minutes, along with Sandy Goodenough, the barmaid, and landlord's daughter from the Smuggler's Arms. She'd brought along a large tray of sandwiches.

Mr Cobbledick was a short man with a ruddy face and a balding head. He stopped three feet inside the door. His eyes expanded to the size of the round-rimmed spectacles he wore.

Then he froze.

The only sign of movement on his whole body was a pulsing vein on the side of his neck. Sandy Goodenough placed her tray of sandwiches on a nearby table then slid a chair behind Mr Cobbledick's legs. He sat back on it with a barely whispered, "Upon my word!"

Sandy Goodenough reached across, took one of the notes from the nearest pile, and held it up to the light. She made a tear over the silver thread, examined it carefully, and sniffed the note.

"They're genuine, all right." She handed the note to Mr Cobbledick.

Mr Cobbledick held the note up to the light and rubbed it between thumb and forefinger. "Yes, it is. It's quite genuine. Yes, indeed. Upon my word." He pulled a red silk handkerchief from his breast pocket and flapped it in front of his face.

"Well, what now?" asked Mrs Pomfrey of the assembled group. "Do we hand it in? Or, do we keep it?"

Chapter 2

Charles Tremayne returned to his Belgravia flat. His daily help had been in and the place reeked of floor polish. He poured himself a scotch then settled down on his white leather sofa to enjoy the view of the sun setting over St Paul's.

The room reflected a lifestyle rather than taste. Possessions were sparse and functional. The only concession to ornamentation was a pair of carved African wooden heads on either end of the mahogany mantelpiece. Minimalist, was the way Charles always described it when challenged. The reality was different though. Used to a life of moving on at a moment's notice, acquisitiveness had never been a desirable trait. Too many possessions slowed one down; they also gave clues about a person. Leaving clues or being slow were definite disadvantages in Charles' trade.

He picked up a multi-function remote control from the marble coffee table and aimed it at the Hi Fi. The dramatic sound of Strauss's Salome instantly filled the room. He closed his eyes and let the haunting soprano gather up his soul and transport him to La Scala in Milan. A world of harmony and solitude. A world where precision and order were the only things that mattered.

***

"Will you all shut up and sit down!" Barry's voice boomed around the church hall. For the last twenty minutes the sound of shouting had risen up to rafter banging levels. Each new decibel in volume had also attracted more visitors.

Jerry Richards had heard the commotion drifting down the street and had followed his instincts for an angle. He'd slid in the back door of the church hall and behind the stage curtain. There he'd listened and waited.

Every so often he risked a peep through the gap. He couldn't remember so many people being jammed in the church hall since the BBC had done the Antiques Roadshow from here two years ago, and the whole village had brought along the contents of their garden sheds. It seemed everybody had an opinion. And in the main, those opinions coincided. The majority were in favour of the money being kept. Even Reverend Featherstone supported hanging on to it. He'd decided it was a gift from the Almighty and should be put to use restoring the church. However, there were still dissenters. The noise had been created when ideas were called for as to where, and by whom it should be kept.

Jerry gave a start as Barry slapped his hand on one of the tables and repeated his request. Gradually the noise subsided.
"That's better," he said. "I've been thinking about this problem. It seems we all feel the money should be looked after by somebody responsible, right?" Murmurs of approval. "The problem is, who is best suited to the task? Now, as finder, I think I should look after it until—" The rest of his words were drowned under a fresh cacophony of shouts. The most common word in the hall at that moment was "Me!"

The main door swung open with a bang, and Police Constable Albert Muchmore entered the room. "Now then. What's going on…" His jaw stopped working as he took in the piles of money that littered each of the tables. A draught from the door caught several of the nearest piles, and a flurry of fifty-pound notes fluttered around the now silent church hall like autumn leaves.

He made some practise movements with his mouth before any sounds finally emerged. "You're all under arrest," he said with authority.
The door banged shut in the wind and the floating notes

drifted gracefully to the floor.

"Why?" somebody called.

"Because I said so! And because this amount of money can't possibly be legal."

"Mr Muchmore," Reverend Featherstone said. "We were just counting it. It appears somebody has mislaid it, and we wanted to be sure that it could be correctly identified in the event of somebody making a claim. After all, we wouldn't want the wrong person to wind up with this just because of some administrative error, would we?"

"Who could mislay this? There must be a million pounds here."

"Two hundred million, two hundred thousand pounds," said Mr Babcock. "Give or take a thousand. I've been doing a recount while you lot were arguing. There's ninety cases, and two point five million in each one."

Barry fell on the floor again.

"We were just going to bring it over to you, Constable," Reverend Featherstone said.

"Well, it ain't no good you bringing it over to me. My lost property cupboard's not big enough for that lot. I need to get onto County."

Time to take control, thought Jerry.

"Tell me, Albert," he said as he slid from behind the curtain at the back of the stage. "What's a copper's pension like these days?"

The silence in the room was so intense Jerry felt he could almost hear the turning of heads as everybody looked towards PC Muchmore. Despite the uniform, the persona of policeman slipped and the real Albert Muchmore, confused and underpaid civil servant, sat down on the edge of one of the tables.

"How much you say is there?" he asked, eventually.

"Two hundred million, two hundred thousand pounds," Mr Babcock repeated.

"By my calculations," said Jerry, "that makes just a little

over a quarter of a million pounds for each resident... or... around ten million for each person in this room."

The room fell silent and Jerry watched their faces, trying to identify allies or potential opponents.

The silence was finally broken be Mr Cobbledick. "Look that's absurd!" he shouted. "We can't keep it... Can we?"

"Who's to know?" Jerry asked. "Mr Muchmore, have you been contacted by your superiors about any large sums of money gone walk-about?"

"No, no!"

"Mr Cobbledick, has anybody asked you about any unusual deposits or transfers?"

"No."

"Now, why do you think that is?" Jerry walked to the front of the stage. He was enjoying the performance. His eyes scanned the audience, but nobody offered a solution, so he continued, "Either it's gang money, in which case this place will soon be swarming with gentleman in suits and violin cases, or, more likely, it belongs to the government's department of dirty deals."

A sea of blank looks told Jerry they hadn't a clue what he was talking about.

"I'll explain," he continued. "From time to time, various government departments find it necessary to move large sums of cash around. It could be anything from a dodgy property deal, reorganisation of local government boundaries before an election or flogging arms to both sides in the same conflict. Either way, they're not exactly going to own up to this."

"Ten million pounds each, you say?" PC Muchmore stared at the nearest pile of money.

"Well," the vicar said, "I suppose... If the money is tainted, it behoves us to ensure it is put to a good use, and not allowed to continue corrupting people or spreading unhappiness."

"Ten million, you reckon?" PC Muchmore said.

"Exactly," said Jerry. "We'll be removing this money from temptation. It's the best thing to do with it."

Everybody nodded in agreement. Everybody wanted to do their bit for society.

"Of course," Mr Cobbledick said, "I couldn't countenance Her Majesty's currency being put to nefarious uses. So I suppose, we'll just have to keep it."

"I've never had a million pounds before." PC Muchmore said. "Let alone ten million."

Jerry stood with his hands on his hips and a big smile across his face. He felt like a character in pantomime. He had an overwhelming urge to slap his thigh and shout. 'Come on children, let's find the pirates!'

Mrs Pomfrey came to her feet and waved a finger in Jerry's direction. "How come you know so much about this sort of thing then, young Mr Richards?"

"I grew up in the East End of London, Luv, and my uncle was on the Greater London Council. He used to tell me stories that would make your teeth blush."

"Ten million pounds," PC Muchmore said, still trying to get a handle on things. "That's a thousand, thousands, isn't it? Five noughts?"

Okay, thought Jerry. Now the tricky bit.

"So, we have established that we're keeping it, how do we divide it up then?"

"Well," surprisingly, the vicar was the first from the starting block. "I think we should put it into a communal fund and keep it for the benefit of all. We could restore the church roof or build a hostel for the single mothers—"

"What single mothers?" Mrs. Pomfrey called. "The only single mother we've got in this village is Mrs. Brierly, and she's sixty three. And courting again! I think we should divide it up into shares. One share for each year that your family has spent in the community." She made a pointed nod in Jerry's direction.

"Well, I think it should be equally divided among every person." Jerry noticed that Bill Painter had suggested that idea. There were seventeen in Bill's family. Enough to ensure Bill a lion's share of the pot.

"We should build a new community centre," Mr Cobbledick said. "That would benefit everybody."

Jerry sat back onto one of the crates on the edge of the stage. He let the ideas bounce around the room. When he was satisfied that the latest round of 'Me' and 'Mine' had died away he stood up and clapped his hands together.
"Listen," he shouted. "There's only one sensible solution to this. We divide the money equally. One share for each family."

He waited again for the shouts to die down to a low murmur. Gradually, nods of assent circulated. It seemed they agreed with him. Good.
"Now," he continued. "What we have to do is to make sure we can hang onto it."
"What do you mean," somebody shouted.
"Very soon, somebody's going to come looking for this. Police, gangsters, government agents. You name it. First, we need to divide this up. Then hide it. We also need to make a promise that we don't spend any of it for a very long time. Because whoever comes looking for it is going to be looking for signs of spending."

Mr Cobbledick stood up with a big smile on his face, but before he could speak, Jerry continued. "No, Mr Cobbledick. It can't be invested in your bank either. That would be the first place anybody would look."
Mr Cobbledick sat down again; his smile replaced with a frown.
"If they can't find us, they can't have their money back, can they?" Barry piped up.
"What do you mean?" Jerry asked.
"Well, my Granddad told me that in the war, they changed all the street signs to confuse the German paratroopers."
"I think we should have some of those walkie-talkie radio things." Mrs Pomfrey shouted. "So we could warn

each other, when visitors come."

"I think we should set up roadblocks," somebody shouted.

Jerry felt he was losing control of this. They seemed to be even more excited about the prospect of fending off invaders than they were about the money.

"We could set up a control centre in the back of my Post Office. I've got a spare room."

"I think we should set up spotters on top of the church tower."

Jerry sat down on the crate again, and dropped his head into his hands.

"My brother's got some camouflage gear from when he was in the army."

"I got a load of barbed wire left over from fencing off the top field."

"How about a sniper on the pub roof?"

Chapter 3

Charles Tremayne clicked off the cruise control as the motorway ended; allowing his speed to drop to a level more suited for Cornwall's narrow lanes. The satellite navigation system attached to the dashboard of his Mercedes informed him that Little Didney was twenty-one point eight miles to the south west of his current position. A synthesised female voice announced there was a left-hand turn coming up in precisely one hundred and eighty-seven metres.

For the last 150 miles, he'd been thinking about his future. He'd finally crystallised the thoughts that had been drifting around his head for many months. This was going to be his last assignment. The world had changed too much. Surveillance missions that used to require a run deep into some foreign, and hostile country were now carried out by Spy-in-the-sky satellites that could read a newspaper from 5,000 miles. Gone also were the adrenaline-pumping defector rescues. There was nowhere left to defect from. And as most state secrets these days were held on computer, it seemed you needed to be under twelve years of age to hack into those. No, this was a different world. A world that no longer had the need for a pen-radio or a poisoned dart disguised as a cigarette.

Now, this seemed the best he could hope for. Being sent to the back of beyond in search of a truckload of grubby money. He had made his decision. This case should take no longer than two or three days, after which he'd retire and move to Geneva. He had always loved Geneva. It was one of the cleanest cities he'd ever seen and operated with meticulous efficiency and a level of precision only matched by the superb engineering of the indigenous timepieces.

Needing to stretch his legs, he pulled off the road onto a large gravelled parking area and switched off the engine, leaving the air conditioning running. The cooling breeze blew across his face.

The rolling Cornish moors spread out in front of him, criss-crossed by low stone walls and the random undulations of a narrow stream. A hundred yards from where he was parked, a collection of granite rocks had been heaved upright and carefully placed in what was long ago probably a highly significant pattern. But now, their meaning could only be guessed at. A few ragged sheep tore at the juiciest strands of long grass that protruded from the bottom of the stones.

Tremayne reached into the back seat and retrieved his stainless steel Thermos flask. He gave it a little shake near his ear, checking to see if the ice cubes had survived, and poured a cup of iced tea. He pressed a button on the door panel and the window hissed down. The interior of the car was at once filled with the most pungent and tear-bringing fumes imaginable. The quaint English farming tradition of muck-spreading was obviously well underway in a nearby field. Charles pulled a white linen handkerchief from his shirt pocket and pressed it to his mouth while his other hand stabbed the 'up' button on the door panel. The window seemed to take an eternity to close, and even when shut the air inside the car was still thick with the noxious smell. Unsure now whether he had just trapped the smell inside the car, or if it was still permeating through, he wound the air conditioning up to full and restarted the engine. The rear wheels threw gravel and dust into the air as he swung out of the parking area in search of cleaner air.

***

Charles followed the advice of his onboard computer until he came to a crossroads. The computer had just told him to turn left at this particular junction, but the sign clearly indicated Little Didney to the right. He tapped the machine and pressed the refresh button. It repeated its previous directions. Not clear as to what to do, he regretted momentarily his over-dependence on technology, and wished he'd brought a traditional paper map with him. He decided to follow the road signs on the basis that the locals probably knew where Little Didney was better than some Taiwanese microchip.

For twenty minutes, he followed the convoluted route suggested to him by the road signs and steadfastly ignored all protestations of his computer, which kept telling him he was going in the wrong direction. Eventually, he found himself in the centre of a small village. He pulled over next to the green where an old man sat on a wooden bench.

"Excuse me," said Charles as he poked his head out of the window. "Can you tell me where I am?"

"Well, you're here of course!"

Charles sighed. "Yes, I know that. What's the name of this place?"

"Why, this is Upper Downing. Everybody knows that."

"And I suppose Lower Downing is just down the road, is it?" Charles couldn't resist it.

"No, don't be silly." The man had clearly missed the humour. "You go down there, you get to Down Downing. Lower Downing's up the hill!"

Charles wondered if the man was winding him up. "Can you tell me where Little Didney is please?"

The man poked his head through the window and into the car's interior. Charles' nose, still recovering from the muck-spreading encounter, was once more invaded. This time the aroma resembled old wet straw.

"Broke, is he?" The man waved a knotted finger at Charles' computer.

The West Country habit of using the male pronoun when indicating inanimate objects was as mysterious to Charles as the London rhyming slang.

"How did you know..."

"Saw one on the Discovery Channel. Not a lot of use if he won't tell you where Little Didney is, though. Is he?"

"Teething troubles," Charles said.

The man gave a rattly, coughing laugh, pulled his false teeth from his mouth and waved them in front of Tremayne's face. "I've got those," he said before re-inserting them into the cackling orifice.

"Little Didney?" Charles reminded him.

"Well, for Little Didney, you're best off not being here at all."

"Yes, I'm beginning to realise that," Charles replied.

"But seeing as how you're here, you need to set off down this road," He waved a weather-beaten hand in the direction from which Charles had just come. "Keep on 'til you get to old Mrs. Stephens' cottage on the corner. Then make a right. That will take you down past Tom's top meadow. Then there'll be a left turning, that's Tinker's Lane. That ain't marked, mind you. But you'll know it, 'cause it's right opposite Badgers walk. Course, that ain't marked neither. Now, you follow that on down, about two miles, brings you right into Little Didney. And if you find your feet are wet, you've gone too far!"

He burst into such a loud, wheezing laugh that Charles felt in fear of the man's teeth being ejected onto his lap.

Tremayne waved his arm and smiled, "Thank you." He swung the car round on the road and headed in the direction indicated. He drove for fifteen minutes. But nowhere could he see anything that said either Tinker's Lane or Badger's Walk.

He tried to follow a combination of the man's directions and GPS instructions and within another fifteen minutes, he was back at the village green in Upper Downing. Even before he'd come near to the man, Charles could see the man was laughing again. He spun the car around the green and headed back down the hill without stopping.

This time, he thought, I'm going to put my trust in modern technology and follow the GPS system. For another ten minutes he followed the directions given by the mechanical voice. All seemed to be going well, until he found himself staring at a sign that said, 'Upper Downing welcomes careful drivers'. In a flurry of anger completely out of keeping with his normally calm manner, he ripped the GPS system off the dashboard and threw it into the back seat. How is it, he wondered, that he could be dropped off the coast of some East European country on a moonless night with little more than a flashlight and a compass, and still find his target 200 miles across country. Yet here, these little Cornish lanes were defeating the hell out of him.

Leafy high banked lanes were not conducive to three point turns, and by the time he had finished, there were pieces of hedge entangled in both the front and rear of the car. On the basis that he at least knew the main roads through Cornwall ran east to west, Charles decided to head north until he crossed one, find a garage and a buy a map. Utilising the same set of skills that in the past had seen him safely through some of the more remote parts of Russia, he quickly found his way onto the A380. Ten miles further on, he came to a sizeable petrol station where he refilled his tank and purchased the largest scale map he could find along with a car compass.

He sat in the car for ten minutes studying the map and committing each turn to memory. As his finger retraced the route back towards Little Didney, he realised the GPS system had been right as it agreed with the map. The signposts were wrong.

He set out, and this time ignored the signposts. Before long he found himself again staring at the sign that welcomed careful drivers to Upper Downing. He ignored that also and put it down to just another one of the mysteries of Cornwall.

He drove on.

Too late he realised he was driving faster than he should have been. His frustration had transferred itself to his right foot. He rounded a sharp corner and caught a glimpse of something bright and metallic before it disappeared underneath his car. A loud scraping sound tore through the car, followed by two sharp bangs. The vehicle veered wildly from side to side, completely confusing the anti lock braking system. The Mercedes slewed to a halt at a 45-degree angle across the road.

He flung the door open and walked round to the front of the vehicle. Tangled in the radiator grill, round both tyres and all underneath the car was a mass of barbed wire. Both front tyres were shredded and deep gouges ran across each wing. He kicked the front of the car.
"What bloody maniac leaves barbed wire in the middle of the road?"

He climbed back into the car, thumped the steering wheel then reclined the seat and closed his eyes. Deep breathing. With great deliberation, he set his mind into mokuso, the condition of no mindedness taught to him by his karate master. He felt his heart rate reduce and the surfeit of adrenaline diffuse through his system.

Once happy he'd recovered his equilibrium, he took the satellite phone from his briefcase and called the breakdown service. He told them exactly which road he was on, as well as providing them with a grid reference. They informed him they'd be with him within forty minutes. He settled back to wait.

An hour later, his phone rang.

"Hello, Sir. Auto Rescue here. I can't find you."
"Where are you?"
"I appear to be in a place called Upper Downing. It's like the bloody twilight zone. I can't seem to leave."

Tremayne explained to him the problem with the road signs and told him just follow the map instead. Ten minutes later, the breakdown truck appeared. The mechanic jumped down and went round to the front of Tremayne's car. He stood with his hands in his pockets, drew in a deep breath through his teeth, and shook his head.

"Well, that's a new one on me. How many spare wheels have you got?"

"Just the one."

"I'm going to have to tow you in then."

"Can't you repair it?"

"Not here. Those tyres have had it. There's a Kwik-Fit centre in Truro, that's about thirty miles away. I'll give you a tow there, shall I?"

"Wouldn't there be a place in Little Didney?"

"I don't know. I have to take you somewhere we're registered with. That would be the Kwik-Fit centre in Truro."

Charles resigned himself to the situation and climbed into the cab alongside the mechanic. They set off for Truro.

Four hours later, Charles Tremayne, complete with two new tyres, was for the third time driving past the sign that welcomed him to Upper Downing. This time however, he was a bit more circumspect in his driving, which was just as well, because just over the brow of a blind hill, he had to brake hard to avoid hitting a tractor parked across the road.

He remembered once having to flee from East Berlin in a thirty year old Trabant. How the Spetsnaz had pursued him along the forest roads. In retrospect, that seemed like a picnic compared to this. He climbed on the tractor. It looked as though it had just been abandoned, and of course, there were no keys. A quick rewiring job and the vehicle burst into life. He drove it into a nearby field, left it there then returned to his car.

Five hundred yards further down the road he came to a large hand-painted cardboard sign that announced; "This is not Little Didney."

Most strange, he thought. Two hundred yards beyond that, another sign, "If you're looking for Little Didney, you're going the wrong way". It seemed the residents of Little Didney didn't exactly welcome visitors.

The road dipped down a steep hill, and there at the bottom, the village of Little Didney nestled in a small cove. The road ended abruptly in a large gravel car park. Of course, Charles remembered, no vehicles within the village.

He removed his suitcase from the boot, set the alarm then went in search of the Smugglers Arms. As he left the gate at the bottom of the car park, he heard some scrabbling noises in a nearby bush. His hand automatically went for his pistol. He stopped as soon as his fingers touched the handle. Don't be silly, he told himself this is Cornwall, not Berlin. He remained still and listened, ears straining for the slightest clue. He was just about to give up when he heard a muffled voice saying, "Cinderella, Cinderella. This is Buttons, come back ten four. Intruder alert."
Must be kids, Charles thought. He listened again. "Cinderella, Cinderella. Are you there, Cinderella? This is Buttons."
A brief silence, then, "No, *I'm* Buttons, you're Cinderella."
More silence.
"No, that's not what we agreed. I didn't want these bloody silly code words anyway. And if we *were* going to have them, I wanted to be Flying Fox."
Charles listened hard to see if he could hear the other end of this strange conversation, but it was too muffled.
"Anyway, there's a bloke here with a posh car and a suitcase. Better pass it on."

Most curious, Charles thought. He decided to pretend he hadn't noticed and to carry on. But obviously something unusual was happening around here.

What passed for the main street was little more than a cobbled walkway, and the severe downward slope it took would make walking highly treacherous in wet weather. White washed, terraced cottages pressed in from both sides. Painted slatted shutters on each side of the windows gave protection against the English Channel storms. Flower baskets hung from under the eves of each cottage, mingling the scent of flowers with that of the sea. It seemed that every third cottage had been turned into a shop of some description. A fish shop, a chandlers and even one devoted to nothing but fudge.

At the bottom of the hill, the street forked, and the smell of the sea became distinctly stronger. The left fork appeared to reach straight down onto a shingle beach, while the right, snaked along, forming a narrow promenade with fishing boats along the seaward side. He followed the path, until eventually he found the Smugglers Arms. It was a surprisingly large building, constructed of a mixture of black timber and cob stone.

Charles pushed open the door, stepped into the gloomy interior. Wood smoke and last night's beer still drifted in the air. He planted his suitcase on the floor and scanned the room. Despite the heat outside, a log fire blazed in the hearth, and a selection of wooden tables and chairs, all from different eras, were scattered across the well worn oak floor.

"We're closed," announced a deep, burred voice from behind the counter.
The barman was tall and slim. Thick black curly hair extended down past his ears and round underneath his chin, but the face itself was cleanly shaven.

"But it's only two o'clock in the afternoon," Charles said. "What time do you open?"
The man looked at his watch then tipped his head to one side as if in deep thought. "Tomorrow," he said, and went back to polishing a glass.
"I've come to check in." Charles walked over to the bar.
"We're full," said the man.
"No, you don't understand. My office booked. I have a reservation, Tremayne, Charles Tremayne?"
"I'll just have a look for you then, sir." He set the glass on the counter and reached underneath pulling out a huge, dusty leather-bound book. He flopped it open and ran his forefinger across the yellowing pages. As far as Charles

could see, there was only one line of writing. And even upside down, he could read the word, Tremayne.

"No," said the man. "No record. Sorry."

He started to close the book, but Charles was quick. He slid his hand into the page preventing it from shutting. "No, look, there!" He said, pointing to the word Tremayne.

The man looked down at the writing. "No, sir. That says *Giles* Tremayne. You said your name was Charles Tremayne."

"Yes, but that's clearly a mistake. Somebody's written it down wrong, or misheard."

"Ah, I can't let you have that room. What happens if Giles Tremayne turns up? And I've let his room go."

"There is no Giles Tremayne. It's Charles Tremayne. That's my room. Prepaid for, over the phone on a Visa card. I can give you the number if you want to check."

"No, that won't be necessary, sir. It seems there's been a slight slip of the pen there. Welcome to the Smugglers Arms. I'll get Sandy to show you up to your room, sir." He turned to face a door behind the bar, "Sandy!" he called.

Sandy Goodenough appeared from the doorway. "Yes, Dad?"

"Show this gentleman up to the bridal suite."

"The bridal suite?" Charles asked.

"It's the only room we've got, sir."

Charles made to pick up his suitcase.

"No, sir. Leave that there, I'll get the boy to fetch that up for you."

"No trouble," Charles said.

"No, you leave it to the boy. That's his job."

Sandy Goodenough shared her father's stature, being nearly five foot ten. She had slim hips and small breasts that she was doing her best to accentuate with a low-cut white blouse. But the real difference was the hair. In contrast to her father's thick black curls, hers was fiery red with strands of gold where the sun had bleached it. It hung straight across her shoulders and curled up underneath her chin.

She came out from behind the bar and led Charles over to a wooden staircase in the corner of the room.

"If you would like to follow me, please Mr Tremayne, sir."

"Charles, please."

"As you wish, Charles."

She walked ahead of him up the uneven staircase. She wore tight, faded jeans, and Charles found himself hypnotised by the graceful movements of her limbs as she climbed the steps. The muscles in her legs were clearly visible through the denim. At the top of the staircase, she led him along a narrow corridor that wasn't quite straight.

"Mind your head, Charles." She pointed at the low oak beams that spanned the passage.

Charles duly ducked as she pointed to each one.

Sandy inserted a large iron key into a door that would have looked more at home in the side of a barn rather than in a hotel. She pushed the door open and stood back, allowing Charles to enter.

If somebody had wanted a room with too many flowery bits, excessive lace, huge numbers of ornaments and other unnecessary trimmings then this room must have been paradise. But for Charles, it was a kaleidoscopic hellhole of trivial fluffiness. A constant source of irritation for the eye, ensuring it never had anywhere to rest. There was also a distinct lack of flat surfaces for Charles to place any of his belongings. Each available flat area had been taken up by some completely unnecessary ornament, carefully placed on its own lace doily.

A huge, four-poster bed dominated the room, and a surfeit of red velvet curtains cascaded from the overhead canopy.

"What do think?" she asked.

"Very... er... bridal."

"Dad designed this. He based it on a picture of Queen

Anne's room in Hampton Court. It was only a black-and-white photo though, so we're not sure if he got the colours right."

Charles scanned the hopelessly clashing deep red walls and bright yellow carpet.

"I'm sure Queen Anne would have felt quite at home here."

"Are you here on business, or pleasure, Charles?" She gave a little roll to the R in his name that he found quite endearing.

"You could say a bit of both, really. I work for a film company. We're looking for a location for a scene set in the eighteenth century."

"Oh, I see. Will you be looking for any extras?" She said it in such a way that Charles couldn't work out whether she meant extras for the film, or extras with the room. He decided he was probably safer opting for the former.

"That would be up to the Casting Department. They usually like to hire some local people."

"Well, tell them not to forget me. I'm good enough."

"I'm sure you are. But that's down to them."

"No," she laughed. "That's my name. Goodenough, Sandra Goodenough. But everybody calls me Sandy."

"Oh, right, Sandy it is then."

"If there's anything I can do to make your stay more comfortable, just call me."

"Right now all I need is my suitcase. Any sign of that?"

"I'll find out what's happened to it, Charles." She smiled as she said his name, as if trying it out.

When she'd gone, he relaxed back on the bed. The mattress was so soft he sank right down into it. He let his eyes wander round the room. Lace hung from every place possible to hang lace from. The brocade wallpaper could hardly be seen underneath a plethora of pictures. Ships in distress appeared to be the common theme in each of them. An old-fashioned white telephone with a dial sat on a lace doily on the bedside table. He yearned for the functional simplicity of a Travel Inn.

Tremayne relaxed, closed his eyes, and began thinking through how he was going to tackle the problem of the missing money. He decided the best approach was to engage the locals in conversation and find out if they'd seen anything unusual, or had any strange visitors. There was certainly something unusual about this place. But it may just be a natural reticence towards visitors. A place that hadn't changed much in 200 years might breed a certain kind of parochialism. He glanced at his watch. It had been fifteen minutes, and there was still no sign of his suitcase.

On his way down the stairs to enquire after his missing luggage, he bumped his head twice on the low beams.

He found Mr Goodenough in the bar still polishing glasses. Mr Goodenough noticed the red marks on Charles' forehead. "You need to watch those beams, Sir. Otherwise you're head's going to wind up looking like a dozen eggs in a crate."

Charles rubbed at his head. "Any sign of my suitcase?"

"Ah, I'm afraid that's got lost in transit, Sir."

"Lost in transit? He only had to bring it up stairs!"

"Well, that's baggage-handlers for you. I think it's probably gone to the wrong hotel."

"What other hotel? There *are* no other hotels!"

"Not here, Sir. It might have gone to the Smugglers Haunt, in Westlyn. Easy mistake to make you see, them both being called Smugglers."

"But Westlyn is twenty miles away. How can you ask somebody to take a suitcase upstairs and it turns up twenty miles away?"

"That's staff for you, sir. Same thing happened to me once on my holidays. I was on my way to Paris, and my luggage ended up in Rome."

"Well, can you ring them please. Find out if it's there? If it is, I'll drive over to collect it."

"Right you are. As soon as the phone lines have been mended."

"What?"

"Phones are all down."

Charles resisted an urge to wrap his hands around Goodenough's neck and squeeze tightly. But he needed to maintain his persona of a naive location scout. Instead, he said, "Just let me know when it arrives, okay?"

"Right you are, sir."

Charles returned to his room and slid the bolt across the door. He removed his satellite phone from the briefcase. Directory enquiries gave him the number for the Smugglers Haunt in Westlyn. And no, they hadn't seen his luggage. He then rang the number for the Smugglers Arms.

Goodenough answered, "Hello, Smugglers Arms."

"Seems the phone lines are working again then?" Tremayne hung up.

He attached the satellite phone to his belt clip, set the alarm on his briefcase and heaved it up onto the top of the wardrobe. He set off downstairs again, this time only bumping his head once.

Goodenough was nowhere to be seen. Charles let himself out the front door.

A row of fishing boats bobbed at their moorings across the narrow promenade, and seagulls skimmed the surface of the water in search of food.

He'd only been walking along the seafront a couple of minutes, but already his hair felt sticky with sea spray. Perhaps the harbour had been used as a getaway for whoever had taken the money. A fast boat across the Channel, then once into France the money could be in any one of half a dozen different countries within a matter of hours.

He stopped to have a better look at the harbour. Footsteps behind him that he'd only been dimly aware of stopped also. Decades of conditioning triggered the alert signals within his brain. He turned quickly, just in time to catch a glimpse of somebody disappearing into the doorway of a newsagent's. The man had been about five-eight, average build except for an oversized midriff that made him look as though he were hiding a pillow under his threadbare red jumper. Unwilling to put it down to coincidence, Tremayne continued west along the promenade then slipped into an alley between two cottages. He waited. A few seconds later, the sound of footsteps reappeared. They hesitated for a while then continued again, this time more briskly.

Charles pushed himself further into the shadows just as he saw the man in the red jumper scurry past the end of the alley. Charles slid out behind him and matched his step, foot for foot. The man appeared flustered at having lost his prey. Charles closed the distance. The man didn't appear to represent a threat, and was probably just some harmless crank. But Charles wasn't about to take any risks.

The man stopped, hesitated then turned. As soon as he saw Charles not two feet away from him, he let out a high-pitched squeal, threw his hands to his face, and fell to the ground.
"Are you all right?" Tremayne asked.
"I wasn't following you, Mr Tremayne, sir, honest. I mean... I don't know who you are even. So why should I be following you?"
"And you are...?"
"Barry Penwrith, sir."
Charles noticed the watch on Barry's arm. If it wasn't genuine, it was an extremely good imitation of a gold Rolex Oyster Perpetual.
"I didn't think you were following me for one minute… Barry, you say?"
"Yes, sir. Mr Tremayne, sir."
"Call me Charles. After all, why would anybody want to follow me? Can you think of any reasons, Barry?"
"No, sir, Mr Tremayne... Charles, sir." His feet scuffed at the pavement, betraying his desire to be somewhere else.

Charles turned his gaze to the harbour. "Pretty harbour," he said.

"Yes, I suppose it is."

"Do only fishing boats use it, or do you get any visitors? Yachts, cruisers or such like?"

"No, just fishing boats. I have got to... I need to go to... I must... They're waiting for me. Nice meeting you, sir... Mr Tremayne, Charles."

"You too, Barry."

Tremayne watched as Barry tried to walk away in a controlled manner. He ended up looking like an Olympic speed walker. *So, it looks like the town already knows me by name.*

As he watched Barry disappear into the distance, another figure emerged from the corner of the high street. Charles scanned her as she approached. She was in her mid-sixties; her grey hair was tied in buns on each side of her head making her look as if she was wearing headphones. She was pushing a twenty-four-gear titanium framed racing-bike. With a wicker basket attached to the front drop-handlebars.

She nodded as she walked past him. "Afternoon, Mr Tremayne." And walked on.

Charles Tremayne had always been a very private man, and he was finding this familiarity disconcerting. It seemed the whole town had the jump on him, which was something else he didn't like.

"Er, excuse me!" He called after the woman. "Do you live around here? Miss... er... "

"Pomfrey," the woman said. "And it's Mrs. And no, I don't live anywhere near here. I live at the top of the high street."

"Do you know much about the town?"

"I know a little bit."

"I wonder if you can help me?"

Mrs. Pomfrey rested her weight onto the handlebars of her bicycle.

Charles continued, "I represent a film company, and we're planning on filming some scenes for a period drama here. I was just wondering if you had many strangers wandering around. I mean, we wouldn't want tourists walking into shot and ruining it, would we? Do you get many tourists, or other sort of strangers here?"

"Just the odd sightseer. They don't stay long though. Just run in with their cameras, take a few photos, and off they go again."

"Thank you, Mrs. Pomfrey."

"You're welcome, Mr Tremayne."

As he watched her push her bike to the end of the promenade and around the corner, he wondered about the communications system that allowed the whole town to know all about him within two hours of his arrival.

The smell of cooking caught Tremayne's attention, and he realised he hadn't eaten for several hours. His normal regime was to eat little and often. Never overloading his system. He followed the inviting aroma to a seafront cafe, The Fishermans Plaice. As soon as he set foot inside the place, he realised how deceptive the smell had been. The Cafe was small, and the eight tables strategically placed around the room were about all the place could handle. Each table was covered in a red and white plastic tablecloth, and in the centre of each one was a salt and pepper set with a heavily encrusted tomato-ketchup bottle.

The walls and ceiling were co-ordinated in nicotine yellow. A bearded old man sat in the corner, puffing furiously at a pipe, adding the next layer. Just above his left shoulder a small sign dangled from a red plastic chain, bravely announcing, 'It is illegal to smoke on these premises.'

Tremayne hesitated just inside the door. He fought with the twin desires of trying to fill his stomach and preserving the interior of his lungs. Hunger won. He approached the counter with the same degree of caution he would have afforded a border post at the East German frontier.

A nearly clean glass cabinet on the counter displayed some decidedly curly sandwiches and several mysterious pastry parcels. A woman appeared through some bead curtains behind the counter. She was about five-two and probably in her mid fifties. Her grey hair was tied into long plaits that fell forward over her shoulders.

"What can I get you, love?" she asked.

"Do you have any salmon, and perhaps some boiled potatoes?"

"No, but I can do you fish and chips if you like, love."

"No, no thank you. A salad?"

"No, I haven't got any salad as such. How about some baked beans if it's vegetables that you're after, love?"

"What else have you got?"

"Cornish pasty, Stilton cheese and cider pasty, chips, steak and ale pie. I could do that with some nice fried potatoes and fried onions if you liked."

Tremayne could feel his arteries clogging as she spoke. "Do you have anything that isn't either fried or wrapped in pastry?"

"Pizza?"

He decided to give in. "Go on, then. I'll have a Cornish pasty."

"Do you want chips with that?"

"Why not."

"Anything to drink?"

"A glass of dry white wine?"

"Sorry, we're not licensed. Nice cup of tea?"

"Okay, nice cup of tea."

"How many sugars?"

"Er, none, thank you."

He settled down at the table nearest the door. At least that way, he felt he could gain some fresh air. The pipe smoking man nodded at him. "Another fine day!"

"Yes it is, isn't it?"

"If this keeps up, it'll soon be time to get the onions out."

"Yes, I suppose it will." He hadn't the faintest idea what the man was talking about.

The meal arrived, a bit too quickly, meaning it was probably courtesy of the microwave. As he cut open the pasty, clouds of steam escaped confirming his fears. He stabbed a forkful of chips while waiting for the pasty to become slightly less radioactive. Chips were not a normal part of Charles' diet, and he'd forgotten quite how good they tasted. And even better once he'd managed to bring himself to apply some tomato ketchup. Time for the pasty. The meat inside was lean, tender, and mixed in with crunchy onion and lightly spiced potato. The overall effect was delightfully tasty. He surprised himself by finishing the meal. He'd intended to eat only just enough to sate his appetite.

The woman reappeared the moment he pushed his plate to one side. She must have been watching him from behind the curtains.
"Want some pudding, love?"
"Do you have any fruit?"
"No, but I've got some tinned peaches and custard. Or as a special treat, some nice treacle tart."
Treacle tart... he hadn't had that since he was a boy. Oh, what the hell! "Yes, that will do fine. Treacle tart."
"And cream?"
"Oh, in for a penny..."

By the time he'd finished, an uncomfortable, bloated feeling had settled around his stomach. Although he had to admit to having enjoyed every mouthful of his meal. He handed over the ridiculously small amount of money requested then headed back to the hotel to see if there was any sign of his errant suitcase.

***

"I've got some good news for you," Mr Goodenough said from behind the bar."Your suitcase has turned up."
"Oh, good. Where was it?"

"It'd got taken to the wrong room."
"But I thought you only had one room?"
"That's why it took so long to find it."
"But... never mind. Where is it now?"
"We took it up to your room, Sir."

The suitcase was waiting for him on the bed. It had sunk into the soft mattress so far that the top was just level with the candlewick bed cover. A cursory inspection was all that was needed to reveal that the lock had been forced. He checked through the contents. Although still neatly folded, his clothes were not in the order in which he had originally placed them. As a frequent traveller, Charles had developed his own methodology about how his clothes were packed and layered. Fortunately, there was nothing of any significance within the case. His important possessions were in the alarmed briefcase on the top of the wardrobe, which a quick check revealed had not been disturbed.

He removed the suitcase from the bed and lay back. For some reason, he was feeling unaccountably sleepy. He briefly wondered if his food had been drugged but decided that was taking caution to the point of paranoia. He drifted into sleep.

Chapter 4

Tom Trevellick stretched his feet out and rested them on the opposite seat of the first-class train compartment. It had been a long time since he'd last left Little Didney, and even then, he never usually ventured further than Truro. Or Plymouth for the big adventure. This was his first journey ever to London. It wasn't that he hadn't wanted to visit London before, it was just that he'd never felt able to leave the farm. But now, things were a bit different. The farm would survive without him for a day or two.

The ticket inspector caught his eye as he entered the carriage. He strode along pulling out his report pad on the way.
"Come along," he said. "Sling your hook!"
"I got a ticket, you know." Trevellick pulled a screwed up piece of paper from his shirt pocket and handed it to the inspector.
"Well, you can get your boots off the seat anyway."
Tom did as requested, leaving a muddy stain on the opposite seat.
"This is only a standard fare ticket," the inspector said as he straightened out the crumpled piece of paper on his pad. "This is a first class compartment, you know. You'll have to move back to the other carriage or pay the excess."
"That's all right," Tom said. He dipped into a brown paper bag that was parked on the seat next to him and pulled out a handful of crumpled notes. "How much is it then?"

The inspector wrote out a receipt and amended Tom's ticket. His expression never moved above sour.
Tom settled back into his seat and watched the countryside roll by. He was fascinated by the way the carelessly defined Cornish fields gave way to the more tightly arranged Devon and Somerset farms, which in turn, became more and more regimented the further east he travelled.

His rumbling stomach told him it was time for supper, and he set off in search of the dining car. The waiter's gaze scoured him as he waited to be seated. He was glad he'd put on his Sunday best clothes before setting out, but he *was* beginning to regret the fact he'd stopped to help them get the tractor out of the mud just before leaving the farm. He was well aware that his green cord trousers were not quite as smart as when he had first put them on, and his white cotton shirt was no longer white. But he couldn't for the life of him understand why everybody kept staring and making funny faces. The waiter made a particularly funny face. Almost as if there were a unpleasant smell in the room.

He was shown to a double table at the far end of the carriage. A middle-aged woman was already seated in the opposite chair. He lifted his hat in acknowledgement.
"Good day to you, ma'am."
She smiled, and said, "Good afternoon to you." Then wrinkled her nose.

Tom sat down, and the waiter passed him a menu. He was just about to leave when Tom grabbed his arm.
"Hang on there, me old mate. I haven't told you what I want yet."
"If you'd care to review the menu, sir, I'll call back and collect your order shortly."
"No need for that. I'll tell you now." Tom opened the menu and stared uncomprehendingly at the page. "This is all foreign!"
"Yes, sir. It's in French."
"Is this a French train then?"
"No, sir."
"Well, why is all this in French then? I don't want any bloody French food. I want English food. What's wrong with English food anyway? I grow as good a cow as any bloody Frenchman"
"This *is* English food, sir. It's just written in French."
"All right then. I'll have some soup and a meat pie."
"What sort of soup would Sir like?"

"Brown soup."

"Very good, sir. I'm afraid we don't have any meat pies, sir. We do have a nice Beef Wellington though."

"What's that, then?"

"It's a prime fillet of beef, with pate de foie gras, coated in a light puff pastry crust and served with Madeira laced gravy "

"Sounds like a meat pie to me. I'll have that with roast potatoes and lots of your dear gravy."

"My dear gravy?… Oh, I see, Madeira gravy…As you wish, Sir."

***

By the time he'd finished his meal, he'd added a few touches of French Onion soup and Madeira gravy to the mess already on his shirt. He just hadn't been able to get the hang of the swaying motion of the train. It seemed that every time he raised a spoon or a fork to his mouth, the train would hurtle around a fresh bend causing the contents to flop onto his shirt. The woman sitting opposite him watched in fascination as Trevellick's clothes gathered more and more debris.

***

Once he'd arrived at London Paddington, he found a taxi and offered the only hotel name he knew. The Ritz. The taxi driver scanned him up and down, sniffed the air and said, "The Ritz? Are you sure, pal? "

He showed the cabby his paper bag full of money. "I can pay the fare, look!"

"You want to be careful with that, pal. Flash that in the wrong place and you'll lose the lot. Your clothes as well, probably."

"Oh, right, thank you." He clutched the paper bag tightly to him and the cab driver set off for the Ritz.

The doorman took some convincing before he would let Trevellick inside. But once inside, the reception staff were much more accommodating. They were well used to dealing with the quirks and foibles of England's eccentrics. Especially when they paid three days up front and in crumpled fifty-pound notes. The porter showed him upstairs to a huge suite with a balcony overlooking Green Park. He tipped the porter a pound coin. As soon as he was on his own, he rushed round the suite, poking and trying everything.

The mini bar was the first item to catch his interest. Within a few minutes, he'd seen off the two bottles of German lager, three miniature whiskies and both miniature gins. He abandoned the champagne after the first sip, deciding that it was a poor substitute for cider.

He next turned his attention to the huge oval Jacuzzi bath. He turned both taps on full then emptied the entire contents of a bottle of bubble bath into it.

He switched the Jacuzzi jet control to maximum then went back into the main room to play with the television.

***

Charles Tremayne dragged himself into wakefulness. He clawed his way off the bed that seemed to want to suck him deeper into its folds. His back ached, and he was feeling unusually sluggish. He glanced at his watch. Hell! Seven o'clock in the evening! He'd been asleep for nearly three hours. He'd never done that before. He changed quickly then headed downstairs.

Tremayne's eyes were watering even before he reached the bottom step. Pipe smoking seemed to be a favourite pastime of the villagers. Layers of smoke hung in the air like strands of blue lace.

The bar was nearly full. A folk singer sat on a stool near the fire plucking out a tuneless melody on a battered guitar and wailing in a peculiar high-pitched manner about a girl named Sally-Ann.

Tremayne stopped at the bar, and Sandy gave him a big smile, "What's your pleasure, Charles?" she asked. There always seemed to be another dimension to everything she said.
"I don't know. What does everybody drink around here?"
"That's very generous of you, Charles."
"Huh?"
"This gentleman has just offered to buy everybody here a drink," she called, pointing at Charles as she looked around the room.
"No, I didn't mean..."
"Yes?"
He thought he could detect a sharpness in her eye. Had she purposely misunderstood?
"Oh, go on then."

Within seconds, he was being squashed against the bar by a sea of bodies. People patted him on the back or tried to shake his hand.
"You're a scholar, Sir."
"A real gent."
"Make mine a double Scotch, Sandy."
"Brandy please."
"Two pints of cider."
"Good health to you, Sir."
"I'll have a packet of pork scratchings with that!"

Despite the annoyance he felt at being conned like this he maintained his smile, and nodded politely at each complement paid him.
"Seems like a nice, quiet little village," he said to Sandy as he settled the bill.
"Yes, it is nice and peaceful."
"I don't suppose you get much excitement here, do you?"
"Ah, we did have some excitement the other day."
Tremayne was careful to avoid letting the interest he felt show in his expression. "Oh, yes," he said. "What was that?"

"Barry ran over Mrs Pomfrey's bike in his new car. Such a to-do there was." Her eyes narrowed, as if studying him for a response. Was she playing with him? Testing him? If so, why?

This village had another layer to it. A hidden level. Was it anything to do with the missing money, or were they all just worried he was a tax inspector who might uncover one of their little scams.
"I hope nobody was hurt."
"Oh, no." Her head jerked up as somebody across the bar snagged her attention. "Look, Old Bill wants you." She pointed over to a corner table where the pipe smoking man from the Cafe was seated. Old Bill waved his arm, beckoning Tremayne to join him. Charles weaved his way through the pressing crowd, receiving a few more pats on the back as he went. He settled himself in the seat opposite Old Bill.

The smoke from Bill's pipe gathered around his head like clouds on a mountaintop. He held up his glass of brown, frothy liquid in Tremayne's direction. "Cheers!"
Charles returned the gesture.
"So, you're making a film then?" Old Bill said between sucks on his pipe.
"Yes, it's based on a novel by Thomas Hardy."
"Oh, right. You're not a gangster, then?"
"No, not at all. What makes you ask something like that?"

Old Bill sucked on his pipe. It gave a deep gurgling noise, but no smoke appeared. He pulled a gold Dunhill lighter from his tweed coat pocket and poked his finger into the bowl of the pipe as he sucked the flame in. Tremayne wondered why his finger didn't burn. He also wondered where he'd come by a gold Dunhill lighter. Tremayne waited patiently while Old Bill sucked, prodded, and gurgled. Although what he really wanted to do, was to snatch the pipe away from him, throw it out of the window, and grab him by the neck to wring the information out of him.

Once satisfied the pipe was under way again, Bill slid the lighter back in his pocket and relaxed back into his seat.

"This is not my usual tobacco, you know, this one."

"Oh, really?" Tremayne hoped his frustration didn't show.

"No, I used to smoke Rough Cut. But this is Black Shag. It's quite nice for a change. Here, have a try." He thrust the pipe towards Tremayne.

"No, thank you. I don't smoke."

"Go on. It'll clear your tubes out. You look like you could use your tubes clearing out."

Tremayne didn't want to upset the man. Not now he felt near to actually getting some useful information. Oh well, for Queen and Country! He took the pipe. At least he managed to surreptitiously wipe the end of it with his hand.

He took a deep pull, and the pipe gurgled noisily. The acrid smoke seemed to roll round the whole of his insides, setting off cough reactions in every corner of his lungs. He held his breath to try to suppress the spasms, but in doing so, managed to increase the level of nicotine hitting his blood stream. He didn't know whether to cough, vomit, or fall over. He thrust the pipe back towards Old Bill. "Very good, thank you," he managed to say. A blue cloud accompanied each word. "You were telling me about gangsters."

He felt a movement alongside him and caught sight of Sandy sliding into the seat next to his.

"Oh, you don't want to pay too much attention to Old Bill," she said. "He's had a thing about gangsters ever since the community centre film club ran a James Cagney season."

"Oh, yes," Old Bill said. "Jimmy Cagney. Here's looking at you, you rat!" He gave a loud wheezing laugh that exposed most of his few remaining teeth.

"Yes, but…" Charles was reluctant to let this go just yet. "Maybe he did—"

"Have you heard of the village secret yet?" Sandy asked.

"No, what's that?" Charles' curiosity levels were running high once more.

"I'll show you tomorrow, if you like."

"Can't you tell me now?"

"No, I need to show you. Meet me here in the bar at ten o'clock tomorrow morning." She stood, gathered a few empty glasses, and headed back for the bar.

Old Bill pointed his finger, pistol-style, and aimed it at Tremayne. He hissed, "You killed my brother. You dirty rat." He erupted into fresh giggles.

The noise and smoke in the bar was providing an assault on his senses that he didn't feel able to tolerate any longer. He left the bar and headed down to the seafront, once more following the promenade west. The earlier aromas of diesel and fish had been replaced with a fresh ozone smell drifting in from the Channel. The sun was just beginning its descent below the horizon, and the water sparkled with reflected reds and oranges of the sky above.

He sat for a while on the end of a concrete breakwater and watched the waves as they tugged at the shingle. Not for the first time, he found himself wondering if the villagers were being intentionally cantankerous, or was this just their strange way. He was still inclined to believe they were probably just concerned about whether he was a tax inspector. Despite the outward signs of a village struggling to survive, the little pockets of extravagance he'd noticed indicated a thriving black economy.

A little flutter of hunger demanded his attention. *That's funny*, he thought, *I had a huge late lunch.* I shouldn't be hungry again already. As he straightened up, he wondered if the little Cafe was still open. He continued along the promenade. And yes, it was. The same woman was still on duty.

"Have you got any more of that treacle tart?" he asked.

***

The electronic chirping of his satellite phone jerked Charles awake. His hand reached for the phone as he sat up, at least as upright as the cloying mattress would allow. He checked the display on the phone before stabbing the answer button. It was Elaine.

"Elaine," he said. "Why so early?"

"Early, Charles? Its twenty past nine."

"What?"

"Don't tell me you've over-slept!" He heard laughter in her voice.

His bleary eyes searched for the bedside clock and confirmed Elaine was indeed telling the truth.

"I must be going down with something." He normally snapped awake at seven o'clock sharp. Never needing an alarm clock.

"Sure you've not been up all night partying?"

"I don't think there's much chance of that. This place goes to bed at ten o'clock. Anyway, why did you ring?"

"Just thought you'd be interested to know one of your villagers has been picked up by the police here in London."

"In London?"

"Yes. A character called Tom Trevellick. Owns a farm down there somewhere."

"Yes, I've heard the name. What's he been up to? And why's he up in London?"

"He's been arrested for trashing a suite at the Ritz."

"The Ritz? Sounds like an odd place for a farmer to be staying?"

"That's what the police thought. Which is why it came to our attention. Apparently he checked in yesterday evening, and within a couple of hours, he'd seen off the contents of his mini bar, flooded the place, and blasted the television set with a twelve-bore shotgun."

Charles pulled himself free of the bed. "Any explanation given?"

"He claimed the television was the spawn of the devil and the doorway into hell itself."

"I guess he found the in-house movie channel then?"
"Probably."
"Is this just coincidence, do you think?"
"Well, he had a large amount of cash on him. Although that in itself is not unusual for some elements of the farming community. But I thought it worth flagging."
"Yes, thanks."
He slid the phone back in his case.

***

Sandy was waiting for him in the bar. "Sleep well?"
"Yes, surprisingly well, thank you."
"Sea air and good food. Talking of which, do you want some breakfast?"
"I don't usually bother."
"That's no way to carry on. You'll never grow up to be big and strong if you don't eat your breakfast. You wait there, I'll fix you something." She disappeared into the kitchen. A few minutes later, the smell of cooking bacon drifted through the bar.

He sat down at a table next to the window. Bright sunlight streamed in through the lead latticework and cast a geometric pattern on the oak table. He looked around the bar. The place was spotless. Sandy had obviously been busy for several hours already.

She reappeared with a large tray, which she placed on the table in front of him. "There you go. Get yourself outside that!"
Charles cast his gaze over the mountain of food in front of him. Bacon, eggs, fried potatoes, fried-bread, sausages, baked beans, and that was just the surface layer. Goodness knows what lay underneath.
"That's not a breakfast," he said. "That's a murder weapon. If I eat this, I'm likely to be committed to a psychiatric ward for attempted suicide."
"Get on with it. That'll set you up for the day."
He speared the nearest sausage. "Are you still going to

let me go out to play even if I don't eat it all?"

She smiled and picked up the tray. "I'm just going to finish clearing up in the kitchen. See you in a minute."

Fifteen minutes later, Charles pushed the remains of his breakfast to one side. Sandy appeared as if out of nowhere and collected the plate.

"Well, you ate most of it!"

"That," he said, "was extraordinarily good."

"All local produce. None of your water injected, genetically modified mono-sodium glutamate here. You ready then?"

"Yes, I must say I am rather intrigued by this town secret."

"We'll take your car then, shall we?"

"Why mine?"

"Because I haven't got one."

Even by eleven o'clock, the interior of his car had reached a high enough temperature to make the leather seat uncomfortable to sit on. As soon as he'd started the engine, he switched the air conditioning unit up to full.

"Ooh, that's nice," Sandy said, as the chill breeze washed across her face.

As they pulled out of the car park, he flicked on the CD player, and the sound of Rigoletto rolled around the interior.

"Yuck! What's that?" Sandy asked. "How can you listen to that stuff?"

"Opera? It's relaxing."

"There's nothing relaxing about opera. It's violent music."

"Violent music?"

"Yes. Take any opera you care to name, and I guarantee the body-count will be far higher than in any Quentin Tarantino movie!"

He laughed and conceded she probably had a point.

"What sort of music do you like then, Sandy?"

"Rock. Something with guitars and drums. Something with attitude. Dire Straits, they're my favourite. Romeo and

Juliet. Have you ever listened to that? It's beautiful and passionate."

"That's not bad I suppose," Tremayne said. It was one of the few bands of that type he actually liked.

Sandy guided him round the increasingly narrowing lanes that eventually gave way to a steep, downward-sloping gravel track. They came to a small grassy pull-in.

"That's as far as we can go," Sandy said.

He locked the car and set the alarm. Sandy led the way down the steep path that dropped into a narrow gorge. At the bottom of the gorge, they followed a twisting trail, and then, as he rounded a corner, they emerged into a small sandy cove no more than fifty feet wide. High rocky cliffs flanked them on three sides. Granite and sandstone layered into the cliffs and displayed the aeons that had gone before. From the centre of the gorge, a clear stream ran through to the sea. It tumbled over a bed of pebbles, rounded by the millennia.

"What do you think?" she asked.
"Of what?"
"The village secret. Here, look." She waved her arms indicating the cove. "That. That's the village secret."
"That?"
"Yes, it's only the villagers that know it's here. No tourists, no families with screaming kids and no ghetto-blasters. Just peace and seclusion."

That small part of him that had been hoping beyond reason that the village secret would in some way be related to the missing money, sank back into its cave.

"It's great," he said. Trying to feel it.
"Come and sit down." Sandy planted herself onto the shingle.

Charles did as he was told. Sandy opened her leather shoulder bag and removed a bottle of wine and two glasses. She passed him the bottle. "You do the honours?"
"Do you have a corkscrew?"
"Nothing that sophisticated. It's a twist-off top."

"Oh, how unusual!" He opened the bottle and poured the wine into their glasses. "Cheers," he said.

"Cheers!"

The wine was warm and sweet but still quite pleasant. He stretched his feet out, enjoying the warmth of the sun.

***

Jerry Richards slammed a phone book on the table with as loud a bang as he could manage.

"Will you all shut up!" he shouted.

The noise in the church hall subsided to mumble-level.

"Thank you. Now we don't have much time. We're not sure how long Sandy can keep him occupied for. I've called in a favour from an old pal of mine in the London Police, and he can find no trace of this Charles Tremayne. He doesn't exist. That means he's government"

"Oh dear," said the Reverend Featherstone. He adjusted his new toupee. It was just a little too brown, and just a little too large. "I think we should give it back."

"That's not an option any more, vicar," said Jerry. "Despite what we agreed two days ago, everybody's been running around spending this money like it's Christmas."

"Oh, dear. Oh, dear."

"We're all right as long as we don't panic. But we mustn't spend any more. That's bound to give the game away. Look at the mess Tom's got himself into. I mean, fancy getting arrested. How unsubtle can you get?"

"He didn't mean to do it," insisted Mrs. Trevellick. "He was just going up to London to buy me a present. He didn't realise how strong that fancy alcohol was. That's all. He's a cider man at heart."

"That's not the point, Mrs. Trevellick. Everybody, the only way this is going to work is if we all put the money away for a few years. Just forget we've got it. Mr Cobbledick will tell you. You can't just suddenly dump two hundred million into circulation without raising a few eyebrows. Isn't that right, Mr Cobbledick?" He looked around the room. "Mr Cobbledick? Where's Mr

Cobbledick?"

***

Mr Cobbledick was at that moment taking possession of his new powerboat. He'd caught the early morning train to Falmouth, and from the station taken a taxi to Poseidon Powerboats in the docks. His only previous experience with boating had been when he had hired out a small cabin-cruiser to explore the Norfolk Broads some five years ago. He remembered being disappointed with the lack of power and had always promised himself a more powerful boat, if he could ever afford it.

In his mind, the word powerful boat, and powerboat were interchangeable. But not to the designers of Poseidon Powerboats. They took great pride in creating some of the most powerful machines that ever graced the water. They were particularly proud of the Mark III Trident that had caught Mr Cobbledick's eye.

"Twin Mercury engines with titanium screws kicking out a total of over four hundred horse-power..."
The salesman waffled on. Nonsense words and meaningless jumble. What Mr Cobbledick saw was a sleek blue shape, with a bow sharp enough to cut silk, and body-hugging leather seats.
"I'll have that, then!" he said stopping the salesman mid-flow.
"What?"
"This one. I'll take it. Thank you very much."
"Right... Yes, well. If you'd just like to step into the office for a moment, sir, we'll complete the paperwork and arrange delivery."
"No need to deliver it. I'll drive it away."
"I'm afraid that won't be possible, sir. Not until we've completed the financial formalities."
"What financial formalities are those, then? There shouldn't be any financial formalities. I'll be paying cash." He patted his briefcase.

Twenty minutes later, he was sitting in one of the leather seats while the salesman showed him the controls.

"These are the throttle levers, Gaffrig design, pull them back and that controls the power. It has Keikhaefer Trim Tabs. Here's the fuel mixture control..."

Mr Cobbledick tried to take it all in. But most of it just sounded like gobbledegook. No doubt he'd get the hang of it. Trial and error was all that was needed. That was the way he worked out how to use the cabin cruiser on The Norfolk Broads.

"Do you want me to come with you while you try it out, sir?"

"No, that won't be necessary, son."

"Well, there you are then. She's all yours."

They shook hands, and the salesman climbed ashore.

Mr Cobbledick turned the key, and the engines exploded into life. He eased the throttle levers back ever so gently and the water boiled behind the boat, the nose lifted into the air. Now that's what he called a powerful boat! The thrum of the engines vibrated through his seat. He could feel the restrained power just waiting to be unleashed. With surgical precision, he guided the boat out from Falmouth harbour and into open water.

He pointed the needle-sharp bow to the west then pulled back on the throttles. The rear of the boat dug into the water, lifting the craft to an angle of thirty degrees. Mr Cobbledick toppled backwards out of his seat and was only saved from disappearing into the water by a manic grip with his right hand on the steering wheel. His left hand flailed out, frantically looking for something to hang onto. It eventually settled on the throttle levers causing the power to increase even further. The boat skimmed across the surface of the water like a flat pebble thrown by a child. Cobbledick's feet trailed in the air behind the boat. Physical exertion of this type was a new experience. Hands that usually gripped nothing more demanding than a fountain pen or a teacup were now being asked to keep him safe from the whirling propellers not twenty inches away from his flailing feet.

As the boat hurtled away from the shore, the waves became larger. Each one hit the boat with a loud bang then threw it into the air briefly before landing on the next. A constant torrent of water washed over the side and across the top of Mr Cobbledick. The buffeting knocked him from side to side. Each inch of lateral movement caused him to swing more violently on the steering wheel, which in turn caused an even more violent yawing motion of the boat. He consciously fought to hold the steering wheel straight and gradually the yawing subsided. Dragging on reserves of strength he didn't know he had, he pulled on both the steering wheel and the throttle levers, and managed to bring himself far enough forward to brace his feet against the rear guard-rail. He crouched on all fours with his backside raised into the air and his back arched in the manner of a frightened cat. But at least he was on board. With his left hand, he tried to push forward on the throttle levers. They were jammed. The severe pounding they'd taken had probably bent something. They were locked on full power setting. But at least he had some slight control over the steering.

***

"So," Charles said. "Have you lived in Little Didney all your life?"
"Not yet!" She grinned.
"You know what I mean."
"I was born here, and I expect I'll die here. I can't honestly think of anywhere else I'd rather be." She lay back on the shingle and closed her eyes against the sun.
"You've never fancied travelling abroad?"
"Nice to visit. But I'd always want to come home."
"What if you had a lot of money? Say you won the lottery. Would you still live here?"
She sat up and locked her eyes with his. He felt as if she were searching his mind.

"What a strange question to ask, Mr Tremayne."

The sound of a screaming engine and loud bangs took their attention out to sea. A sleek, blue powerboat bounced across the waves not a hundred metres from the shore. Each time the propellers left the water, the engine noise increased, culminating in a loud thump when it hit the next wave. A figure crouched on the rear of the boat. He seemed to be trying to stand, as though on a surfboard.

"Bloody idiot!" Sandy said. "What *does* he think he's doing?"

"Well, whoever it is, he's certainly got a feel for adventure. That's quite some stunt, trying to stand up on the back of one of those. That thing must be doing sixty knots."

As the boat disappeared around the headland, the sound of the engine faded.

"I'd better get back," Charles said. "I've got some scenes to plan."

"Can't you stay a little longer? It's so nice here." She tipped her head to one side and raised an eyebrow. Charles felt his normal single-mindedness waver. Either the money was here, or it wasn't. Whichever, an hour or so wasn't going to make a lot of difference.

"What do you suggest we do?"

Her head jerked backwards a fraction, as if she'd been startled by his question.

"Do? I'm not suggesting we do anything. Just relax. Enjoy the day." She lay back on the stones again.

Charles struggled for a moment to make sense of her stop-go behaviour. He gave up and lay back himself, enjoying the feeling of the warm sunlight penetrating his clothes. There *was* something quite pleasant about this place. A natural isolation.

"Where are all the people, Sandy?" he asked after a while.

"What do you mean?" She propped herself up on one elbow to study him.

"Well, there must be seven or eight hundred houses in this village but I've only seen a handful of people."

"This is a ghost village, Charles You heard of those?"

"Probably not in the context you mean." He smiled.

"Grockles, weekenders, ghosts, call them what you like. Half the property in this village is owned by 'Second Homers'. People who live in London then visit their cottage- by-the-sea for four weekends a year. They're tearing the heart out of the place."

"But surely they bring money in?"

"Money! They turn up here in their people-carriers stuffed with Marks and Spencer's food. They may have they odd pint in the beer garden while they grumble about the price of beer. They put *nothing* in, Charles. The village is dying because they don't buy in the shops yet they push the property prices out of reach of families here."

Charles realised he'd touched a nerve. "Perhaps they could be persuaded to fit in a bit more. You know, invite them to the next hog roast or something?"

Sandy said nothing, just gave him a scathing look then lay back with her hands behind her head, squinting at the sky. Her silence told Charles that the subject was over and that he'd crossed a line somewhere.

"Smoking that pipe suited you, you know," she said after a short while. "Made you look sort of... macho, more relaxed."

"I didn't feel more relaxed. I felt as though there were a tiger inside my lungs clawing his way out."

"Perhaps you should start with a milder tobacco."

"I have no intention of starting at all. I am very fussy about what I put into my body."

"So why did you smoke it in the first place? Or were you just trying to butter up Old Bill to get him to talk?" She sat up and once more he felt those eyes searching his face.

He'd been trained to withstand interrogation by everyone up to the KGB. But he found it difficult to withstand Sandy's particular brand of questioning. He made a conscious effort to control his expression.

"Not at all, just being sociable."

She lowered her face and looked at him as if she were peering across the top of half-moon spectacles. He knew she didn't believe him. "Come on, I really have to get back."

They scrambled up the gravel-strewn path. At one point she slipped, Tremayne's hand reached out instinctively, catching her on the elbow. She turned briefly, closing her hand on his for added support as she regained her balance. In that transient moment of body contact, he felt a spike of energy flash through his system.

***

By the time they'd reached the car, Tremayne was breaking a sweat. Too much soft living of late. He sank gratefully into the leather interior and flicked the switch for the air conditioning.

Nothing.

He tried a few other controls and turned the ignition key. Dead. He grabbed the steering wheel with such ferocity that his hands shook. Sandy touched his arm. "What's wrong, Charles?"

" Bloody car won't start. Damned heap of junk!"

"Calm down. You don't need to get into such a state. The sun will still rise tomorrow whether your car starts or not."

"I don't need home-spun philosophy right now, thank you!" He said, then instantly regretted the anger in his voice. "What I need is a mechanic."

"We'll have to walk back, I guess," she said. "It will only take an hour or so."

"I'll ring for a break-down truck." He unclipped his phone.

"Mobile phones don't work here, you know. The companies haven't got round to putting masts up yet."

"No, this is not cellular. This is a satellite phone. It will work anywhere on earth."

"Isn't that a bit over the top for a location scout?"

Hell, she was astute!

"Well you never know when they're going to send me out to the wilds of some jungle or other in search of a location." Had he got away with it? A quick glance at her face told him no.

He dialled the number of his breakdown service and gave his details.

"Where are we?" he asked her.

"Cannard's Cove. Here, let me, I'll explain." She reached for his phone and gave precise directions to the operator. When she had finished, she looked at the face of the phone, pressed the off button, and said, "Very smart. And how much would something like this cost then?"

The breakdown truck arrived after about thirty minutes. It was the same repairman as before.

"You're not having a lot of luck, are you, sir? Perhaps you ought to stick to English cars. Stay away from this German stuff."

"Yes, thank you. I'll keep that in mind."

As the mechanic worked inside the engine he gave Charles a running commentary, which due to Charles' lack of interest in all things mechanical, the only words he picked out were, "Wire", "Dislodged" and "Knackered."

"Can you fix it?"

"Oh yes, sir. Just a matter of re-attaching this cable here, and..." the engine sprang into life. "There we go."

"What would cause something like that?" Tremayne asked.

"Any number of things, sir. It might have happened when you got tangled up in that barbed wire the other day. Or squirrels."

"Squirrels?"

"Yes, squirrels sometimes get inside engines and try to make a nest of the wires."

"Could it have been intentional?"

"Well they usually just build their nests without much

fore-thought!"

"No! I meant could *somebody* have done it intentionally?"

"I suppose. But usually the little sods who tinker with cars do it to make them go, not to make them stop."

Unless, Charles thought, somebody wants to stop me being somewhere. Perhaps it's time I had a word with the local constable.

***

When they arrived back in the village, Charles asked Sandy to show him where the Police Station was situated. She led him up a narrow alley that ran between two shops, pointed to a hand painted sign that said 'Police' then left him to it.

The door to the police station appeared to be the back entrance to a Baker's shop. When he saw the shape of police constable Muchmore, he wondered if that was just coincidence, or careful planning.

The constable prised his bulk out of the too-small desk chair as Tremayne entered the room.

"Ah, hello, Mr Tremayne. I was wondering when you'd pay me a visit."

Tremayne's eyes scanned the office. The wooden desk at which Muchmore had been seated wore a faded leather cover. It was littered in paper. Pride of place, at the centre of the desk was devoted to a plate of biscuits. Obviously one of the perks of working behind a Baker's shop. A portable television set flickered football results from the top of a filing cabinet.

Tremayne closed the door behind himself. "Mind if I sit down?" He pointed to a wooden chair opposite the desk.

"Be my guest. What can I do for you, Mr Tremayne?"

"I assume you're aware of the Official Secrets Act?"

"Yes." Muchmore's voice was laden with suspicion.

"Well, what I'm about to tell you, falls within the scope of that act."

"Why would a film company be covered by the Official Secrets Act?" Muchmore sat down and relaxed back into his chair.

"That's just my cover. I'm actually an agent for MI6."

"What could possibly be of interest to MI6 in Little Didney?" The constable didn't look surprised enough.

"Did you hear the helicopters over here the other day?"

"Yes, that happens all the time. There's a Navy air base not fifty miles away."

"Well, those helicopters were there to track down a gang of truck hijackers."

"We've not seen any of them around here. I'll let you know if we do." Muchmore started to rise out of his seat. An indication that in his mind, the conversation was over.

Tremayne held out his hand, motioning that Muchmore should remain seated. The constable settled back again

"No, we've got the hijackers. What we didn't get, was the lorry they'd hijacked. That just disappeared not three miles away from here."

"Not seen any lorries either. What was in it?"

Charles studied Muchmore's face closely, waiting for a reaction to his next words. "Two hundred and fifty million pounds in cash." The reaction was there. Muchmore was genuinely surprised. A quick jerk of the head, a querulous eyebrow, and the unmistakable slight dilation of the pupils.

"Two hundred and fifty million, you say?"

Tremayne felt that he'd emphasised the fifty part a little too much, but dismissed it.

"Yes, in one hundred packing cases marked 'Books for Pulping."

"Definitely two hundred and fifty million? In one *hundred* cases?"

"Yes," Tremayne said.

"Do you mean approximately two hundred and fifty, give or take say fifty million or so?"

"No, I mean two hundred and fifty million."

"I suppose whoever counted it could have made a mistake though, couldn't they? I mean, a few million either way, easily done?"

"No," Tremayne said, becoming exasperated. "It was two hundred and fifty million. Exactly two hundred and fifty million. It had been counted several times. People given charge of two hundred and fifty million don't make mistakes like that."

"Right." Muchmore cast his eyes upwards as if in deep thought. Tremayne decided it must be the sheer quantity of money involved that had thrown Muchmore.

The constable seemed to recover his senses.

"And what did you say this money was for?"

"I didn't. And that's beyond your 'need-to-know' basis."

"Well, where do you think it's gone, then?"

"My guess is that there was a third party involved, and that the money was transported from here by boat over to the continent. This is where you come in. I need to know what strangers have been seen around here over the last few days. Any boats you've never noticed before? "

"Okay, I'll have an ask around then. I'll come back to you if I hear anything." Muchmore rose from his seat again, this time, Tremayne didn't stop him. Things hadn't gone quite the way he'd hoped, or anticipated. Although he could quite see how mention of two hundred and fifty million going missing would likely unsettle a country copper.

Just as Tremayne was leaving Muchmore caught him by the elbow. "Definitely two hundred and fifty million then?"

"Yes," Tremayne said.

"In one hundred cases? Not ninety?

"Two hundred and fifty million in one hundred cases. But you will let me know if two hundred million turns up in ninety cases won't you? I mean, it just might be the same money!"

"Oh, aye," said Muchmore, his eyes still held an unfocused look. Tremayne's sarcasm was clearly wasted.

***

The Money That Never Was

Despite the huge breakfast he'd eaten, a morning spent in the fresh air, scrambling steep paths had created quite an appetite. He decided to see what was on offer at the Cafe.

As soon as he turned onto the little promenade, he was caught with such a strange sight that his feet almost slid to a halt. The rear end of a blue powerboat protruded from the Fish Shop next door to the Cafe. Scratches all along the boat's surface corresponded with gouges in the promenade, showing where the boat had leapt out of the water, straight into the front of the shop. Pieces of glass and splinters of timber lay scattered across the pavement.

He peered in through the window. The pointed nose of the boat was skewered into the shop's counter. The shopkeeper, a small man with a blue and white striped apron, was sweeping the floor.
"What happened here?" Tremayne asked.
The man looked at him with an expression that managed to convey total scorn.
"This here boat came through my window."
I suppose I asked for that one, thought Tremayne. "Sorry, I meant how did it happen?"
"I don't know. I was out back at the time. I just heard this huge crash. I came through to see what was going on, and this is what I find." He waved his arm around the devastation.

Charles ran his hand along the edge of the boat. "This is brand new," he said.
"Not any more, he isn't."
"You didn't see who was driving it?"
"No, probably yobs."
"Yobs with expensive tastes."

Tremayne left the shopkeeper to his clearing up and went next door to the Cafe. He was the only customer. He wondered how this place made any money. The woman appeared from the beaded curtains just as he arrived at the counter.

"Oh, good afternoon, Mr Tremayne. What would you like today? I have got some treacle tart put by for you for afters. I know how much you like that."

"Ah, right, thank you."

"How about some fish and chips? Got some nice fresh cod just come in."

The portion, when it arrived was anything but small. Chips spilled over onto the table as she put the plate down in front of him.

"There you are, that will feed the inner man."

Why is it, he wondered, that everybody round here has to give a pithy little saying whenever they present him with food?

"Thank you, wonderful." And it did look wonderful. The chips glistened golden-brown. The batter was even-coloured and beautifully crisp. He decided to go traditional and liberally sprinkled salt and vinegar across the meal.

"You ought to open up a place in London," he called as he cut into the cod. "You'd make a fortune."

"Oh, I can't be having any truck with the big city."

The cod was flaky, white, and beautifully moist. The chips were just the right texture. Crispy on the outside and beautifully soft inside.

He finished the meal and slid the plate to one side, patting his stomach. "I couldn't eat another thing."

"Oh, that's a shame," she said as she reappeared with his treacle tart and custard.

It really did look delicious.

"Well, perhaps I can find a corner for that."

By the time he'd left the Cafe, he once more had the bloated feeling he'd remembered from his last visit. However, this time, it didn't seem quite so uncomfortable. In fact, it felt rather pleasant.

The Money That Never Was

He skirted around the stern of the Powerboat still protruding from the fishmonger's window then turned into the high street.

He heard the commotion even before he saw where it was coming from. Raised voices, in amongst which, something that sounded like a frightened pig. What new delights did this village hold now? Pig-baiting?

A crowd of people gathered around at the far end of the high street, some three hundred yards away. They were oblivious to his presence. They were grouped around a lamp post from which something large dangled, although at this distance, he couldn't make out what it was. He stayed close to the buildings for cover as he continued walking. He wanted to get as close as possible before they noticed him.

He'd only covered about half the distance when he heard his name being called. Faces turned in his direction, and hands pointed. The group dispersed like smoke in a draught, melting back into the narrow streets. They left the dark shape swinging from the lamppost.

As he approached, the lump resolved itself into a person hanging upside down by his ankles.

Barry Penwrith.

He was making a strange, high-pitched squealing noise. Tremayne quickened his pace. As soon as he arrived at the scene he slipped a knife from his pocket, grabbed hold of Barry, lifted his weight, and slit the rope. Barry tumbled unceremoniously into a heap on the ground.

When Barry had sufficiently gathered his senses enough to stand, Tremayne asked him, "What was all that about, Barry?"
"Just friendly joshing, Mr Tremayne, sir, Charles. High spirits. I have got to go now... The er... the things ready... I'm meeting... I'll be late."

This time, Barry made no pretence at walking. He ran as fast as his short legs and wobbling stomach would allow.

Tremayne had no difficulty in following him. Barry's cottage was situated about a mile out of town, at the end of a short muddy drive. Tremayne stayed in the shadows of some trees while he observed it. The walls were cob-stone and topped with a thatched roof. The front door was missing. Lawn flanked the cottage on the three sides that Tremayne could see. The front lawn was a mixture of long grass, cut grass and gouged earth. In the centre, sat a brand new sit-upon lawnmower.

A bright blue shape protruding from the right-hand wall caught his attention. He moved in for a closer look. About twelve inches of what appeared to be a corner bath poked out of a rough hole in the upstairs wall. Bright gold taps sparkled from the top of it.

Tremayne slid back into the shadows then made his way back to the pub.

Chapter 5

Sandy was already behind the bar when Tremayne returned. "What kept you?" she asked.

"Oh, just wandering."

"What can I get you?"

Tremayne weighed the question carefully. Was this going to cost him drinks for the whole village again? Very clearly he enunciated, "I'll try a pint of cider, please." There, that couldn't be taken the wrong way.

"Local, or bottled?"

He only just stopped himself in time from asking, 'What do people usually drink?' instead, "Local, please."

He paid for the drink then turned to look for somewhere to sit. It had only just turned five, and most of the tables were empty. He needed to make contacts, get under the skin of this place. He noticed a man with a bandaged head sitting at the window table. He wore a blue pin-stripe suit, something Tremayne had not seen in this village before where green cords and Wellington boots were the normal order of the day.

"May I join you?" Tremayne asked.

The man looked up. His bandage slipped to cover half of one eye. He adjusted it quickly.

"Oh, yes. If you like."

Tremayne held out his hand as he sat down. "Tremayne, Charles Tremayne."

"Yes, I know. My name is Mr Cobbledick. Rupert Cobbledick. But everybody calls me Mr Cobbledick."

"Everybody?"

"Yes. Even my wife calls me Mr Cobbledick." He cast his eyes down to the table as if remembering great sadness.

"What happened?" Tremayne tapped his own head while looking at Cobbledick's bandage.

"Oh, that... I... I fell down the stairs."

"Nasty!" Tremayne took a long pull on his glass of cider. It was sweet and sharp at the same time, with a strong taste

of apples. Really quite pleasant in an earthy sort of way.
"What do you do?" Tremayne asked.

"I'm the manager of the local branch of the Western Counties Bank."

Aha! Here was an in. Could be worth digging around. Bank managers tend to know a lot about small communities. Very often more than the local policeman.

"May I get you another?" Tremayne nodded at Cobbledick's empty glass.

"Oh, yes. Thank you. Shandy please. Just a small one."

Tremayne sank the last of his cider and stood up. "Are you sure you wouldn't like to make it a pint?"

"Well, if you insist."

A few minutes later, Tremayne returned with two pints spilling over the edges of their glasses.

"There you go," he said. "Get the inner man set up around that."

"Pardon me?"

Tremayne replayed the tape inside his head of what he'd just said and realised it was complete and utter rubbish.

"I meant, cheers."

"Good health," Cobbledick said.

"So, how long have you been the manager?"

"I really don't remember. I seem to have been there all my life." He looked up at Tremayne, his eyes reddened, his expression hung loose like a terminally depressed bloodhound.

"Excuse me for mentioning this, but you seem less than satisfied. Why don't you change?"

"Change? In Little Didney, Mr Tremayne?" A flash of anger dashed across Cobbledick's eyes. "You don't change in Little Didney, Mr Tremayne. You survive. Here, you're born into your job, and stay there till you die. You'll find no career guidance centres here. No recruitment agencies. Who would want an ex-banker in Little Didney? I can't cook and I can't turn soil."

"Have you ever thought of leaving the village?

"Nobody leaves Little Didney, Mr Tremayne."

The Money That Never Was

Tremayne took a long sip on his cider as he pondered Cobbledick's last statement. Maybe it was his old paranoia, but he felt there was almost a threat in there somewhere.

Realising his glass was empty Tremayne stood. "Can I get you another?"

"Goodness! You seem to have taken rather a liking to our local brew, Mr Tremayne," Cobbledick said, pointing at Tremayne's empty glass. "My round, I do believe."

Cobbledick gathered the empty glasses and took them to the bar for re-filling.

Tremayne gazed out of the window and watched the shop opposite going in and out of focus. Ironically, it was an optician's. He vaguely wondered if they were doing it on purpose. Hearing a double click on the table, he turned to see Cobbledick had returned with two overflowing glasses.

"There you are then. That'll curl your hair!" Cobbledick said.

"Thank you. I must say, that once one becomes used to it, it is rather a pleasant drink."

"Ah, you need to be careful, Mr Tremayne. It's a bit like a woman. Soft and sweet to draw you in, but then she will take control of you the moment you relax."

"That's a very cynical view."

"A lifetime of banking tends to make a man rather cynical." He took a measured sip of his drink that left a foam dot on the end of his nose.

Tremayne felt a giggle rising inside him. He fought to suppress it.

"Surely you can't have too many problems around here. This looks like quite a prosperous little village." Good, back on track.

"Prosperous? Whatever gave you that idea? Most of the villagers here are just one step ahead of the bailiffs. I see their bank accounts, remember."

Tremayne felt his chair move. A slight wobbling movement as if the legs had turned to foam rubber. He bent down to investigate and instantly regretted it as the floor rotated around his head in a lazy circle.

"Are you all right, Mr Tremayne?"

"No, I seem to have come over all... sort of... Whoops! Oh dear, what's that all over my shoes? "

***

Barry Penwrith was sulking. As soon as the rest of the villagers had cottoned on to the fact that he had an extra ten cases of money squirreled away, it hadn't taken them long to extract the information as to their whereabouts from Barry. He knew which way the crops were growing. In another day or two they'd be round here for the rest of his money. Well, they weren't going to have it. He was going to get away from here while he still had the chance, and a few pennies to his name. He was going to take Maisie and the boy to Disney World. He'd seen it on the television. They could stay at the Magic Kingdom for a couple of days, and when they got bored, they would hire a Cadillac and spend the next week looking at the rest of America. After that, he'd take whatever money they had left and move to Argentina. He'd heard they didn't have extradition, so even PC Muchmore would be unable to get hold of him there.

Maisie and Tommy sat in the back of Barry's Capri, surrounded by a myriad of assorted baggage. The boot of the car had been entirely taken up by four crates of money. He was just pulling out of his drive when a green Jaguar XJS slid across the entrance, blocking his way. He recognised it as Jerry Richards' car.

Barry leapt out of his Capri. "What's your game, then?"

"Easy now, Barry," Jerry said, climbing out of his Jag. "Where are you off too?"

"Holiday. If it's any business of yours. I'm taking them to Disneyland. And if I like it, we may even live there."

"Barry, we all agreed we would stay put. We wouldn't go on a spending spree until things calmed down."

"Well, you should've thought about that, before you strung me up on the lamp post."

"Ah, maybe you shouldn't have tried to keep back an extra stash for yourself."

"It was all mine before you lot got your hands on it. Now you just want to take the rest of it away from me, don't you? You won't be happy 'til it's all gone. Well you're not having it."

"We can't let you leave, Barry. You do know that, don't you?"

***

"Good morning! I thought you might like some coffee."

Tremayne couldn't understand why the KGB agent, who currently had him in a stranglehold, should be offering him coffee. And in such a cheery voice too. He tried to kick out at the big Russian, but his legs weren't working properly.

"You'll never get away with this, Boris," he shouted.

"Come along, sleepyhead!" Boris said.

Huh? He grabbed at the corners of reality and pulled himself up into semi-consciousness.

"What?"

"Who was in a bit of a state last night then?"

Even through his fug, Tremayne realised this was probably a rhetorical question, and that whoever had asked it, was quite possibly referring to him. He told his eyelids to open. They didn't. He gave them a gentle massage with his fingertips and tried again.

Strands of white drifted across violent reds and oranges. Was he hallucinating? He knew some eastern countries still used LSD in preference to sodium pentothal. He remembered his training. Pick a point and focus on it. He chose to focus on Sandy Goodenough's face.

Sandy Goodenough?

What was she doing here?

"So, what do you think of our local cider then, Charles?"

He scanned the room. No, he wasn't hallucinating. The reds, oranges, and wispy lace were all still there. All just part of the normal decor of the Smuggler's Inn bridal suite. He was lying in the ridiculously soft bed with the overstuffed quilt in a tangle around his midriff. It looked like the Russian had got a good kicking after all. Sandy Goodenough stood by the foot of the bed with a large tray in her hand. A quick glance told Tremayne it probably contained three days allowance of saturated fats and caffeine.

"Huh? Oh... cider... Yes. I think I must be allergic to cider."

"Nothing to do with being drunk then?"

"Drunk? No!" He lifted the edge of the quilt to his chest, risking a glance underneath as he did so. He was naked. "No, I haven't been drunk since university. I don't get drunk."

"Rolling down the street with Mr Cobbledick singing Eskimo Nell was all part of this strange allergic reaction then, was it?" Sandy placed the tray on the bedside table.

"Eskimo Nell? I don't even know the words to Eskimo Nell!"

"Yes, that much was apparent." A grin on her face clearly reflected her memory of last night's performance.

Tremayne took another peep under the bedclothes.

"Did I..."

"I put you to bed."

"But I haven't... You didn't..."

"I've got three older brothers, Charles. You've certainly got nothing that was going to surprise me." She looked straight at him. "Why, Charles, I do believe you're blushing!"

"No, it's just a bit hot in here, that's all." He examined her face for signs of disbelief. A raised eyebrow was all he needed.

"Anyway," she said. "I had a chaperone. You were quite safe." She straightened the quilt across his bed, unhooked the legs from the bottom of the tray, and settled it firmly in front of him.

"Oh, who was that then?"
"Mrs. Pomfrey."
"Oh, good! That's perfect then!"
"Put that lot inside you. It'll make a true man of you." She made a point of staring at his groin area, winked, and said, "On the other hand... Perhaps you don't need it!"

Tremayne pulled the quilt more tightly around his neck. For some unaccountable reason, he suddenly felt vulnerable.

Just as she reached the door, she stopped and said, "Oh, by the way, we're having a skittles night tonight. Old Bill is the captain of the 'Otters' team. He's asked for you to be his 'Number one'. It seems he's taken rather a shine to you. I think he regards you as the son he never had."
"But I can't play skittles."
"Shouldn't let that worry you, neither can Old Bill." She pulled the door closed behind her.

Charles let his head drop back into the depths of the fluffy pillow. It closed in around his face as if trying to suffocate him, the lace trimming tickled his nose.

His head felt like a bell that had struck twelve, and his tongue was three sizes too big.

He had just decided to allow himself another ten minutes sleep when his satellite phone squawked with such violence that it felt like a steel shaft of sound running through his head. He snatched it from the bedside table and dragged it down into the depths of the pillow in search of an ear.

"Hrmph?"
"Charles?"
"Huh? Oh, sorry, Elaine. Good morning."
"You sound very croaky. Are you all right? I've been trying to ring you for the last hour."
"What's the time then?"
"Just gone eleven."

"It can't be!" He pushed himself into a sitting position. Or as much of a sitting position as this quagmire of a mattress would allow. He felt is though he was in quicksand. His every movement sucked him deeper into the depths of the bed.

"Did you oversleep again, Charles? This is becoming a habit."

"I had a late night. I was trying to soften up the local banker."

"Oh, I see." The microwave link between them fizzled with her scepticism.

"Anyway, why the call?"

"Well, since the Trevellick incident, we've had worms inserted into all the major computer systems. They're set to flag us on any mention of Little Didney."

"And?"

"And, a family in the name of Penwrith failed to turn up at Heathrow Airport for their Virgin Atlantic flight to Los Angeles."

"Now, that is interesting. I'm beginning to think these villagers are more involved with the disappearing money than I'd first thought. Maybe they've been paid off for the use of their harbour by whoever's behind this. I think it's time I upped the pressure a bit."

"Are you sure you don't need some help down there, Charles? You do seem to be having some difficulties." He could feel her patronising smile oozing through the phone.

"Very funny. No, I think I can manage this bunch on my own."

He clicked the phone off and tried to replace it on the bedside table. The aerial tangled in the lace doily and the phone fell to the floor, dragging a china nymph along with it. The sound of breaking porcelain scraped through Tremayne's head.

That was it!

He lifted his untouched breakfast tray to the floor then fought his way free of the bed. On his way to the shower, he flicked the switch to the radio. The sound of folk music filled the room.

He turned the shower's thermostat to minimum and stepped underneath the spluttering spray. Lukewarm water dribbled over his body. He'd been in many hotels where he couldn't get a hot shower, but being unable to obtain a cold one was something new. But slowly his head cleared and a sense of normality threaded its way through his system.

He dressed in a white Armani shirt and cream trousers then headed downstairs, remembering to avoid each beam on the way.

Goodenough was in his usual place, behind the bar polishing glasses. "Morning, Mr Tremayne. Going to be another grand day today!"
"Yes, I think it probably is, Mr Goodenough. Glad I caught you. While I'm out, there's a couple of things I'd like you to get for me, please."
"Oh yes. What would that be?"
"I'd like four large packing crates and a kettle, please. Oh, and a door."
"A door?"
"Yes, a door."
"But you've already got a door. That one not to your liking, Mr Tremayne?"
"That one's fine, I just want another one please. Just a door. I don't want it attached."
"Right you are."

As he followed the main road up the hill, a selection of familiar faces wished him, 'Good Morning'. He was now beginning to recognise most of the locals.

He turned off onto 'Leafy Lane', retracing his route of yesterday to Barry's cottage.

Empty buildings have a feel about them. Something intangible, a sort of deeper silence. He knew from two hundred metres away there was nobody home, but he was not about to take chances. Years of conditioning lightened his step and he disturbed the ground no more than a shadow as he approached.

The lock on the rear door sprang open under the first touch of Tremayne's lock-pick. He paused for a few seconds while his ears filtered out nature's noises in search of anything more human-like.

Once satisfied the house was empty, he stepped into the kitchen.

The kitchen was a testament to Barry's home-improvements enthusiasm. Lopsided cupboards clung tenaciously to interestingly shaped walls and tiles drifted across the floor in seemingly random patterns. The overall effect made Tremayne feel slightly seasick.

A huge oak table in the centre of the room lay almost buried under a mountain of travel brochures. Mainly relating to Disney Land.

A slightly skewed pine door led into the lounge. The room was dark, heavy brocade curtains effectively blocking the light from two tiny windows. He waited until his eyes adjusted.

As his vision returned, he congratulated himself on his decision to stay still. Six inches in front of his nose, a huge chandelier dangled from the low ceiling. He ducked his head around it and as he did so, his foot scuffed on something soft. He looked down to see a washed silk Chinese rug sprawled across a threadbare carpet.

Satisfied that no light could escape through the curtains, he switched on his torch and scanned of the rest of the room. Cob-stone walls played host to a variety of overly ornate oil paintings. Portraits of austere Victorian gentlemen in formal poses comprised of most of the paintings. Clearly family portraits, but also clearly not Barry's family.

He reached for the light switch and his hand froze just above it. A yellowing cable snaked over the wall from the switch, across the ceiling to the chandelier. It was secured to the wall with heavy iron nails. He decided to rely on the torchlight.

In the corner of the room, a new computer sat on top of a mahogany desk. Freshly discarded cardboard boxes lay scattered across the floor. As he drew nearer, Tremayne noticed a large wooden handled screwdriver skewered upright through the keyboard. One way of dealing with Windows crashes, thought Tremayne.

An examination of the upper floor revealed more of the same. Years of neglect, overlaid with a flurry of unrestrained expenditure. High-tech radio alarm clocks nestled alongside the pre-war table lamps. Black silk sheets peeped over the top of a faded blue eiderdown.

Tremayne decided he'd seen enough. Wherever he was, Barry was up to his scruffy little neck in this. Fortunately, if past performance were anything to go by, it wouldn't be too difficult to extract information from him. Once he'd been found.

He headed back to the hotel, stopping briefly at the local store to buy coffee and fresh vegetables.

***

"I put your door in your room," Goodenough greeted, as Tremayne stepped into the bar. "It's a light olive green with a big brass handle."
"Thank you, Mr Goodenough, you'll add it to the bill of course."
"Already done. Talking of which, how long were you planning on staying?"
"I don't think it will be too long now, and you'll be the first to know, Mr Goodenough, I assure you."

The door matched Goodenough's description perfectly. Tremayne opened his multi-function penknife, removed the brass handle then dragged the bag of fluff that passed for a mattress to one side as he slid the door directly onto the bed base. He replaced the mattress on top of door and sat down on it to test his improvements. Good, as firm as any Holiday Lodge bed. Only the slightest bit of give. The kettle Goodenough had provided was an old fashioned metal one with a Bakelite handle. But it would do the job. It meant his mornings would be back to black coffee instead of cholesterol on toast.

He dragged the first of the packing cases to the dressing table then carefully filled it with porcelain bells, gilt picture frames, and lace doilies. Once the first case was full, he started on the next, and it wasn't long before all four cases overflowed with whimsy and trivia.

He stepped back to admire his new room. Clean, naked surfaces shone under the bare light bulb. At last, a room he could relax in.

He picked up the bag of vegetables and opened the door to leave. He was slightly taken aback when he saw Sandy standing in the entrance way, her hand raised ready to knock.
"Oh," she said. "Knock- knock."
"What is it?"
"No, you're supposed to say, who's there?"
"Why?"
"Sort of a joke, you see."
"Oh, I'm not very good at jokes."
"I know!"
"You wanted something?" He resisted the desire to snap.
"I was just curious about the kettle and the door. I wondered what you wanted them for." Her eyes peered around Tremayne.
"Come in." He gave a sweeping gesture with his right arm which ended up pointing at the bed. "There, try it!"

"Mr Tremayne! How forward of you."

"No! I meant—"

"It all right, I know what you meant. I was just pulling your leg." She sat down on the bed. "Ooh, that's hard!"

He scanned her eyes, trying to determine if this was another one of her double-entendres. But he still couldn't see through the crystal maze that lay somewhere between her eyes and her soul.

"I was having trouble sleeping. The mattress was so soft."

"Trouble sleeping? Can't say I noticed. The kettle?"

"I wanted to boil water."

"Yes, I figured that."

"Coffee... I like coffee in the morning."

"You don't like my coffee?" She made an exaggerated frown.

"Your coffee is lovely..." Why did he always feel wrong-footed whenever Sandy was around. "But it usually comes complete with a do-it-yourself coronary kit."

"So, it's my cooking that you don't like?" This time her face could maintain the frown no longer, and broke into a grin.

"I love your coffee. I love your cooking. It just... I just surprised myself by how soft I'd become over the last couple of days. That's all."

"Wouldn't want you to go soft on us now, would we?" Her smile widened. She stood and made for the door. "Don't forget the skittles tonight, Charles."

"I'll try not to."

After she'd left, Tremayne lay back on the bed. For the last twenty years he had relied on his quick thinking to keep him alive. So why was it, within a few minutes of being near Sandy, he felt like his brain was running in slow motion? He replayed the conversation in his head, trying to sort out just where he'd lost control. But he still couldn't work it out and gave up.

The next thing of which he needed to regain control was his diet. He collected his pack of groceries and left the room.

***

The powerboat was still embedded in the fish shop counter. The difference was that now the front deck was almost buried under trays of fish with plastic seaweed draped across the gunwales. Clearly the shopkeeper had decided to make a feature out of it.

"Very ingenious," Tremayne said.

"Well, the constable said it'd have to stay there until he'd completed his investigation. I couldn't have good shop space going to waste now, could I?"

"No, indeed you couldn't."

"What can I do for you then Mr Tremayne? Nice piece of rock-salmon?"

"Sounds interesting. I've not heard of that before. Show me."

The fishmonger held up what appeared to be a baby shark.

"That looks nothing like a salmon!"

"It's a dog fish actually. But we seem to sell much more of it when we call it rock salmon."

"I can't imagine why! Do you have any plaice?"

"Came in this morning. Look at this." The shopkeeper pulled a plastic tray down from the bow of the powerboat. It contained several large and very fresh plaice.

"Excellent! I'll have that one." Tremayne pointed to a particularly large specimen. "Thank you."

After he had paid for his fish, Tremayne went next door to the café.

"Oh, hello Charlie!" The woman behind the counter greeted him like a long lost friend.

Tremayne cringed inwardly at the distortion of his name.

"What will you have today then?" she continued. "I've got a nice steak and kidney pudding on the go."

"No thank you. Delightful as that sounds I think I'll pass on that. Could you do me a favour?" He opened his bag on

The Money That Never Was

the counter to reveal the plaice, fresh green beans, tomatoes, and new potatoes.

"What would you like me to do with that lot then, Charlie? Pop them in the deep fat fryer for you shall I?"

"No!" He hoped the sudden shock he felt at her intended desecration didn't show. "I do not want you to pop those in the deep fat fryer. I'd rather they went nowhere near a deep fat fryer. Could you please lightly brush the fish with olive oil then grill for a few minutes only, boil the potatoes, and just blanch the beans? Of course, I'll pay you for a full meal."

"As you want. It just seems a dreadful waste of nice fish and potatoes. Can I at least put the fish in some batter for you?"

"No. Just lightly grilled, thank you."

The meal when it arrived, was almost everything he'd hoped it would be. The only shortfall was that he felt sure she'd used lard instead of olive oil. But he could forgive that. At least it had escaped the deep fat fryer.

He finished the meal a little too quickly then pushed the plate to one side. His stomach still insisted it was hungry. He'd become used to that pleasantly full feeling over the last few days. He would have to retrain himself. Switch off the false signals his system was generating. He turned in his seat to look out of the window. Think about something else. He gazed across the tiny harbour. What sort of boat would they have used? How many crew would it take?

A clattering of china onto Formica returned his attention to the table. The café owner had just deposited a huge bowl of treacle tart and custard in front of him.

"There you go," she said. "Get your juices working on that!"

Chapter 6

Mrs Pomfrey sat back in the wooden rocking chair and watched as the huge machine that took up most of her garage gurgled and clanked. She hadn't realised how much sugar and butter that contraption would hold, and she had quite worn herself out filling it up. But now, as the machine was doing its bit, grinding, churning, and mixing, she was able to relax.

She poured herself another glass of sherry. The combination of sherry and self-satisfaction drew a smile across her glowing face.

She'd only gone to visit Marlowe's Confectionery Products on the off-chance they'd take a few bags of the village fudge. Her disappointment at being told she couldn't produce in large enough quantities for them, was quickly dispelled when they'd offered to sell her one of their redundant machines. They'd even delivered and installed it the same day. Now, she could produce fudge by the hundredweight.

She could even begin exporting. Little Didney fudge would become as famous as Cheddar cheese, or Pontefract cakes. And where in the world was Pontefract anyway?

She let her sherry-coloured mind drift through the world's cultures. She imagined an American Thanksgiving table with a silver tray of Little Didney fudge as the centrepiece. Or Australians, sharing a box of it around the barbecue. A Japanese fudge-vendor walking the aisles at a Sumo match. Yes, Little Didney was about to become the centre of the world of fudge making. The very heart of real confectionery.

She realised her bottle of sherry was empty and tossed it into the bin before reaching for a fresh one. The machine made a rather pleasant whirring noise as it churned together the ingredients for the first batch of the world's favourite fudge.

What about different flavours? She could experiment. After all, there was no need to stick to vanilla. As the world's leading fudge producer, she would set the pace. Hers would be the standard by which all other fudges were judged. She could produce it in any flavour she liked. She glanced at the bottle of sherry in her hand. Now, there's an idea!

***

"This dial here, controls the frequency of the current waveform in the 'A' file."
"I see." Reverend Featherstone didn't see. In fact, he hadn't the faintest idea what the young man with the ponytail was talking about. He might as well have been trying to explain the intricacies of quantum theory. But what Reverend Featherstone did know, was that the instrument made a lot of noise. And the young man had assured him that it would never go out of tune on a wet autumn morning the way his fifty-year-old pipe organ did.

He would also be able to 'Set up a sequence', the young man had explained. Featherstone wasn't sure what a sequence was either, but he just knew that the machine could play itself if Mrs. Pomfrey failed to turn up for her Sunday morning stint at the keyboard. Mrs. Pomfrey failing to turn up was a fairly regular occurrence at St. Mary's parish church, and due in no small part to her liking for the sherry.

"Now," said the young man. "Do you want me to tune it to the acoustic properties of the church?"
"Yes, I think that would be a good idea, don't you?"

A high pitched tone filled the church and seemed to pierce Featherstone's head. The engineer hunched over his equipment and studied the oscilloscope. Reverend Featherstone watched with interest as a spiky green line drifted across the screen. The spikes gradually levelled out and settled into a single straight line.

"Last time I saw that happen," Featherstone said. "was when I was called in to hospital to administer the last rites!"

The man stared at Featherstone's face for a moment then returned his attention to the monitor. "Never thought of it like that. But this doesn't mean it's dead. This is now perfectly tuned. Do you want to hear it play?"

"I'll have to fetch Mrs. Pomfrey. I can't play a note."

"No problem. It's pre-programmed. What would you like? Bach?"

"You mean this machine can play Bach all by itself?"

"Yes, Bach, Beethoven, Wagner, even Iron Maiden if you like. Watch"

He flicked a switch, and Bach's gloriously overblown Fugue thundered across the rafters of the four-hundred-year-old church.

"My word! I haven't heard anything like that since I was a curate at Westminster Abbey!"

"That's the organ this program is based on."

"Most impressive, young man. Most impressive indeed."

"And if you need to give your flock a shake out of bed on a Sunday morning, you've got fifty megawatts of power to play with."

"I see, fifty mega…thingys. That would be…?"

"I'll show you."

***

Charles Tremayne was about to step across the gangplank leading to Old Bill's boat, when he heard the music drifting down across the village.

Bach? Some classical music fan must have their hi-fi up full with all their windows open. He continued across the wobbling platform then knocked on the door of the dilapidated motor launch that served as Old Bill's home.

"Come on in, Mr Tremayne. It's not locked."

Tremayne stepped into the surprisingly spacious interior. Old Bill was sitting in a white leather recliner, watching a huge, wall-hung, plasma TV screen.

"How did you know it was me?" Tremayne asked.
"Nobody else bothers to knock. They just walk in."
"But I could have been a burglar or something."
"Do burglars usually knock where you come from then?" Old Bill's lips widened into a smile, but his teeth remained clamped on the pipe that was a permanent part of his features.
"Come along, son. Sit down." Bill waved towards a grease-stained armchair that sat leaking stuffing into the corner of the room.
Tremayne's gaze flitted between the chair and his own cream coloured trousers. "No thanks. I'm not stopping. I just wanted to check the arrangements for tonight. Sandy tells me I'm in your team. How many of us are there?"
"What, including both of us?"
"Yes."
"Erm... two!"
"And you're the captain?"
"Unless you want the job."
"No, thank you. What time does it start?"
"Tonight! Didn't young Sandy tell you that?"
"Yes, but she didn't tell me what time."
"Well, it starts when everybody gets there of course."
"Yes, I suppose I should have worked that one out." Tremayne let his gaze wander around Bill's cabin. It seemed quite homely in a rustic sort of way. There was little furniture to clutter the room apart from the two chairs and a circular plastic table just inside the door. A continuous shelf ran all around the room and contained an assortment of brightly coloured bottles and jars. A deep amber rug brought warmth to the scuffed pine floorboards.

"Do you ever go anywhere in this boat, Bill?" Tremayne hoped his voice was light-hearted and conversational.

"No, I'm not inclined to travel much in this anymore."

"Oh, why's that?"

"Well, he hasn't got an engine for one thing."

***

Tremayne swung open the door to his hotel room and froze. When he had left the room, not three hours earlier, it had been devoid of all superfluous artefacts. All of the assorted items of porcelain and glass had been packed neatly into the crates. But now it was all back again. Lace dangled once more from the light fitting. A china milkmaid swung glass buckets from her outstretched arms. They tinkled in the draught from the open door. Crystal picture frames once more contained whimsical little poems about friends or gardens.

And everything sat on its own little doily.

He sat down on the bed and sank deeply into the mattress. They'd even taken his door. This was a plot. He knew it now. The village was riddled with conspiracy, and it was becoming increasingly clear that several people in the village had come into some new found wealth. The evidence was all here. Barry Penwrith's spending, the powerboat that nobody wanted to own up to, and even Old Bill looked like he'd received a payoff of some kind.

What was also becoming clear, was that the villagers were trying to destroy his resolve. They were plotting to make his life as uncomfortable as possible, so he'd leave quickly.

Well, they were about to find out whom they were up against.

He set off down the stairs at such a pace that when he cracked his head on the beam, it gave him such a jolt that he had to sit down on the steps while he waited for his eyes to regain focus.

A blurry shape coming up the steps in front of him resolved itself into the form of Mr Goodenough.

"Are you alright, Mr Tremayne? I heard that one from the cellar."
"Yes, I'm fine, thank you." Tremayne's fingers probed his forehead searching for lumps or blood.
"You want to put a piece of steak on that. "
"Why did you put all the ornaments back?"
"We didn't."
"Well, who did then? The ornament fairy?"
"No, your ornaments are all downstairs in the boxes where we left them."
"What's all that in my room again?"
"They're new ornaments. I thought you didn't like the last lot, so I got you some new ones."
"But they look exactly the same! And where's my door?"
"Oh, I'm looking after that for you. It's downstairs. You don't need to hide it under your bed, Mr Tremayne. Nobody will steal it around here."

Tremayne felt his system flushing with adrenaline as his body readied itself for kill or be killed. He couldn't ever remember feeling this level of frustration before. He was used to clear-cut danger. Go in, kill the bad guy or rescue the good guy, then get out again. But here, these people were frustrating him at every turn. They were making a mockery of an unblemished career that spanned three decades.

He straightened up as far as the low beams would allow then jabbed his forefinger into the air between himself and Goodenough.

"Right!" The word exploded through clenched teeth, but he was unsure how to follow it up, so he jabbed the air again and repeated the word, "Right!"

"Yes, Mr Tremayne?"

Tremayne visualised a china milkmaid skewered through the top of Goodenough's head. "Oh... Nothing"

***

P.C. Muchmore jolted back in his chair when he heard Tremayne enter the office. He quickly removed his feet from the desk and sat forward in what he clearly hoped was a posture of keen intent.

"Mr Tremayne, sir. What can I do for you?"

"Sorry, did I disturb your siesta?"

"No, I was meditating. It takes my mind to a higher level."

"Yes, I can see how that would help."

"All part of a police officer's armoury, you know." Muchmore rubbed his eyes free of the last traces of meditation.

"What particular crime were you meditating on?"

"The mystery of this boat of course!"

"And the disappearance of two hundred and fifty million has been relegated to second place by a joy rider in a powerboat?"

"No, sir. That's part of our ongoing investigation."

Right, I'd like you to make a list of everybody in the village who's spending more than usual,"

"Why's that?"

"Because I think the money came through the village, and I think some of the people here have been paid off. Do you think you can manage that?"

"No problem, sir. Leave it to me and I'll have it ready for you by next week."

"How about tomorrow morning?"

"That's what I meant."

"Oh, and one other thing. Have you seen Barry Penwrith? He seems to have disappeared."

The constable shifted in his chair. There was something about that question that disturbed him.

"Is he not at home?"

"No he's not."

That's strange, he never usually goes very far, does our Barry."

Tremayne left Muchmore to return to his meditations. He was sure there wouldn't be much help from that quarter. Not only did Muchmore seem not in the slightest bit interested in helping to locate the missing money, but Tremayne had also noticed a Berber coat hanging behind the door.

Chapter 7

The venue for the skittles evening was a converted stable behind the Smuggler's Arms. Although 'converted' was probably too optimistic a word as most of the stalls were still in place. One of which now served as a makeshift bar. A couple of benches had been laid on their side to form the skittle alley itself, and nine heavy wooden skittles were in place at the far end. The air was already thick with smoke and the smell of beer and rock music drifted from the ancient PA system. Sandy's choice of music no doubt. Tremayne wondered how long he'd be able to put up with it.

"I've kept a seat for you, son," Old Bill called from a table near the bar.
"I'll just fetch us some drinks. What would you like?" Tremayne asked.
"Seeing's how it's a special occasion, I'll have a Creme de Menthe."

The bar consisted of little more than a couple of planks supported by two barrels. What appeared to be a large tray of fudge sat prominently in the centre of the planks. A hand written sign lying in amongst the little brown cubes offered a free sample.

"May I?" Tremayne enquired of Sandy, behind the bar. She wore a white cotton shirt , with one too many buttons open.
"Help yourself," she said.

He rolled the piece of fudge around his mouth with as much care as if it were a fine Bordeaux. The sickly sweet goo attached itself to the roof of his mouth. There was something most unusual about the flavour; it took him a moment to place it.

"Sherry?"

The Money That Never Was

"Yes." Sandy smiled. "Mrs. Pomfrey's latest creation."

"Sherry flavoured fudge?" He scraped at the roof of his mouth with his tongue, trying to dislodge the sticky mess. "Unusual. Makes an interesting change." As he swallowed, the fudge left a warm trail down the back of his throat. "But this still has alcohol in it! How did she do that?"

"She says it's an industrial secret."

"I think it's probably best if it stays that way."

"Would you like to buy some, Charles?" Sandy dangled a little plastic bag in front of him.

"No thank you. I think that's one little pleasure I shall deprive myself of. For Lent or something. I'll just have a pint of cider and a Crème de Menthe, please."

As Sandy poured Tremayne's cider she said, "Don't expect me to put you to bed again tonight!"

"I'll be fine. I know my limit with this stuff now."

"Oh, yes?" Sandy poured the best part of a quarter bottle of Crème de Menthe into a large tumbler.

"What the hell's that?"

"It's for Old Bill isn't it? That's how he takes it." She dropped a couple of ice cubes and a cherry into the glass.

He paid for the drinks then turned to head back to the table.

"Good luck!" Sandy called.

"What?"

"Good luck. Your team, in the skittles. Good luck!"

"Oh, thank you."

Tremayne sat opposite Bill and placed the drinks on the wooden table, completely failing to think of a pithy saying.

Old Bill immediately grabbed his glass and took a large pull on his drink. The switch between pipe, glass, and back again was so swift, that Tremayne hardly noticed.

"So," Tremayne said. "What's the plan?"

"Huh?"

"The plan, the strategy?"

Old Bill still looked vacant.

"Our plan of attack for winning the skittles match?" Tremayne persisted.

"Oh, right. It's in two parts you see. Part one, I go over there," Bill pointed a gnarled finger at the alley. "Pick up the ball, and chuck it at those wooden things to knock down as many as I can. That's the first part."

"And the second part?"

"The second part? Oh, you come along and do the same."

Tremayne had been hoping for something a bit more strategic. With maybe even some psychological planning to unnerve his opponents.

"So, who're our main rivals?" He took a cautious sip of his cider. He was going to make this pint last all night.

"That would be Sandy's Angels"

"Sandy Goodenough?"

"Yes, and Jeannie Featherstone, the vicar's daughter. That's her over there." The gnarled finger waved to a woman talking to Sandy. She appeared to be in her mid thirties. She wore the kind of skin-tight jodhpurs and tight jumper that a vicar's daughter should never wear.

"They're good, are they?"

"They win every season." Old Bill sank the rest of his drink. "Come on, son. You've hardly touched yours. Time for a top up." Without awaiting Tremayne's approval, he creaked over to the bar to re-stock.

Tremayne scanned the room. He'd decided this would be a good opportunity to see who was spending.

The rock music had increased in volume. He recognised Dire Straits playing and remembered his outing with Sandy to the cove. His eyes coasted around the room and quickly homed in on the little pockets of abnormality.

Danny Trevellick, Tom's 'little boy' and all six foot three of him, stood near the door. He wore a Paul Smith suit and green wellingtons. A gold medallion dangled over what was clearly a very expensive white silk shirt. He was deep

The Money That Never Was

in conversation with the Reverend Featherstone. The vicar nursed a large brandy. An obvious toupee clung precariously to his head.

As Tremayne's eyes became more attuned to what he was looking for, he found more and more evidence of sudden wealth. A Gucci handbag, a handheld television. A mobile phone bleeped from one corner of the room.

A man answered it, "Hello? Hello? Hello?"
Giggles from the opposite end of the bar snatched Tremayne's attention. He looked towards the sound and saw two youths at a corner table. One of them held a mobile phone and was stabbing at the buttons.

Another phone rang in a different part of the room. Somebody else reached for his pocket. "Hello? Hello?"

More giggles.

Mobile telephones had become such an ordinary part of the world that it took a moment to realise what was happening here. He hadn't seen any cellphones here before. And for a very good reason. There were no signals here. These had to be satellite phones, and all of a sudden, there seemed to be a lot of them.

Old Bill arrived back and planted the fresh drinks on the table.
"Liquid sunshine," he said. His hands rummaged through his coat pockets then emerged with two large bags of fudge. "Bought these for us. It was on special offer."

He dropped one of the plastic packets on the table in front of Tremayne then ripped open his own.

"Thank you. I'll... er... save it for later."
"No need to worry about that. I bought plenty." He pulled another four packets out of his packets.

"Oh, good. I'd just hate to think of us running out of fudge halfway through the evening."

Old Bill squeezed a piece of fudge past his pipe and began chewing.

"Nearly forgot," he said, between puffing and chewing. "Bought you a present."

Another rummage through old Bill's pockets produced a brown paper bag which he passed to Tremayne. It bore the legend, Canon's, Purveyors of fine smoking materials to the aristocracy since 1782.

Tremayne opened the bag with the same delicacy he would have afforded a potential letter bomb. One by one, at fingertips, he extracted the contents and placed them on the table. A fine, ornately carved Meerschaum pipe. A leather tobacco pouch. A packet of something calling itself 'Black shag' and a metal contraption somewhat resembling a Swiss army knife. He couldn't for the life of him see what that was supposed to do.

"I don't know what to say, Bill. That's very kind of you."
"You seemed to enjoy smoking so much the other night, I thought I'd buy you one."
"But you really shouldn't have...I..."
"No need to thank me. Here, why don't you load it up? Give it a try."

Tremayne picked up the pipe and turned it around in his hands. "It seems a shame to spoil their newness of it really. Perhaps I'll just keep it for a special occasion."
"This *is* a special occasion. Come on. Pipes are for smoking, not for looking at. You want me to start it up for you?"
"No!" Tremayne looked around the room, desperately hoping for some chance of escape. For some reason, his eyes locked with Sandy's. She smiled. He knew what was behind the smile. He remembered her challenging him about the last time he'd smoked with old Bill. Whether he'd

The Money That Never Was

just done it to pump Bill for information. Her eyes held his just a moment longer, challenging him. Then the link was broken and she returned her attention to a waiting customer.

Tremayne felt trapped. As slowly as he could, he filled the pipe. Bill watched his every move expectantly. Each time Tremayne slowed down, Bill's hands twitched as if eager to help.

Eventually, when all delaying tactics seemed exhausted, he had to light the pipe. Smoke curled from the bowl and drifted upwards to join the growing cloud that had collected six inches under the ceiling. The taste was surprisingly sweet. Not what he'd been expecting. Not too unpleasant. Experimentally, he inhaled. Immediately, it felt as though there were an angry cat trapped inside his chest. His eyes filled with tears as the cat exploded up through his throat. His lungs convulsed violently in an attempt to expel the source of the irritation. He coughed with such violence that he felt sure he must have damaged his larynx.

As the spasm subsided, and his vision returned, Old Bill said, "You don't want to inhale that! Not Black shag you don't. Here, take a drink." Old Bill pushed Tremayne's glass towards him.

Tremayne drank a large gulp of cider, and immediately coughed most of it straight out again. Gradually, the coughing subsided. He removed a white linen handkerchief from his pocket and mopped the cider froth from his face.

"Now, take it a bit more slowly this time," Old Bill said. "You youngsters always rush headlong into everything."
It had been a long time since anybody had called Tremayne a youngster. Despite himself, he warmed to Bill. Under his mentor's watchful gaze, Tremayne drew the warm smoke into his mouth. This time he was careful not to inhale. Old Bill looked pleased.

Another phone rang. Fresh giggling erupted from a

corner table. There was something about this business with the satellite phones that was just eluding Tremayne's logic processes. There was a connection he wasn't making. It irritated him.

Three loud knocks from the corner of the bar brought silence to the room. Goodenough puffed out his chest in best sergeant major fashion. "Good evening ladies and gentlemen. Proceedings will get underway shortly in the usual manner. With the opening team being last times winners. Sandy's Angels."

Claps and mumbles circled the room. Sandy blushed slightly and pretended to ignore it.
"Usual rules apply," Goodenough continued. "Loser of each round buys the drinks for the other teams."

"Er, Bill?" Tremayne asked.
"Yes, son?"
"How many rounds are there?"
"Ten."
"And how many teams?"
"Five."
"And what would you estimate our chances are of winning any of these rounds?"
"As in winning, you mean... Not losing? Honestly?"
"Honestly."
"About zero, I would think."
"That's about where I had it figured. So, by my calculation, between the two of us, we are going to be paying for about fifty drinks."
"Oh, ah," Old Bills busied himself with his packet of fudge. "We might get lucky." He slipped a particularly large piece of fudge past his pipe stem and chewed thoughtfully. "Even Sandy's got to have an off day once in a while."

A movement of people towards the skittle area indicated the start of the match. Tremayne pressed forward in order to gain a good view and hopefully some tips. A ball spun from Sandy's grip and skittered across the floor, knocking all nine

The Money That Never Was

of the pins into the air. This procedure was repeated a few moments later by Jeannie Featherstone. She shook her fist into the air and shouted, "Yes!" In a very unvicar's daughter-like way. They followed this up with another turn each, where the result was repeated.

Okay, thought Tremayne, it can't be that hard. It's all a matter of angles and trajectory. Same basic principles as a rifle. His turn came and he picked up the heavy wooden ball. He squinted along the floor, looking for deviations that would nudge the ball off course. He drew his arm back and slid the ball forward trying to emulate Sandy's movement. The ball bounced twice on the floor, skipped across to the bench on the left, and slid harmlessly between bench and skittles.

"Oh, that's good!" Old Bill said.
"Why?"
"I thought I was the only one that did that."
True to his prediction, he repeated Tremayne's manoeuvre perfectly.

They fared little better in the second round. Scoring three points between them. Their disgrace was further heightened by the ignominy of having to buy the drinks. The next round was no improvement, although the ever-encroaching alcoholic haze seemed to make the defeat slightly less offensive.

It was only half way through the third round, when Tremayne suddenly realised his pipe had gone out that it dawned on him he'd been smoking at all. He pulled it from his mouth and looked at it as if seeing it for the first time. He gave a little shudder and stuffed the pipe in his pocket. A few minutes later, he realised he'd eaten the best part of his packet of sherry fudge.

The room folded in around him like a warm duvet on a cold winter's night. People smiled and joked. They seemed genuinely pleased for him when he managed to knock over a few skittles. Or perhaps, it was just that they knew there was more alcohol heading their way at his defeat. No, that was unfair. They even bought him drinks in return. And that *wasn't* in the rules.

The noise level increased with each passing round. Clinking glasses and mumbled voices.

And above all, laughter.

A constant, underlying laughter rolled across the room like waves on a beach.

Tremayne took his place for his next and final attempt at the skittles. Taking a bead on the centre skittle, he forced his shoulders to relax. He began the back swing.

He felt a presence behind him and stopped.

The nape of his neck tingled and the muscles in his legs tightened. His heart rate doubled. This sensation usually told him danger was threatening. But, this was different. He certainly didn't feel afraid. No, he felt a strange sense of warmth.

He turned.

Sandy's face was not three inches away from his.
"Oh!" he said.
The babble in the room retreated and he suddenly realised Dire Straits were playing Romeo and Juliet. His visual range narrowed focus until Sandy was the only thing he saw. The rest of the room fuzzed into blurry shapes. Senses in full overdrive. The last time that had happened had been when he was about to kill an Armenian terrorist who was trying to dynamite a busload of children. But that response didn't seem appropriate here. His mind fumbled for matching patterns and found none.

"Do you need some help?" Sandy's gaze danced across

his face. His sudden intake of breath pulled the scent of Opium into his nose.

"What?" He realised as soon as he'd opened his mouth just how inarticulate that sounded but his brain was still struggling with its heightened senses and refused to co-operate in the speech department.

"That!"

He followed her eyes down and saw she was looking at his bowling ball.

"Is that allowed? Within the rules?" he asked.

"I don't see why not. You're going to lose any way."

"Thank you. Was that supposed to make me feel better by any chance?"

"No. Winning isn't everything, it's how you play the game that matters."

"I don't understand."

"*That* was designed to make you feel better. Now, do you want a hand or what?"

"Thank you, I'm sure there's probably a knack to it." He looked again at the bowling ball that he held like a barrier between them

"It's all in the wrist." Sandy's hand slid over his wrist.

The room stopped.

The universe existed only in a single point of contact between them. Something flowed across the touch and spread through his body. Like the warmth from a summer's day seeping through his skin and waking each cell in a rush of sensation. He resisted the urge to break the contact and pull away.

Her eyes locked on his. Deep, bottomless eyes. Drawing him in. Two singularities, pulling at the new sensations, drawing them back and forming a complete circle.

"Oh," he said then instantly regretted it. The last time he'd felt anything even remotely similar had been at La Scala when listening to Elisabeth Soenderstroem sing Martern aller Arten. How the pure notes had swept through him.

But that had been a soft breeze and this was a whirlwind.
"Oh?" she echoed.
"The wrist." He looked down to where her hand still covered his. "I expect you're right, it's all in wrist." He wondered if she felt the same thing.
"Come on, let me show you," she said.

She guided him to the end of the alley. The room came back and he realised the noise had been there all along. And that very probably, nobody else had actually noticed. She showed him how to hold the ball and where to place his feet. He followed her instructions obediently, willingly.
"You need to relax, Charles. Let the ball take control. It's like life, you can only guide it, you mustn't fight the direction."
Under her guidance, the ball slid from his fingertips with the delicacy of a butterfly lifting into the air. The ball struck the centre pin, sending all but one of the pins into a heap at the back of the alley.
"Not bad," she said.
Tremayne felt a slight glow of pleasure at the compliment then quickly suppressed it.

***

The match ended as Tremayne knew it would. Sandy's Angels taking first place, and the 'Otters' struggling to secure last.

He sat back in his chair, and for the moment just enjoyed being there. His senses swirled under a cider and fudge induced haze. But beneath that haze, a spark burned. A spark of something he thought had died many years ago. Strangely, he could still feel Sandy's touch on his hand. His gaze went in search of her. He found her stacking glasses on a shelf behind the bar. She had her back to him, but even then, she looked different. More sensual almost. As if sensing his gaze, she turned and looked directly at him. At the same time, another mobile phone rang.

The piece slotted into position.

And the spark settled back into the dark recesses that formed the more natural order of his mind.

Chapter 8

Jerry Richards looked around the room. The villagers were more subdued at this time in the morning, with only Tom Trevellick appearing comfortable with 6.30am. Probably milking time.

"Are we all here?" he asked.
"All except Barry," Constable Muchmore answered. Jerry thought he could detect an edge in Muchmore's voice.
"I think Barry's gone away, Constable. I thought I heard him mention something about Disneyland."
"I see."

They sat on folding wooden seats in a loose circle in the village hall. Although the circle was supposed to indicate no hierarchy, Jerry's position in front of the stage gave him natural control.

"Okay, then," Jerry started. "I called this meeting so we could assess the damage and work out how best to deal with our visitor. So far, Sandy's done a great job in keeping him occupied. But from what Constable Muchmore says, it seems our government man is on the track. Although hopefully, he doesn't know the full extent."
"I think he just believes we've been paid off for handling the money." Muchmore said.
"Can we keep him amused until he becomes bored and leaves?" Reverend Featherstone asked.
"Sandy?" Jerry raised an eyebrow as he looked towards her. "Over to you."
"No!" Sandy snapped. "I don't think I can do it any more."
"We can help," Reverend Featherstone said. "It's about time we had a village fete anyway."
"No, it's not that." Sandy turned her attention to her fingernails. "It's dishonest."
"Interesting point of view," Jerry said. "Depriving Her

Majesty's government of two hundred and fifty million isn't dishonest?"

"Yes it is. But in a different way. It's not people. It's not personal. It's not... Oh, I don't know. I just know I'm not going to do it any more. Make your plans without me." She jumped out of her chair with such a start that it clattered backwards to the floor. She headed for the door then slammed it behind her.

Mrs Pomfrey caught up with Sandy at the lych-gate on the edge of the church grounds. Sandy held onto the gate, fingers digging into the century old wood. Only her shoulders moved, rising rhythmically in time with her controlled breaths.

"Are you alright, my dear?" Mrs. Pomfrey asked.

Sandy continued to stare out across the graveyard. Motionless, almost a part of the lych-gate itself. The early morning breeze flicked at her hair. Mrs. Pomfrey reached out and touched her shoulder. Sandy flinched.

"What's wrong, Sandy?"

"Nothing. It was just very smoky in there. I needed a break. How's the fudge going?" "Sometimes, when I'm making my fudge, an unexpected ingredient gets added in by mistake. It doesn't mean I have to throw it all away though. I just follow it through to see how it turns out. Very often, it turns out nicer than the way I'd intended."

"Thank you, Mrs. Pomfrey."

"You're welcome, my dear."

Sandy turned to face Mrs. Pomfrey. Her eyes tight with suppressed tears. "I just—"

"Ah! There you both are!" Reverend Featherstone bowled up the path towards the gate in a way that Mrs. Pomfrey found reminiscent of the White Rabbit from Alice. "Woman talk is it? Jolly good!"

"Meeting finished?" Sandy asked.

"Oh, yes. I have to start the organ. Call the faithful!" He breezed through the gate and headed up the narrow path that wove through the gravestones towards the church entrance.

"You were about to say?" Mrs Pomfrey asked.

"Nothing. I have a breakfast to sort."

***

The first chord of Metallica's 'Blackened' seared through Tremayne's sleep. By the second chord, he was sitting upright. The music burst in through the walls. His hand reached for the radio switch. It was already in the off position. He staggered out of bed and followed the sound to the window. He fought his way through the seemingly endless array of lace curtains that separated him from the glass. Most odd. The noise appeared to be coming from the direction of the church.

He checked his watch. 8am. He went into the bathroom and stepped under the shower. The pummelling water drove out the noise. By the time he emerged, Metallica had been replaced by the funeral march.

Just as he'd finished slipping his trousers on, he heard a knock on the door.
He opened it to find Sandy there with a tray in her hand.
"Oh!" he said. "I didn't expect breakfast."
"I know. It's only toast and coffee."

The music outside changed to the peal of church bells. The more usual Sunday output of a village church.
"What's with the music?" Tremayne cocked his head towards the window.
"I think the vicar's still getting used to his new toy."
"Oh, I see."
"Well? You going to take the tray or are you going to make me stand here all day?"
"Of course. Sorry!" He took the tray from her and carried it into the room.

Sandy followed him. Her eyes scanned the room, clearly finding the unadorned surfaces somewhat of a mystery.
"What happened to all the ornaments this time?"
"Ah, they fell out of the window."

The Money That Never Was

"Even the lampshades?"

"Yes, they went first. It was while I was looking to see where they'd gone. Everything else fell out. Must have been the wind."

"I expect Dad will give you the bill for those you know." She sat down on the edge of the bed.

"I'll pay happily, as long as I never have to set eyes on another porcelain nymph."

"Mum used to like ornaments. I think that's why Dad keeps so many of them about."

Although Tremayne had seen his fair share of dead people, even having dispatched a few of them himself, he had always been uncomfortable talking about bereavement.

"Sandy?"

"Yes?"

"What do you know about satellite phones?" He watched her pupils carefully waiting for the telltale dilation.

As if aware that her eyes might betray her, she turned towards the window. "Isn't that what you have? A satellite phone?"

"Yes, I just wondered why there were suddenly so many of them around this village now."

"Oh, I hadn't noticed." She stood up, keeping her back to him.

"How many people did you tell about the way satellite phones work?"

She turned to face him with what she obviously hoped was a light-hearted toss of the head. "I don't know. I might have mentioned it a few times. Not important, is it? Anyway, I've got things to do Mr Tremayne. I can't stand around here chatting all day."

Without even asking whether he still wanted his breakfast, she picked up the tray and left the room.

As soon as he was alone, Tremayne picked up his phone and pressed the button that gave him a secure, scrambled line to his office.

"Elaine?"

"Good morning, Charles. How is the country life treating you? Not eating too many pasties I hope?"

"No, no pasties. You know me, Elaine."

"That's just as well then. You know what Gemini's like about his agents being lean and fit."

"Lean and fit as ever."

"What can I do for you, Charles?"

"Jerry Richards. I was expecting to have come across him by now. But he seems to be keeping a low profile. Where am I likely to find him?"

"Hold on a second." He imagined her tapping at her computer keys. "Details coming across to you in a text message now, Charles."

His phone gave two short bleeps to indicate the message had arrived.

"Thank you, Elaine."

"How's it going down there anyway?"

"Fine! Nearly wrapped up I think. I'm fairly sure I know where the money is."

"You going to tell me?"

"Not till I return to London. I want to be sure first. I'll speak to you later." He closed the connection then thumbed the button that brought up the text message. He committed to memory the details of Jerry Richards' address.

He picked up the jacket he'd been wearing to the skittles match to transfer the items to the pockets of the leather coat he'd just put on. He felt slightly puzzled as his hands closed around an unfamiliar object. He pulled out the pipe. Giving a quick shudder, he tossed it in the rubbish bin.

He double-checked the lock on his suitcase, clipped the phone to his belt then left the room. He was just about to pull the door closed when he paused for a moment.

He returned to the bedroom, retrieved the pipe from the bin, and stuffed it in his pocket.

***

Jerry Richards' Used Car Emporium lay three miles out of town in what appeared to have once been the car park to a quarry. Two lines of cars stretched across the gravel forecourt. Banners fluttered overhead proclaiming 'Quality pre-Owned Vehicles at discount prices.' Each car was further adorned with Day-Glo orange signs offering attractive finance terms and full guarantees on selected mechanical parts.

Jerry was crouched next to the front wheel of a blue Audi when Tremayne pulled onto the gravelled forecourt. Jerry looked up as he heard the car arrive. He held a pot of paint and a brush and appeared to be painting the front tyre of the car. He stood up as Tremayne's car stopped, leaving the paint pot on the ground. His foot worked at nudging it under the vehicle.

Tremayne climbed out of his car just as Jerry Richards reached him.
"Hello," Jerry said. He nodded at Tremayne's car. "Looking to trade up? Not much call for Mercs these days. The market's dropped. What with the Euro and so on. But if you want to trade it in against a Ford, I'll do you a good deal."

Tremayne studied the man in front of him. Richards was a good six-foot three. His shoulders hunched slightly, giving him a lean, hawkish look. His receding blond hair swept back in a naturally flamboyant wave.

"No," Tremayne said. "I'm not looking for a car. I'm looking for a location. I'm a location scout for a film company."
"You want a car showroom for your film?"
No, not exactly. We're filming an eighteenth century romance. A car showroom might be a bit out of place. But the area looks good for some of our shots."
"Well, If you made me the right offer, I'd sell up and you

can tear this down and do what you like."

"Thank you, but that won't be necessary. My name's Tremayne, by the way. Charles Tremayne." He held his hand out.

"Jerry Richards. Call me Jerry. Call me anything! Just as long as you call me when you want a new car!"

Jerry's handshake was firm but not exaggerated.

The sound of a car arriving caught Tremayne's attention. A red Ford Fiesta pulled up to a stop not three metres away. A young couple climbed out followed by a cloud of cigarette smoke.

"Be back with you in a minute, Mr Tremayne. Real punters."

His relaxed, easy gait told of high confidence.

"Good morning! Looking to trade up? Not much call for Fords these days. The market's dropped. What with the Euro and so on. But if you want to upgrade to say an Audi, I'll do you a good deal."

His arm snaked around the woman's shoulder, and he guided her towards the Audi whose tyres he'd been painting.

"I could do you a special on this one if you like. I've only just taken this in as a part exchange. As I made a nice profit on the original deal, I'm prepared to let this go at what it cost me."

"How much do you want for it?" the woman asked.

"Well, I was going to clean it up a bit then put it out at four thousand. But if you take it as seen… oh… go on… I'll let you have it for three."

"You hear that Darren?" the woman said. "It sounds like a bargain!"

"That's more than we were planning on spending, Tracey. I think it's too much."

Jerry opened the door for them. "Here, sit inside. No hurry. Get the feel of it. Have a chat."

The couple climbed into the car, and Jerry returned to

Tremayne. "Let's go into my office."

Jerry's office consisted of a converted caravan. Inside, a wooden, paper strewn desk took up central position. A selection of metal-framed chairs filled most of the rest of the floor space. A green metal filing cabinet sat in the corner and supported a kettle, a milk bottle, and a packet of sugar.

Jerry indicated one of the chairs. "Sit down." He sat down behind the desk, opened a drawer, and removed a small black radio receiver. He planted it on the desk and switched it on.

At once, Darren and Tracey's voices could be heard through the tiny speaker.

"You have a microphone in the car?" Tremayne queried.
"I have in all of them."
"But isn't that slightly unethical?"
"Of course not. Punters are shy people. They won't tell me what they really want. If I listen in on them and find out what they really want, I can fill their needs. What's unethical about that?"
"But surely—"
"Shhh! Listen!"
The tinny speaker crackled, "But, Darren, it is a lovely car. Look it's got an electric sunroof."
"Yes, Tracey, but three thousand pounds is a lot of money."
"We can afford it."
"Well, I suppose. If you really want it. But we'll see if we can knock him down. Let's offer him two."

Jerry switched off the radio and returned it to the drawer. "There, see! Now I know they want the car, I can help them buy it."

Footsteps in the gravel just outside the caravan announced the return of Darren and Tracey. Jerry picked up his telephone and put it to his ear just as the couple entered.

"Yes... yes," Jerry said into the mouthpiece. He waved the couple to the seats opposite. "I know... but I've got somebody looking at it right now.... I know you want it... Yes, four thousand... No, I can't. No... not even for four and a half. I've got to let these people have first option now. If they don't want it, I'll come back to you. Bye."

Jerry replaced the handset and turned his attention to Darren and Tracey. "Well? What do you think?"

"It's all right I suppose," Darren said, in what he clearly hoped was his best nonchalant voice. "But I don't think we can afford three thousand. Will you take two?"

"No can do, I'm afraid." Jerry stood up ready to shake Darren's hand. "I was going to sell it just then to somebody else. But I'm a man of honour. I wanted to give you first go. I'll let you know if I get anything cheaper in."

"Darren?" Tracey whispered loudly.

"Oh, okay then."

Five minutes of paperwork later, Darren and Tracey left with their new Audi.

"Very smooth," Tremayne said. "Just one thing that puzzles me."

"What's that, Mr Tremayne?

"Why were you so confident I wouldn't give the game away?"

"Because we all have our secrets, don't we, Mr Tremayne?" Jerry leaned forward across the table and rested his chin on his entwined fingers. The posture was relaxed, but the eyes were alive.

Tremayne knew that look. He'd seen that one many times before. He'd just never expected to see it here in Little Didney.

"I'm not sure what you mean, Jerry."

"What I mean is..." Jerry sat back in his chair and slipped his hands behind his neck. "Is that if my secrets aren't safe with a Ministry of Defence field operative, then

The Money That Never Was

who could I trust?

For the first time since his arrival in Little Didney, Tremayne felt the presence of a very real threat. His body readied itself for action. Blood left the digestive system and flushed into his limbs. His focal range narrowed, and the heart rate increased, ready to pump extra supplies when needed.

"I think you must have me confused with somebody else." Tremayne weighed the distance between them. Richards was out of range, so no attack was imminent. "I'm a location scout for Trojan Films."

"Mr Tremayne, let's cut the bullshit. You're a field operative for MI6"

"What makes you think that?" How on earth had his cover been blown? Had PC Muchmore been talking? How much did this man know?

"I'm in the motor trade, Mr Tremayne. Your car is registered to Mayfair Exports. Not Trojan Films."

"How does that connect to MI6?"

"The car was purchased from Blenheim Motors six months ago. Paid for with a government cheque! Now, I wondered which government department would possibly want to conceal ownership of a vehicle? And if you are driving a government car, why are you telling porky-pies about who you are? Which government departments lie so fluently, I asked myself. You see my point?"

"Very astute, Jerry." Tremayne relaxed back in his chair. Jerry Richards was clearly a very clever and resourceful man. But at least it seemed the real reason for Tremayne's visit was still secure.

"Now," Jerry said. "Suppose we talk about money!"

Chapter 9

"He wants how much?" Gemini's voice had lost none of its strength in the fifty-thousand mile round trip via the telecom satellite. "A hundred thousand? For half a dozen dodgy motors and a caravan?"

"And his silence." Tremayne leant against the roof of his car. The metal felt warm through the sleeve of his jacket. He had left Jerry inside the office while he went to consult with Gemini over this somewhat unusual transaction. "You see, sir, his logic is that if we are a film company then a hundred grand for a location is only a little steep. However, if we are M16 then the same amount for his silence is extremely cheap. In his mind, the deal is fair either way."

"What would your recommendation be then, Charles? And no, you don't have permission to kill him."

"Well, in that case, plan B would be to play along with him for a while. Give me time to establish whether or not he does actually know anything."

"So, what do you need? Some cash I assume?"

"Ten thousand should do it, sir."

"Well, I suppose as we've already lost two hundred and fifty million losing another ten thousand's not going to make a lot of difference."

"Thank you for the vote of confidence, sir."

"Just get it sorted, Charles." The phone went dead.

Tremayne returned to Jerry's office. "Looks like you've got yourself a deal Jerry."

"It's a pleasure doing business with you. Whoever you are." Richards gave an exaggerated wink that made Tremayne want to poke his eye with something hard and pointy.

"I'll have a cheque for you in a couple of days."

"A cheque? Oh, no! I don't think a cheque will do at all. Folding stuff is good enough for me."

***

The Money That Never Was

"More gravy, Charles?" Sandy slid the gravy boat across the huge pine kitchen table towards Tremayne. He'd never seen so much food together on one plate before in his life. When he'd been invited to share traditional Sunday lunch with Sandy and her father, he'd envisioned a light midday meal. But this was something else.

They'd started with home-made vegetable soup and bread, fresh from the oven. But now the main course just kept coming.

Goodenough set about carving huge chunks of beef with an over elaborate electric carving knife that wouldn't have looked out of place trimming a hedge. A large piece of meat flew off the end of the knife and skidded across the floor.

Sandy dished out the vegetables. Roast potatoes, mash, carrots, green beans, roast turnip, and the whole lot topped off by an enormous Yorkshire pudding then covered in gravy.

"Not often we have a guest for lunch," said Goodenough, as he balanced another ragged chunk of meat onto his plate.

This was the first time Tremayne had been in their kitchen. The pine table took up most of the available floor space with just enough room for four chairs around it. Every time he moved, his chair wobbled on the uneven quarry floor tiles. A huge green Aga oven filled the original fireplace.

Tremayne waved his hand at the gravy boat. "No thanks."

"Here," Goodenough said. "Help yourself to some horseradish sauce. Locally made. None of yer E additives here."

Tremayne managed to manoeuvre some of his potatoes to one side to clear a tiny spot for the sauce.

"Sandy, get Mr Tremayne another beer would you?"

"Yes, Dad."
"No! Really, I have a lot to do this afternoon."
"Do? On a Sunday?" Goodenough sounded shocked. "People don't do things in Little Didney on Sunday afternoons, Mr Tremayne."

Sandy reappeared from the back door to the bar carrying a large pitcher of frothing beer.
"How's Mrs. Pomfrey doing?" Goodenough asked.
"She fine, Dad. There's only a couple of people in the bar."
"Are you always this quiet on a Sunday lunchtime?" Tremayne asked. It seemed strange to him they could afford both of them to be absent from the bar during a Sunday lunchtime. Perhaps though, this wasn't normal. Perhaps this was another stage-managed event.
"We're a very traditional village, Mr Tremayne." Goodenough refilled the glasses from the jug. "Most people are at home having their lunch as we are. None of those fancy gastro pubs here." He picked up his knife and fork and waggled them at Tremayne. "Start away then. We don't stand on ceremony here."

Tremayne looked at his mountain of food and wondered just where to start. He decided to start at the top and work his way in. The Yorkshire pudding was crisp, light, and brought back memories of his lodging days at university.

"Tell me," Goodenough said. "Where are you from?"
"London"
"No, I mean originally? Your family?"
"They were Londoners too."
"What, with a name like Tremayne? That's a good old Cornish name, that is. Looks like you've come home!"
"I never thought of my name as Cornish."
"Oh, yes. Lots of Tremaynes down this part of the world. There's three of them in our graveyard."
"Now, Dad! I'm sure Charles isn't interested in who's in the graveyard."
"Nothing wrong with graveyards," Goodenough said.

"We're all going to end up there one day. I was saying the same thing to Mrs Goodenough the day before she went."

Tremayne felt that was probably a great comfort to her. "Yes, Sandy told me you'd lost your wife, Mr Goodenough. I am sorry."

"No I didn't!"

"Sorry?"

"I didn't lose her at all! She died, Mr Tremayne! If I'd lost here, I'd have sent somebody out to look for her."

"Dad!" Sandy scolded. Then, in a transparent attempt to change the subject, "So, Charles, what have you been doing with yourself today?"

"I went to see Jerry Richards."

"Oh, yes," Goodenough said. "And how much did that cost you then?"

"Er, About a hundred thousand."

"Ah right. I'd say you got off lightly then!"

***

Tremayne pushed his nearly empty plate to one side. "That was delicious, thank you."

"More potatoes?" Sandy offered.

"No. Thank you, I couldn't eat another thing." He slid his chair back and tugged at his waistband to test the free space. There was none.

"I'll just get the pudding. Hang on."

"Pudding? No, I really couldn't."

"Oh!" Sandy looked dismayed. "I made it specially. It's your favourite, treacle tart!" She wrapped a white linen tea towel around her hands and extracted from the oven a beautifully browned treacle tart the size of a dinner plate. A lattice of golden pastry criss-crossed the surface. The sweet smell hit Tremayne's nose, and his resolve disappeared.

After two large portions of treacle tart and another beer, they adjourned to the lounge. More evidence of Goodenough's passion for ornamental whimsy filled the room. A glass fronted dresser contained an inordinate number of souvenir china plates. Every level surface contained some item of porcelain or carved wood. And every surface that wasn't level held something soft and fluffy.

"Move Shep and sit down then." Goodenough indicated a full sized toy Old English Sheepdog that sat in a huge floral recliner.

Tremayne moved Shep to the floor and settled back in the chair. It seemed to eat him. Goodenough flopped onto the sofa and pointed the remote control at the television set. It burst into life at the point where John Mills was explaining the escape plan to Steve McQueen.

"Ah, lovely!" Goodenough said. "One of my favourites."

The room was too warm, the chair too soft, and Tremayne's stomach too full. Within ten minute, he was fighting a losing battle with the pervasive tendrils of sleep.

He awoke just as Steve McQueen was making a final attempt to leap the barbed wire on his motorbike. No matter how many times he saw this scene, irrationally, he always had a slight hope that this time he'd make it.

Goodenough lay stretched out on the sofa. His head thrown back, and his mouth wide open. A loud gurgling sound, reminiscent of water running from a sink, escaped the gaping orifice each time his chest rose and fell.

Tremayne eased himself free from the clutches of the chair, headed for the back door, and out into the fresh air.

If the Sunday afternoon tradition in Little Didney was to fall asleep in front of the television, then the village should be quiet. On the other hand, if this were a managed project, then the villagers would assume Goodenough was still keeping an eye on him. Either way, it meant a couple of hours freedom.

He parked his car up a narrow track about a quarter of a mile away from Jerry Richards' Used Car Emporium and set off on foot.

Something had bothered Tremayne about Jerry. While most of the village sprouted expensive trinkets like Christmas in Harrods, Jerry Richards had been wearing a fake Rolex, and cheap, gaudy gold plated rings. That meant he either wasn't in on the disappearing money, or he was much cleverer at concealing his involvement.

Tremayne skirted around the rear of the forecourt, staying tight to the hedges that provided some cover at least. Although the forecourt was open for business, there was no sign of Jerry. He was probably in his caravan.

A large green wooden shed stood to the rear of the premises. Tremayne guessed this was some sort of workshop. In a series of short, surreptitious movements, he made his way towards the shed. This was more comfortable ground. Sneaking up on places or people was what Tremayne did best. He'd had enough of this pussyfooting around, being nice to people. He didn't do 'nice' very well. This was much better. All that was missing now, was a Heckler and Koch pistol in his hand.

The window of the shed was caked in dirt. He plucked a handful of long grass and rubbed at the glass to clean a small patch to peer through. The inside was in darkness. He pulled a Mag-Light from his pocket and shone it through the clear patch. The beam of light raked across a bright green vehicle. A familiar vehicle. Barry Penwrith's Ford Capri.

***

Tremayne parked his car in its usual place at the top of the town, then set off on foot through the main road heading towards Leafy Lane, and Barry's cottage. He had only walked about twenty metres down the road when he saw Goodenough heading up the hill towards him. As they drew nearer to each other, it became apparent that Goodenough was in a highly flustered state.

"Where've you been then?" he asked accusingly, between ragged breaths.

"Oh, just for a drive. Still looking for some suitable moorland for the highwayman scene."

"Oh, right! Fancy popping back for another beer then?"

"No thanks, I'm just going for a bit of a walk to blow the cobwebs away"

He continued walking, leaving Goodenough bending over by the side of the road drawing deep, wheezing breaths.

Tremayne was about to turn off into Leafy Lane, when he heard the thrum of a powerful engine approaching from behind. He turned to see a black suited and helmeted figure astride a shiny Harley Davidson Motorcycle. The bike was travelling so slowly that the rider had to keep putting a foot to the floor to stay upright. It drew level with Tremayne and the figure raised a hand and called, "Afternoon, Mr Tremayne"

"Good afternoon..." He struggled to place the voice. Then it clicked. "Mrs. Pomfrey!"

Mrs. Pomfrey continued to wobble her new toy down The High Street and disappeared around the corner.

***

This time, Tremayne wasn't interested in the interior of Barry's house, or even the house itself. He was more concerned with the surrounding area. A quick search of the woods that skirted three sides of Barry's house revealed a well-trodden trail that ran deeper into the woods. In places, the trail was difficult to follow; bramble and hazel pushed in from all sides. After about a quarter of a mile, the nature of the woods changed. Tall, evenly spaced fir and beech made the way clearer. Sunlight speckled in through the green canopy above, giving a kaleidoscopic effect to the ground. The smell of pine permeated the air.

A clearer patch ahead, revealed itself as a wide, driveable track coming in from the north. Recent tyre tracks ran deeper into the wood. Tremayne followed them. Before long, he was standing outside a ramshackle wooden shed. He tugged at the piece of string that held the door closed. It swung open then dangled at a skewed angle from the one remaining hinge. Behind that was another door.

The Money That Never Was

A white metal door.

It bore the legend 'Shifter's Road Transport Services'

Tremayne pulled the back of the van open. It was empty. Well, at least he knew who had hidden the truck in the first place. Barry Penwrith. And the fact that Barry's car was now locked up in Jerry Richards' workshop, meant Jerry was deeply involved in this as well. Along with everybody else who seemed to be spending rather a lot of money at the moment.

He pushed both doors shut then followed the wider trail north. He'd only gone about five hundred metres when he heard footsteps ahead. He slid into a particularly thick patch of woods. Brambles scraped at his face and hands. As soon as the footsteps closed in on his position, he stepped out from his hiding place.

"Charles!"
"Hello, Sandy. What are you doing here?"
"I was... I was looking for you. Mrs. Pomfrey said she saw you going this way."
"I thought she might." He watched her face, noting that the colour she'd lost when she'd first seen him was quickly returning. She had changed since lunchtime and now wore well-faded jeans and a white sweatshirt.
"What are you doing here?" she asked.
"Just thought I'd like to take in the local scenery." He waved his arm, indicating the woods. "Why did you come looking for me?"
"I wanted to..." She closed the distance between them till she was no more than a few inches from his face. Her eyes appeared to search his. "I just thought... thought it would be nice if we walked together for a while." She broke the eye contact and turned her head. "Don't you think the woods are lovely this time of year, Charles?"
"I must confess to never having given much thought to woods before."

"Don't the trees make you feel exhilarated? Perhaps it's the oxygen the leaves put out or something. Do you think that could be it?" She was rambling. She turned to face him again. Her gaze was flitting far too quickly around his face. A sure sign of concealment.

"That's quite possible I suppose. Oxygen can give you a buzz. And yes, I would like to walk with you."

"Oh!" She looked surprised.

Tremayne pointed up the track in the direction of the shed. "Let's see what's up this way, shall we?"

"No! Not much up there. Tell you what, why don't we..." She moved closer and touched his arm. "Why don't we... I mean, we could..."

"Yes?"

"I'm sorry!" She turned away. "I can't do this."

"He touched her shoulder. "It's all right, Sandy. I know."

Her breathing stopped.

"What do you know?" She spun back to face him.

"I know about the truck. I know about the money. And I'm guessing you were sent here to divert me. Whose idea was that? Jerry's?"

Her eyes reddened with suppressed tears. "Mrs. Pomfrey's actually. What do you know? How much? Who are you, Charles?

Chapter 10

Tremayne looked past Sandy and into the woods. He wanted to end the deceit.

"I'm with M.I.6.," he said finally.

"M.I.6?" Sandy's brow wrinkled. "If I remember my spy books correctly, aren't they the ones that are supposed to operate in foreign lands? Preventing World War Three by stealing the secret death ray machine?"

"Not so many death ray machines about these days."

"Isn't Little Didney a bit tame for you?"

"Exceedingly."

"So, just how much trouble are we in, Charles?" Sandy leaned her back against the tree and slid down into a sitting position. Her outstretched feet ploughing two furrows in the soft soil.

"That's not up to me. That will be for the police and the courts to decide." He avoided her gaze.

"We didn't steal the money, you know. We only found it. Perhaps we'll get a reward?"

"I think the best reward you lot can hope for is a lenient judge and a short prison sentence." He knelt down on the ground near her. "Just to fill in a few gaps for me... I take it Barry discovered the money and it's now divided up?"

"Yes," she said. "Pretty much." She kept her gaze firmly on her feet as they kicked at the leafy ground. "Whose money was it?"

"It belonged to the Ministry of Defence. That's as much as I can say. In fact, I shouldn't have told you that."

"Dirty money pay-off, Jerry said." She pushed into the dirt with her heels, piling up a small pile of earth. "Why did they send you, anyway? Aren't you supposed to be rescuing beautiful KGB spies?"

"Not much call for that nowadays. The Russians are our best friends now. Didn't anybody tell you that?"

Sandy forced a smile. "Will they really arrest us all? Send us all to prison?"

Tremayne turned his head away. He was finding her

difficult to look at for some reason. "Come on," he said. "We'd better head back. I have some calls to make."

He made to stand, but she grabbed his arm. "Please don't, Charles. Can't you just forget?"

He turned to face her again. She looked so lost. So upset. "No. I'm sorry, I can't. All my life I've been fighting for what I believe is right. It's not right to steal two hundred and fifty million pounds. Whatever it was meant for."

"Is it right to destroy a village?" Her hand, still gripping his arm, tightened. "What's going to happen to Little Didney when most of the adult population are in prison? You've seen the village, Charles. It's not just a place to live, a collection of houses; it's a community. A family. Is that your version of fighting for right? To destroy it?" She drew her knees up to her chest and wrapped her arms around them. "Before that money, Little Didney was only just surviving. Hanging on. The younger generations have been drifting off for years. Even my own brothers have left. Most of the local businesses, Dad's included, are in hock to the bank. Tom's farm has been hit by one European directive after another. Tourists don't visit anymore. Why should they? They can visit a genuine Cornish Fishing village in a theme park now! That money would have saved this village, Charles. And now, you're going to finally close it down."

"It's not my decision, Sandy. You all made that decision when you kept the money."

She stood up and stared down at him. "I thought you were a decent man. I thought... maybe... I felt...You're not though are you? Don't you realise the world doesn't need you any more? Or Little Didney, we're dinosaurs, you, me, the village. But you're worse. You're cold. There's nothing human in there anymore is there? Just as long as the job gets done. Well do it! Do your fucking job!" She turned and walked away up the track.

Tremayne sat back against the tree, allowing her words to settle in. He watched her disappear through the trees. He wanted to call her back, but he wasn't sure why. What would he say if he did call her back?

He picked up a handful of the dirt that Sandy had been kicking into a pile. A slight musty smell drifted by him.

As Sandy's footsteps had faded into the distance, the woods were once again silent. He let his mind drift. Taking advantage of the solitude. If they hadn't stolen the money, who had? Mr Green and his gang had been paid off by a voice on a telephone. But it still left a third party in all this. Who had hijacked the van? Why had they left the money there to be picked up by Barry? And just where was Barry?

Oh, well. He'd done his bit now. Time to turn it over to the police, hand in his papers and head for Geneva. He took another pull on his pipe, rolling the smoke around his mouth. "What!" He pulled the pipe from his mouth and held it up in front of him. Where the hell had that come from? He didn't remember lighting that.

He smiled as he remembered the first time he'd tried the pipe. How he'd coughed so hard he thought he'd never breath normally again. It was quite funny now, looking back on it.

He heard a rustling to his left and turned his head quickly, wondering if Sandy had returned. A small roe deer stood not three metres from him, Watching him. Its nose twitching. Tremayne stayed absolutely still and the deer ventured closer a few steps. A small trail of smoke drifted in the deer's direction. The deer flicked its head then, as if disgusted by the smell, turned and scampered off into the woods.

Tremayne had never seen one of those creatures that close before. He'd have to remember to mention it to Sandy next time they talked. If they talked. Somehow that thought pinged at something deep within him. Cold, inhuman, she'd called him. Maybe he was. When you've spent your life dealing with the scum of the planet and helping to expedite their reunion with their maker, it might have a tendency to sour on one's world view of humanity. He resolved to do a degree in philosophy or something when he got to Switzerland. Find his soul. There's bound to be a course on that.

***

Tremayne turned out of the end of Leafy Lane and into The High Street with a slight sense of apprehension. Had Sandy told everybody yet? Were they going to conduct one of those upside down lynchings he'd already been witness to? He wasn't even sure why he'd told Sandy as much as he had.

Mrs Pomfrey was waiting for him. "We thought you'd got lost. Those woods can get fair tolgy in places. Man could circle round for days, never be seen again." She slipped her arm through his as if they'd been dating for years.

He found himself being guided down The High Street, a direction he'd not actually planned to take but it didn't seem worth the fight to change course. The street was deserted, the normal everyday and somewhat mysterious meanderings of the villagers strangely absent. Mrs Pomfrey's gentle but insistent guiding veered to cross the narrow cobbled walkway. She hesitated halfway across, seeming to listen before continuing. Charles felt a gentle but firm pressure on his arm.

"Just need to pop into the Post Off ice, my dear. Need a stamp." She dug deep into her handbag as they walked and pulled out a Louis Vitton purse. They were halfway across the road as she opened the purse and the contents fell clinking to the ground. "Oh, drat and darn," she exclaimed as loose change ran in all directions. "That was the last of my pension."

Charles let slip her arm. Years of public school

education have an effect on a man. Without thinking, he dropped to the ground to chase down the errant coins as they spiralled and bounced between the cobbles.

"Don't worry, I'll catch them." He glanced up to smile reassurance only to find Mrs Pomfrey had disappeared from view. Confusion slowed his normally lightning reactions. How had she moved so fast? Why? And what the hell is that noise? The last question was answered instantly as his eyes turned up the steep slope of the High Street. At tractor with some complicated and vicious looking farming attachment on the front was bouncing down the road at an outrageous speed. There seemed to be nobody at the controls as the engine screamed and it swerved from side to side. The contraption on the front, probably a hay turner or similar, seemed to scrape both sides of the street at the same time. Sharp rusty metal spikes dragged across the stone walls of the cottages and ran gouges into the cobbles.

Tremayne had seconds only. There was no way of either slipping to the side of this thing or outrunning it. Even as stood up, his feet were already running. Downhill, he gained speed but not enough. He removed his jacket as he ran, wrapping it round his left arm. A quick glance over his shoulder told him it was either jump now or be torn apart. His eyes scanned the windows to the cottages on either side, finding the largest instantly. White painted frame with small panes of uneven glass, it was going to hurt but it was the best of limited options. His jacketed arm curled in front of his ducking head as he jumped. He felt the impact through his shoulder as he burst headfirst through the window and rolled in a perfect breakfall across the carpeted interior ending in a stable crouch. Even as he stopped, his eyes skinned the room and his hand reached to his waistband in search of his gun. It wasn't there of course, which was just as well for Mrs Petherick who stared across the top of her momentarily interrupted knitting at the newly arrived visitor. She gave him the sort of look probably reserved for the local boys riding their bikes down the pavement.

"You could've knocked you know," she said, resuming the clickity clack of the knitting needles.

"I'm sorry," said Tremayne. "It was a bit of an emergency."

"Always a 'mergencey with you youngsters. Rushing around headlong. Wouldn't rush so fast to your grave now, would you?"

Tremayne straightened up, picking pieces of glass out of his clothes and carefully collecting them in the palm of his hand. "I'll pay for the damage of course." He extracted five ten-pound notes from his wallet and proffered them to Mrs Petherick. "That ought to cover it."

"What would I be wanting with those? I've already some of those." She dipped her hand down the side of the seat on which was sitting and pulled forth a crumpled bundle of fifty-pound notes. "See," she said, holding them aloft."Got lots of them. What I ain't got is a window. Not any more." She shook the handful of notes in the direction of the shattered window.

Tremayne had to pull on his vast reserves of charm to convince her he would arrange immediate repairs before she would let him leave.

As he returned to The High Street people were already beginning to gather around the remains of the tractor, now imbedded in the window of a bookshop where it had failed to negotiate the sharp right hand turn. A copy of '20th Century Farming' was pinned to the wall of the window display by one of the lethal spikes of the hay turner.

Surprisingly enough, Mrs Pomfrey was nowhere to be seen.

"Oi, what you lot done with Old Bess?" Young Danny Trevellick's arms flailed in an effort to stay upright as he ran way too quickly down the cobbled street. He arrived panting and leant heavily against Old Bess, his dad's errant tractor, panting to regain his breath. "Dad'll kill you lot if you've busted his tractor."

The tractor engine still roared and the wheels bucked

suddenly as if trying to push itself deeper into the bookshop. Tremayne jumped into the cab and pressed the engine cutout. Silence. His eyes scanned the inside of the cab, a large piece of wood lay jammed between the seat and the accelerator peddle. He pulled it free and examined it. He'd seen wood like that before.

"How did this happen," he asked Danny.

"Don't ask me." Danny pulled a white table napkin from his dungaree pocket and wiped his brow. It had a Prada logo in one corner. "Just finished turning the Top Field, left Old Bess in the lane to lock up, turned me back a moment like and she's off! Don't know how she got round the corner though." He gazed up the cobbled street to where the sharp right hand bend led out of the village.

Tremayne could hazard a fair guess. Still clutching the piece of wood, he squeezed his way past the tractor and back to the hotel. Goodenough glanced nervously from behind the bar as Tremayne burst through the door.

"Make up the bill please. I'll be leaving first thing."

"Right you are, Mr Tremayne." Goodenough's eyes never left the piece of wood.

Tremayne took the stairs two at a time, automatically ducking and weaving at the appropriate times deftly avoiding the 17th century obstacle course. As soon as he opened the door he could see the room had been searched. Nothing too obvious, the bedside cabinet drawer was now closed instead of the quarter inch gap he'd left. The slight ruffle he'd left in the bedspread resembling the shape of Mont Blanc had been smoothed, a sign that the mattress had been lifted. The angle of the suitcase on the wardrobe was now closer to thirty three degrees rather than the twenty eight to which it had been set. He pulled it down and dumped it on the bed. Everything looked to be there though the signs of a recent search were in evidence.

Time to phone in his report, he was finished here. They'd need to send a team of police in now to search the village properly, although he guessed in the main part the money wouldn't be too difficult to find. It would be under mattresses or in garden sheds, certainly nothing more complicated than under some loose floorboards. Even a bunch of myopic U.N. weapons inspectors shouldn't have too much difficulty there. He felt a slight touch of... What was that...? Sympathy? If only they'd been a bit sharper, they might have got away with it.

He pulled the satphone from its case, stabbed the button and waited for the green display to tell him it had located the satellite. Only it didn't. He plugged in the charger even though he remembered charging it overnight. Still nothing. He prised the back off the phone. Everything looked in place. He tossed it back in the case. Whatever they'd done to it he guessed he wasn't going to be able to fix it.

Goodenough answered the reception phone on the first ring, as if he'd been waiting. "Reception!" he announced.
"I need an outside line."
"Sorry, Mr Tremayne, sir, phones are down."
"Of course they are." Tremayne replaced the receiver without bothering to enter into protracted conversations about when they might be back on. He knew the phones would be out of order until after he'd left the village.
Oh well, there was no real hurry he supposed. These people weren't going anywhere anytime soon. And even if they did, they'd leave a trail behind them the size of the M4.

He showered then went downstairs to the bar.
"What's on the menu this evening?" he asked
"Don't know yet, Mr Tremayne. Chef's not in for another hour yet."
"But you're the chef, aren't you?"
"Not for another hour I'm not. I'm Head of Reception till six."
Tremayne couldn't face another of these circular conversations. "Chef won't mind if I just pop into the kitchen to make myself a sandwich then, will he?" Without waiting for the inevitable protests, he slipped through the beaded curtains and into the kitchen. Half a loaf of bread sat on a wooden board. He picked it up and tapped it on the

breadboard. Two days old at least. He opened a couple of cupboards. The only items he could find that were in anyway appetising were two tins of baked beans and a can of 'Genuine Cornish Lobster Bisque', *'Produce of Gdansk'*. He emptied the contents into a bowl, placed it precisely two thirds off-centre in the microwave and hit 'Start'. The microwave was dead. He checked the lead and plug. The plug was slightly blackened. He removed the soup and looked inside. Black smudges and distorted side panels attested to the fact that somebody had been cooking things in here they shouldn't have. Satellite telephones perhaps?

The bead curtains rustled. Tremayne turned as Goodenough hesitated into the kitchen.

"Ah, yes. Microwave's not working," he said. "There's some bread over there." He nodded towards the breadboard.

"Hmmm, I think I'll pass." Tremayne glanced around the kitchen. The concept of microwaving delicate electronics was clever. It showed a level of subtly beyond Goodenough, who would probably have been more inclined to just take a two-pound lump hammer to the job. He found a saucepan and placed it on the top of the Aga then emptied the bowl of soup into it. A few thinly sliced potatoes and carrots quickly followed. Goodenough watched in fascination as Tremayne added a few herbs, garlic and a sprinkle of grated cheese. He sniffed at an open bottle of red wine, shrugged and added a healthy dash to the mix.

"I'll pay for this of course," he said. He placed the lid on his stew and reached for his wallet.

"That won't be necessary. Fair portion you've made there. Looks like you might have some of it left over."

"You might be right there," Tremayne dipped a spoon and tasted his creation. A dash of pepper. "Would you care to join me?"

"Wouldn't do to waste it, so I suppose it'd be for the best."

The stale bread provided quite passable croutons after being lightly fried with herbs and added to the mix. They sat at the kitchen table and ate.

"Where'd you learn to cook like that?" Goodenough asked between slurps.

"When you've spent most of your life on your own you learn to become adaptable."

"Doesn't do a man good. No, to spend his life on his own, not good for the soul."

"Sometimes it's better that way."

When they'd finished eating Goodenough opened a fifteen year old scotch and they chatted about nothing until the regulars started to drift into the bar. Nobody was overtly hostile to Tremayne but there was sufficient undercurrent to ensure he understood he was no longer welcome here. He wandered along the harbour wall watching the sun setting over the headland in the west. Fishing boats drifted in from a sea that rolled gently through the gap in the harbour wall. Tired but incessantly cheery they unloaded large plastic crates of crabs and other assorted crustaceans onto the dockside.

The sound of approaching footsteps kicked his senses back into place. He whirled round, hands loose, feet braced. Sloppy, Charles. Very sloppy. As his recent encounter with Old Bess would testify, this lot were not as harmless as they seemed. In the past, he'd hired killers who'd work for less money than he'd spend on a ticket for Covent Garden. In some parts of the world two hundred and fifty million would buy you a good sized army and a regime change. As the CIA had proved on several occasions. Do not underestimate these people, Charles.

"Nice evening for it," Mrs Pomfrey announced as she came to lean on the harbour wall not three feet away.

"Yes, it is." Whatever 'it' might be. "Did you manage to buy your stamps?"

"Yes, just as well too. If I hadn't been popping into the Post Office just at that moment... Well, Lord knows what would've happened. Quite a turn up for the bushes indeed."

Yes," said Charles slowly. "Most fortuitous."

"There's talk you're setting about leaving tomorrow. I suppose you got what you came for now then?"

"Yes, there's nothing left for me to do here anymore."

"Well you make sure you ask all your little friends to drop by visit us, won't you? We'll see they're made to feel most welcome."

In his long career, he'd heard many an interesting threat. But that one actually made him feel quite cold. Perhaps it was the incongruity, this harmless old lady inviting the full might of Her Majesty's government to come and 'have a go'.

Chapter 11

He awoke at six-thirty exactly, his internal clock back on track. He showered, shaved and dressed in exactly twenty-three minutes. 'Charles Tremayne Normal Time' has been resumed. No sign of Sandy yet with her morning tray of arterial poison. He packed his suitcase with the precision of a watchmaker, each item in its correct place. He eyed the satphone and wondered briefly if it was worth taking back. He tucked it in the corner of the case, the techie guys could have fun with it if nothing else.

As the clock in reception started to chime seven 'o clock Tremayne hit the bell on the counter.

Goodenough appeared as if he'd been waiting behind the door. "And what can I do for you this morning, sir?"

"You were going to have my bill ready?"

"Ah yes." He lifted a tray of paper onto the counter. "Which room were you in?"

"The Bridal Suite. I thought you only had... Oh, never mind"

Goodenough thumbed through the pile of paper. "B...b...b..." he muttered. "Hmmm... that's odd, doesn't seem to be here. Ah, no wait, here it is! It had been misfiled under T."

"T?"

"For Tremayne, sir.

"Of course it had. How much do I owe you?" Tremayne yearned for simple transactions and understandable conversations.

"Four nights bed and breakfast..." He tapped numbers into an oversized calculator. "That'll be seventy four pounds and eighty nine pence, including the VAT."

Tremayne wondered how Goodenough had managed to come up with a prime number by multiplying anything by four but decided that the ensuing conversation would probably end with Goodenough's blood all over the reception floor. He pulled cash from his wallet.

"Rather have a credit card, if that's alright with you? More reliable in these times."

Tremayne handed over his United European Films Visa card.

"Just write you out a receipt." He located a piece of headed paper and a chewed biro. "To... the... use...of...one...room..Whoops, sorry that's 'Suite'. I'll just do that again... To...the... use—"

"Just leave it! Please! I don't need a receipt." In his mind he had already snatched the pen from Goodenough's hand and it now protruded from the side of his neck.

"Are you sure, sir? I mean we want to keep everything in order don't we?"

"It's fine." He picked up his case and started towards the door.

"And just where the hell do you think you're going?" Sandy's voice demanded from behind him.

He stopped still. He could ignore her. He could just walk on. Leave this hell-hole and these lunatic people. He didn't have to answer. He really didn't. He dropped the suitcase to the floor and slowly turned.

Sandy stood hands on hips, her eyes dark and challenging. "Haven't you forgotten something?"

"It's too late, Sandy. I'm returning to London and washing my hands of this... this..." His arms widened as he struggled for a suitable adjective. "This warp in normality, this land of 'The Fruit Loops', it's time for me to re-enter the real world."

"I'm not talking about your sordid little spy business. You will do what you have to do. I'm talking about simple promises to simple people."

He was puzzled. "I made no promises."

"Ah, but you did. She moved forward, he felt oddly threatened and took a step backwards to maintain distance. "Mrs Petherick, you remember? You trashed her window with your James Bond nonsense. Or did that slip your mind?"

"Oh, yes. I was going—" Another step backwards.

"You were going to fix it for her, that's what you promised her."

"Look, if it hadn't been for—"

"Be a man, Charles. Stick by something for once. Go fix her window for her." A small whirlwind disturbed the papers on the counter as Sandy turned and left.

Tremayne needed to kill something. His frustration levels confused his fight or flight senses, readying them for the sudden explosive violence for which they'd been conditioned. His hands clenched and unclenched rhythmically and his vision narrowed as adrenaline flushed his system.

Goodenough must have picked up on the danger signals. "I'll be... erm... just out here." He slid backwards through the bead curtains, hardly disturbing them, leaving Tremayne alone in the centre of the room vibrating with barely controlled rage. He had dealt with professional assassins, terrorists, third world dictators and the state police of many a totalitarian regime. He dealt with them all with diplomacy when he could and ruthless efficiency when he couldn't. He'd negotiated, traded, blackmailed and tortured to achieve his goals. All with calm and rationality. So what the hell was it about this infernal village and its bewildering inhabitants that continued to push him to the edge of psychopathic fury? A place where he would actually enjoy the violence, feel pleasure as his hands closed around the throat of yet another cantankerous, obstructive yokel. Instead, he kicked his suitcase over. Slowly and with care so as not to damage the contents, he had nonetheless kicked it over.

Damn Gemini and his entourage of scheming, self-serving politicos. Damn the money grubbing illusionists who ran things these days. And damn the Russians, damn them to hell for making peace and so completely destroying his raison d'être. He'd fix the window, Sandy was right and damn her too. He'd fix the window then take the next flight to Geneva. Let them all drown in their own little mud pools of intrigue and corruption. He left his suitcase lying in the middle of the floor and slammed the front door behind him.

Thirty seconds later he re-entered and carefully placed the case behind the counter.

***

Fixing windows was not turning out to be one of Tremayne's natural talents. He'd managed to buy several large planks of wood from the chandlers. It was decking teak but that was all they had, unless he wanted to go to the nearest B&Q about forty miles away. He piled it up outside Mrs Petherick's cottage then went in search of glass. Little Didney seemed to have an acute shortage of glass shops. The best he could manage was the purchase of nine framed pictures of lighthouses from which he removed the glass, discarding the rest in the growing pile of debris at the edge of the cobbled street. Okay, now how to start assembling this lot into a window? Saw, nails and glue. Another trip to the chandler's yard. He gazed at the resulting collection, trying to visualise the finished window and how to get there from here. Strategy, tactics and detail. He'd been brought up on planning, how hard could this be? He was a member of MENSA for God's sake!

He set about sawing the planks of teak into strips that approximated the size of the remains of the original window frame. After twenty minutes sawing he had little to show for his efforts other than another small pile of debris to add to the rest. There had to be an easier way.

Mervyn Liddicoat at Rettalick's Marine & Chandlery was fast becoming his new best friend. Mervyn said; "I knew you'd never cut decking teak with little saw of yorn."

"You didn't think to mention that when you sold it to me?"

"You didn't ask. If you'd said to me 'Mervyn, will this saw cut this here timber?' I'd 've probably said 'Not a chance.' But then you didn't ask. Not my place to push my opinions. Different folks—"

"Do you have anything that *will* cut decking teak?" Tremayne interrupted.

"Got just the thing." He disappeared behind a tarpaulin curtain and re-emerged a few moments later with a handheld electric circular saw. "That ought to do it, no time. Just be careful mind." He held up his left hand to show it was one finger short of a full set. He grinned, "You don't get no second chances with they things there."

The electric saw was certainly efficient. It enabled him to increase the pile of scrap wood in no time at all. But unfortunately, it hadn't helped bring him any closer to a completed window. Tossing the latest piece of mangled wood onto the heap, he started work on the final plank. He was going to need to buy some more timber if this one didn't go right.

He concentrated.

So much did his level of focus narrow that he didn't notice the little trickle of water that meandered out of the Butcher's shop three doors up and trickled down the edge of the cobbles. His eyes saw only the pencilled line along the wood as he struggled to keep the whirling blade on track. They didn't see the flow of water increase to a bubbling stream bouncing over the cobbles, lapping around the electric cable powering the saw. Such was his determination in achieving straight line this time that he didn't even notice when the water started licking around the plug and socket connection in the extension lead Mrs Petherick had loaned. What he *did* notice however was being lifted three inches clear of the floor and thrown against the wall of Mrs Petherick's cottage as two hundred and forty volts made their way through his nervous system. He also noticed lying on the cobbles wrestling with a manic circular saw as it took on a life of its own and seemed determined carve a perfectly straight line through his head. But he didn't notice when everything stopped. The plug and socket went bang, lighting up briefly like a small firework then the saw sat fizzing quietly in an ever growing puddle. His legs and arms twitched spasmodically as if a master puppeteer was testing his strings.

Slowly his eyes opened. He groaned and looked around himself, taking in the small disaster zone that surrounded him. Bits of mangled wood, several pieces of broken glass and a blackened circular saw all tangled in the remains of the extension lead and gradually disappearing under what was beginning to resemble a small pond.

He stood, easing out each limb gently against the protestations of the still twitching muscles. He gave thanks for his hand-made Church's shoes with the custom rubber soles, good for sneaking up on people and now, it seemed, good insulation against runaway electric saws. A small piece of decking teak bumped softly against his ankle as it was lifted by the water and started heading downstream.

"What're you up to now?" Mrs Petherick blustered through her front door. "My knitting light's just gone pop! And look at the mess you've made."

Tremayne was indeed looking at the mess he'd made. He was still in a state of shock, although he wasn't quite sure whether that was due to the vestiges of partial electrocution or to the realisation that these idiots had nearly killed him for a second time.

"You come down here from the big city," she continued. "Runnin' around pokin' yer nose places where noses didn't ought to be poked, then you go smashing up a widow lady's house."

His eyes followed the trail of water upstream to where it disappeared through the entrance to Babcock's Butchery and Game.

"Woke up this morning with a window and a knitting light I did. Thought I'd be going to bed with much the same...."

He left Mrs Petherick poking at the debris with her walking stick and followed the water through the door of the butcher's. A tap in the corner of the shop spilled water onto the tiled floor. He turned it off. Mr Babcock was nowhere in sight.

"Hello," he called. "Shop?"

No reply. He wandered back onto The High Street and glanced up and down. The village seemed deserted.

Apart from Mrs Petherick. "And look at my extension lead." She lifted a loop of the burned out cable on the end of her stick. "How am I supposed to cook the dinner now?"

A quiet calm filled Tremayne. Twice these people had tried to kill him now and he might not survive the next attempt. They were dangerous by their very amateurishness, and highly unpredictable. He'd had enough. In the past he'd been willing to die for what he believed in. Prepared to risk his life to stop a terrorist or protect the innocent. But he wasn't ready to be electrocuted or harvested or whatever else these people had in mind next just for the sake of a pile of dirty money.

He made his way back to the Chandlery. That too was deserted. He cut a large section of clear heavy duty polythene from a roll and left a twenty pound note on the counter. Although he was sure it wouldn't be needed.

When nailed across the open gap where Mrs Petherick's window had once been it made a fair imitation of glass. Billowy and slightly opaque, but passable.

"What d'ya call that?" She called after him as he headed back to The Smuggler's Arms. "That's not a proper window. And what about my knitting light? How's a poor widow lady expected to do her knitting without a knitting light? Her words continued to follow him until he turned the corner at the bottom of The High Street.

Thirty seconds later he was headed back up the cobbled street, suitcase in hand, and en route to car, London then Switzerland.

He checked underneath the car for any home made additions or deletions not specified by Mercedes engineers. All seemed as it should. He turned they key in the ignition and the 2.5 litre V6 engine made exactly the noise he had expected. Silence. Not even a click, let alone a whir.

MI6 training had been highly selective. In the section on motor vehicles and transport, he had learned how to overcome alarms and hotwire just about anything with an engine. He had also learned to identify improvised bombs or sabotaged brakes. But the area sadly missing from the curriculum was how to fix the damn things when they went wrong. He supposed the perceived wisdom was that if one vehicle didn't start then just find yourself another one. That thinking was probably quite sound in downtown Berlin, but in Little Didney?

What he did understand though, was that this car was not going to be easily fixed. Whatever they'd done to it this time he was fairly confident would put it beyond the skills of the average breakdown van. That's even if he had a working phone with which to call them. No, he needed to find alternative transport, and the only place he could be sure of finding a car was Jerry Richards' car sales site, and that was a three mile walk.

"Time I got some exercise anyway." He lifted the suitcase and set out up the winding lane, leaving behind, hopefully forever, the sign that announced 'This Is Not Little Didney'.

Chapter 12

The door to cell twenty-one swung open. Mr Green remained seated on the small bed. "And what do *you* want," he asked, looking up at his visitor. "Keep telling you, I know nothing."

"Yes I know that. Which is why you can leave now," the visitor replied

"Just like that?"

"Yes, just like that."

"What's the catch. You gonna shoot me in the back like I was making an escape or something?"

"My good man, you've been watching far too many war movies."

Mr Green stood up, hesitantly. "You expect me to grass on me mates? Is that it? I ain't no grass."

"I'm sure you are not, indeed, they are free to go with you. However, there is just one very small request I'd ask of you."

Mr Green narrowed his eyes. "What's that then?"

"I'd like you to finish the job you started."

***

Tremayne kept up his standard, timed walking pace. It was a measured and practised pace that allowed him to accurately calculate how far he had walked. He looked at his watch. He had exactly nine tenths of a mile to his target.

He was starting to relax into the exercise now. The past few days of constant frustration and the inability to act within his normal parameters had tired him. But he felt that tiredness slipping away with each raised heartbeat and every yard covered. Perhaps in retrospect this had been just the 'Final Mission' he had needed. It had certainly shown him his time in this line of work was over. Sandy had been right in one ting at least. He *was* a dinosaur. The world no longer needed Russian or Serbian speaking Caucasian spies. It needed Asian looking agents fluent in Arabic or Afghani. The ability to hack past blowfish level encryption was far more valuable than being able to diffuse the timer on a small nuclear device.

A car rounded the corner a hundred and fifty yards ahead of him. As it drew closer he saw it was a police car. Good, maybe his luck was turning. A quick radio contact with control, a helicopter and he'd be on his way to a happy retirement. He stopped in the road and raised his arms up and down. The police car gave a short whoop on the siren, put on the blue lights and pulled alongside him.

Tremayne's briefly risen spirits dashed themselves against the rocks of depression. P.C. Muchmore stepped out of the car. Oh well, nothing for it but to deal with this final level of incompetence and get on with the job.
"I need to use your radio, constable," Tremayne said. "I have to contact London. It's a matter of national security."
"Right you are sir, but it won't work just here. Need to pop up the hill a mite. Hop in." Muchmore held open the rear door and Tremayne slid into the seat with a sigh. The door clunked shut at the exact moment he realised what he'd done. The *back* seat. The one with the doors that only operated from the outside. The one with the wire fence between him and the driver.
"We just need to drop by town first, Mr Tremayne. I'm afraid you've got some serious charges to answer afore you go gallivanting back off to London."
Tremayne watched his hard-won miles rolling back. There went the incongruous little sign again.
"I did tell you I was with MI6, didn't I?"
"MI6, CID, M&S. Got no truck with any organisation that wants to hide behind a bunch of letters. You'll all get the same from me. Good old fashioned policing that's what we need more of. Not your secret societies and funny handshakes." Muchmore threw the police car round blind corners with seemingly total faith in the road ahead being empty
"And does old fashioned policing allow for the theft

government money?"

"Don't know nothing about no money. But I do know you can't go doing criminal damage to an old lady's house and then just walk off like cheese don't smell."

The car clipped a hedge as it turned a particularly sharp bend. Muchmore's driving was becoming more erratic the angrier he became. Tremayne decided it was best not to provoke him again and settled back in his seat.

They bounced through a narrow gap at the back of the car park that looked like nothing more than a footpath and eventually pulled up outside the 'Police Station'. Or the room at the back of the bakery, depending on your point of view. Muchmore opened the back door by no more than six inches, leaving significant bulk pressed up against it.

"Just give us your wrist here, sir." He indicated the gap, leaving Tremayne no chance to push his way free. Tremayne slid his hand through the gap and with admirable dexterity Muchmore clamped his handcuffs on the exposed wrist. This was clearly a well practised routine. Probably the result of years dealing with drunken farm workers.

"Now the other one please," Muchmore opened the gap another couple of inches to allow the other arm access.

It was at that point Muchmore's system fell down. His well proven system of removing drunks from the back his car found itself lacking when up against years of Aikijutsu training. He dropped to his knees with a yelp as Tremayne applied particularly nasty wristlock.

"It's only pain, Mr Muchmore. Nothing's broken... yet."

Within fifteen seconds Muchmore was handcuffed in the back seat of the car and Tremayne was reversing the police car back up the footpath. Or rather attempting to.

"How do you get out of here?" Tremayne asked into the rear view mirror. Muchmore remained silent. For the first time, Tremayne felt a grudging admiration for this man. Anybody who could reverse a car of this size back up here was worthy of some respect at least.

He shuffled the car inches forwards and backwards

The Money That Never Was

trying to negotiate a difficult hairpin bend that cut around a high stone wall. He became impatient, revved a little too hard then the clutch bit. They jolted backwards with the sound of metal on stone behind them. The engine stalled.

"That's it buggered then," announced Muchmore.

Tremayne climbed out of the car to examine the situation. The car's rear end was wedged neatly in a gap in the stone wall.

"Mrs Petherick's gonna be none too pleased."

"Why?" asked Tremayne, already knowing the answer.

"Well, last time this happened, we had to take the wall down. And it's her wall."

Of course it was. It couldn't have been anybody else's wall. It must seem to her that Tremayne had arrived in this village with one goal in mind. To systematically demolish her cottage piece by piece.

He yanked open the passenger door to retrieve his suitcase, paused then said to Muchmore; "You know something? I escaped from Lubianka prison with less difficulty than getting out of this place."

He slammed the door shut and started up the path, paused, then returned and opened the door once more. "And I had half the Russian Spetsnaz after me."

Twenty minutes later he was once more passing the 'Not Little Didney' sign and heading for Jerry Richard's place. This time he hid each time a car passed. Soon he was within fifty metres of the car lot. He hid behind a gorse bush, observing, listening. Nothing. Still not trusting the apparent absence of life he crept closer. Only after many minutes of careful observation did he venture to the door to the caravan that served as an office. The lock offered little resistance to Tremayne's paperclip and he slid inside.

He was hoping to find a small wall cupboard or similar containing the keys to the cars and also the wheel clamps that immobilised each one. Nothing was going to be that simple. What he did find was a safe that would have done the Bank of England proud. He examined the lock. He had no doubt that given time he would be able to open it. He also had no doubt he didn't have the luxury of time. Jerry wouldn't be too far away or it wouldn't be long before Muchmore was found, either way half the village would soon be descending on this place pitchforks in hand.

There was one car that he remembered wasn't clamped. Barry Penwrith's Ford Capri he'd seen locked in the shed behind the forecourt.

A sharp sidekick and the door splintered pleasingly. The inside of the shed was littered with car parts and bits of wood. Bits of wood of the same heritage as the one he'd found jammed against the accelerator pedal of 'Old Bess', Tom Trevellick's beloved tractor currently still parked in the bookshop window. In the centre of the shed stood Barry Penwrith's Capri. And in the corner of the shed sat Barry, Masie and Tommy. Tied and gagged they wriggled and grunted to attract his attention.

"Not quite Disneyland," Tremayne said quietly. He glanced around. Years of dealing with hostage rescues guiding his actions automatically. Look for wires, snipers, explosives strapped to hostage. He scanned his surroundings constantly as he set to work untying the Penwriths.
"Oh, thank you, sir. Mr Tremayne sir."
"My Lord! Thought we'd all be dead by breakfast."
"Where's my bicycle."
They wittered at him incessantly as he untied the nylon ropes.
"Wait till I get my hands on him, I'll..."
"Be quiet," Tremayne said. He thought he'd heard a noise.
"Told Barry it would come to no good..."
"No you didn't! You wanted all them new frocks and stuff"
"Are we still going to see Mickey Mouse?"
"Will you lot shut up!"

The unmistakable sound of a gun being cocked.

The Money That Never Was

Tremayne narrowed his eyes against the glare of sunlight now streaming through the open door. A silhouette of a man moved forward slowly. The silhouette carried a double-barrelled shotgun.

"I thought Muchmore had you sorted," Jerry Richards said as he moved further into the relative gloom of the shed.

"No, he's waiting down the road for me. He's turning Queen's evidence. It's all over, Jerry." He knew the bluff wouldn't work but he just needed time to close the distance slightly.

Jerry took a step forward, the weapon aimed for the centre of Tremayne's chest. "Is that what they teach you in Spy School? How to bullshit? Why don't you just tie these idiots up again then you and I can have a chat?" He waved the gun at the quivering Penwrith family.

Tremayne took a step back, circling slightly as if making for the door. Jerry took the bait and closed the distance between them. In his mind it gave more of an immediate threat to his victim. In Tremayne's mind it showed the stupidity of amateurs. Amateurs who believed their eyes and trigger finger coordination would be faster than Tremayne's hands. By the time Jerry had fired the trigger, Tremayne's fingers had already closed around the barrel and it was now pointing harmlessly to the far wall. As the second barrel fired, Tremayne was pivoting the gun around its fulcrum point, Jerry's hand, and twisting it free of his grip. Jerry stared momentarily at the two barrels as they now faced his head. He had chance for a brief smile in the knowledge they were both empty before the gun pivoted once more and the butt collided with the side of his head. He was unconscious before he hit the ground.

"Why won't you all leave me alone?" he said to the back of Jerry Richards' head as it lay at his feet. "Don't you understand? I've had enough now." He turned to the Penwriths and waved the shotgun in their general direction. "Get in the car." He nodded towards the Capri.

Barry made for the driver's side, stopped briefly at the door to see Tremayne glare at him then dived in the passenger door. Masie and Tommy squashed themselves in the back. Ford had only ever intended this vehicle two be a two-seater, and the rear seats were added at the last minute as a sop to the family market.

Tremayne squeezed his suitcase in the boot alongside the Penwrith's luggage, climbed in and turned the key. The engine sprang instantly to life. Things were beginning to look up.

Chapter 13

Mr Babcock was having no such difficulties leaving Little Didney. He'd filled one holdall with a spare set of clothes and another with his money and set off for London Airport. He wasn't quite sure where London Airport was, but he figured it couldn't be too far from London and that it must be fairly big. So his plan, what there was of it, was to drive to London where he would be sure to find it.

That at least was part 'B' of his plan. Part 'A' had simply been to get the hell out of the village and Cornwall as fast as his little blue van would carry him. He'd just assassinated a government agent and he was sure that constituted treason or something. And wasn't hanging still in vogue for treason?

Not that he'd meant to kill Tremayne. No, only frighten him. Just like they'd all agreed. Keep scaring him until he went away. But when he'd looked out through the door of his shop after hearing the commotion Tremayne was laying twitching in a puddle of fizzing water and Mr Babcock suddenly remembered he had an urgent appointment in Argentina.

Anyway, he'd always meant to travel and they must have a need for a master butcher in Argentina, what with all that cattle. Feeling a little less stressed now he'd put some distance behind him he moved the little van in to the centre lane of the motorway and brought his speed all the way up to forty miles per hour. Wouldn't do to hang around.

***

The Capri drank fuel faster than a space shuttle launch. The first time he'd stopped at the services he expected to return after paying to find the Penwriths had escaped. The second time he actually waited for ten minutes drinking machine delivered coffee-soup from a soggy cardboard mug in the hope they'd take the hint. But no, they doggedly sat hunched in the car awaiting his return. He thought of phoning in for another car and leaving them to it but he wasn't sure he wanted department involvement just yet. So he continued to put up with his passengers.

And the country and western music.

A cassette tape was jammed in the unit and refused to do anything other than play endless dirges about lost horses or dead dogs. He couldn't even turn it off as all the controls were missing. The only solace was the twenty seconds of silence every thirty minutes as the tape went through its automatic rewind cycle. He yearned for his SLR, the sound system, the air conditioning. At least the Penwriths were quiet. A little too quiet perhaps, none of them had uttered a word since they'd set out. Which was slightly disturbing now he came to think about it.

At least the car drove well. It may be ancient, but Ford had built these beasts well and at some point somebody had obviously looked after this one. He had to pull wide into lane three to avoid some idiot in a little blue van doing forty in the centre lane.

For the third time he had to stop for fuel. He filled the tank and poked his head back through the window.
"Anybody need anything? Natural break?"
Blank looks.
"Do you need the washroom?"
"No thank you, sir, Mr Tremayne, sir. We're still all clean from yesterday."
"Do you need the toilet then?" he abandoned the niceties.
"Oh, best do. Masie here has had trouble down below since—"
"Barry!" Masie scolded. "Mr Tremayne doesn't want to know 'bout 'Lady Problems' now does he? He's a proper gentleman." She smiled a yellow toothed smile in Tremayne's direction.

Tremayne certainly did not want to know about Masie's 'Lady Problems'. In fact the very acknowledgment of the existence of such things made him shiver.

By the time he'd paid for the fuel, the Penwriths were once more firmly wedged inside the Capri. He pulled away from the petrol station to the tune of 'Truck-stop Lonesome Blues'. After a quarter of a mile, he pulled over in the emergency lane and went round the back of the car. He opened the top of his suitcase and without looking dipped his hand in. He found what he was looking for instantly. The joys of methodical packing. He opened the driver's door, pointed his Heckler & Koch mark 23 pistol at the dashboard and fired twice in quick succession. Double tap. SAS training. Masie squealed, Tommy started crying but the cassette tape was silent.

He tucked the gun in his waistband and they set off up the motorway once more. This time in blissful silence.

By the time they reached London evening was drawing in. The Penwriths, each with their respective noses against the windows oohed and aahed over the bright lights and hectic bustle that was London in full preparation for the evening shift. Like a rat in a well trodden maze, Tremayne slipped the car in and out of narrow streets and alleys with such dexterity that would have caused a London cabbie to quit on the spot had he witnessed it. He stopped the car at the gates to the parking for his flat, waiting for them to open automatically. They didn't of course as the sensor was in the Mercedes and not in this car.

"Okay," he said to Barry. That's as far as I go. It's all yours now." He climbed out of the car and stretched.

"What're we supposed to do now, Mr Tremayne, sir?"

"This is London, Barry. You have a car and a suitcase full of money. Enjoy!"

"I thought you were going to arrest us or something?"

"I still might if you don't get out of my sight extremely quickly."

"But... why?"

"You heard the man, you dumb nitwit," Masie scolded. "Drive!"

Barry slid into the driver's seat, did a twelve point turn that removed most of an ornamental hedge and three feet of iron railings then burst into the London traffic amidst a torrent of angry horns.

Tremayne watched them go, wondering what would become of them in this strange new world. As it happened, he wouldn't have to wonder for very long.

He swung open the door to his flat, pausing to savour the air, the very faint smell of cleaning chemicals and the slight metallic odour of air conditioning. Heaven. He passed his hand over the light sensor and concealed lighting brought the room to life. Clean, tidy and a distinct lack of 'stuff'. No lampshades or china dolls, no lace doilies or ornamental throws. Just space. The simple beauty of the black low table with dimensions that conformed precisely to the 'Golden Ratio' and the large piece of granite placed on it at the exact focal point recommended by Leonardo da Vinci. Plain clear walls, the only exception, a huge panoramic picture of Lake Geneva separated over three wood blocks.

Hi picked the remote control from its cradle, a couple of key pushes and the inset fire burst into life and the sound of Turandot flooded the room. He unpacked quickly, placing his used clothes, still all neatly folded, into the laundry box. The shower room consisted simply of four marble tiled walls with overhead drench sprays and a selection of body jets at various points. He passed his hand over a metal plate on the wall and the room was filled at once with steam and water jetting in from all angles. For ten minutes, he turned slowly letting the water blast the last remnants of Little Didney from his skin. He passed his hand over the controls once more and a blast of hot air gently and efficiently dried him.

He slipped on a black silk kimono then went through to his office, time to submit his final report. He wondered if he was supposed to be feeling anything at this point. The end of thirty-two years continuous service was no small event. But he felt nothing. Just the simple pleasure of once more being in his own ordered and sane world. The office at first sight would appear incongruous to the casual glance. The only furniture, a leather swivel chair in the centre of the room and a huge set of bookshelves that covered the far wall. It looked incomplete.

He locked the door behind him. The hidden sensors registered that the door was locked from the inside and there was only one occupant in the room. He removed the copy of Robinson Crusoe from the bookshelf .There appeared to be a small plastic circle in the rear of the cupboard. It could easily have been a simple screw cover. He held his thumb against the circle and listened for the tiny click that told him his fingerprint checked out and the lock had opened. He pulled the centre section of the shelves and they swung open revealing a desk with keyboard and large flat screen imbedded in the wall.

He logged on to the secure MI6 servers and began his report:
Money located. Split into various locations in village of Little Didney in the possession of individual residents. Suggest full search team under Section 72 of The Prevention of Terrorism Act. Local Police Constable not to be trusted. On receipt of this report please acknowledge this as my formal resignation from the service.

His finger paused over the 'send' button. Had he covered the main points? His mind scanned the events of the last few days. Jerry Richards, Barry Penwrith's shed, the runaway tractor. He found himself actually smiling as he recalled the image of the power boat with its nose lodged firmly in the counter of the Fishmonger's. The Smuggler's Arms, the cantankerous Goodenough. Sandy. The enigma that was Sandy.

He reread the report. Satisfied that it conveyed the necessary information for Gemini to move it on to the next phase. The clean up. He'd seen that happen in the past. They would descend on the village, probably before dawn, and decimate the place like locusts in a cornfield. Shock and awe. Let Mrs Pomfrey try and stop that lot. There'd be no patience for Goodenough and his infuriating stalling tactics. Or maybe that was just the way he was?

Who cares? He'd done his bit. They were somebody else's problem now. All he had to do was to hit 'send' and the mess would be over. He could forget them all and book his flight to a new life. He could relax in quiet, peaceful order.

He hit delete.

The message disappeared and he stared at the blank screen wondering what just happened. Sod it! He'd rewrite it in the morning. There was probably more detail needed anyway, addresses or something. Couldn't think of them right now. Too late in the day.

He logged on to 'Logistics and Resources'. Erich's face appeared. Erich was always happy and smiling. He spent his life surrounded by half built gadgets, circuit boards and racks of equipment. Just looking at the chaos behind his smiling face on the screen made Tremayne uncomfortable.
"What can I do for Charles?" Erich asked. "Thought you'd got yourself lost in the wilds of Cornwall."
"I'm afraid my satphone's had it."
"What happened this time? Use it to wedge open a cell door again?"
"No, they microwaved it."
"That's a new one." Erich's grin widened. "Easy enough. I'll clone you a new one with all your settings installed again. Courier be round with it in about half an hour. Or is it urgent?"
"Tremayne hesitated. He hadn't thought of a replacement. He was just tidying up loose ends. "No... I don't actually need..." He couldn't tell Erich he was resigning before Gemini. Bad protocol. "Erm, yes that will

be fine."

"Anything else?" Erich was already typing the necessary code for the cloning.

"The SLR. You'll need to send a recovery team to collect it. I don't know what they've done to that."

"Too big for the microwave I guess. Where is it?"

"Top of the village in the car park. Tell the recovery guys to ignore any signs and just ping the GPS transponder."

"Will do." Erich's fingers flew across the keyboard. "I'll get a replacement straight round to you. What do you fancy? Got a nice XKR just come back. Fancy that one?"

"I don't really... I mean...Yes, that's fine." Indecision Tremayne. What's with this indecision? He broke the connection.

He secured the office and returned to the lounge. He settled back in his recliner, letting the music of Puccini wash through him, cleansing his soul.

The intercom buzzer sounded. Tremayne answered it.

The voice of Alfred, the doorman crackled through the tiny speaker. "Package just arrived for you, sir," He said. "Signed for it. Hope that was okay?"

Alfred was a veteran of probably at least one world wars and several minor ones. Tremayne trusted him, perhaps more than any other person alive.

"That's fine, Alfred. I'll be down for it shortly."

Tremayne put on white linen trousers and white short sleeved shirt then headed downstairs. He picked up the new satphone from Alfred and set out to find something to eat.

Takimoto's Sushi Bar was quiet. It was still early though. He settled down at the bar.

"What you want tonight Tremayne-san?"

"As it comes, Chiro. Be creative."

The knives flashed. Blades of exquisite sharpness flew through the air and where they met the fish, slices fell neatly on a small square china plate. Tremayne watched as the dish grew in front of him. Tiny packets of lightly scented rice and asparagus wrapped in unknown leaves finished the ensemble. He savoured each mouthful. Each part of the dish yielding up a new delicate taste that complemented perfectly the preceeding one. Such harmony. Tremayne felt order finally being restored to his world.

He bid sayonara to Takimoto and meandered his way back home through the warm summer evening. He enjoyed watching the chaos and bustle of the city in a way that sometimes seemed slightly voyeuristic. Detached observer watching the ants scurry about their irrelevant business.

As he returned to his building he was greeted by Alfred.
"Somebody dropped a new motor round for you while were gone. Nice wheels." He tossed the keys towards Tremayne.
Tremayne snatched them from the air without breaking his stride. "I'll give you a ride in it one day, Alfred."
"With all due respect, sir, I value my life too much to get in a car with you."
"You're probably very wise, Alfred." Tremayne smiled and closed the lift door.

He had just settled back in his chair and was about to watch 'Newsnight' when the satphone rang.
"Charles?" Elaine's voice sounded perturbed.
He checked his watch. "You're working late."
"Pulling a double shift, Susie called in sick. Are you alright?"
"Of course. Why shouldn't I be?"
"We noticed you'd logged in to the report servers but never filed. Out of the normal parameters of expected behaviour. You know what it's like, Charles, detail saves lives."
"I got sidetracked. I'll file in the morning, there's nothing urgent. Was that all? Not that I'm not flattered by your interest in my welfare of course."
"Only one other thing. Another one of your little chums has turned up."

"Oh? Who's that?"

"Chap called Babcock. Got himself picked up at Heathrow with an out of date passport trying to buy a ticket to Argentina with a suitcase full of money. Tried to bribe the check-in staff."

"He's the local butcher," Tremayne said.

"We guessed that, he parked his van right outside departures. Special Branch destroyed it in a controlled explosion."

"That will please him." Serves him right too.

Well, everybody's twitchy after Glasgow. Anyway, they're holding him there for you to pick up."

"I'm not sure... I was... Can't airport police deal with him?" He felt himself being sucked in again. Damn Babcock!

"Your brief, Charles. You know what the pen pushers are like about loose ends."

Sod their loose ends. Sod Babcock. Sod them all. "I'll pick him up later. Thanks, Elaine"

He put the phone down on the table and stared at it. He'd deal with Babcock tomorrow then he'd file his report and put his papers in. This time tomorrow he'd be a free man. He could put up with just one little bit more piece of aggravation. Nothing to it.

He relaxed back and the intercom crackled again.

"Yes, Alfred?"

"There's a bunch of gypsies down here demanding you arrest them."

Chapter 14

The gypsies turned out to be the Penwrith family of course.

"Never seen nothing like it, honest," Barry said.

"He screamed, Mr Tremayne. Right proper scream it was." Masie nodded towards her husband.

"Didn't scream. It was a shout of anger. All them cars, and them all going so fast, round 'n round they went." Barry made to venture further into the room,

"Stay on the newspaper please, Barry." Tremayne fearing for his white carpet had made them each stand on a sheet of newspaper by the door while he worked out what he was going to do with them.

"Right you are, sir."

"Where was this, Barry?" Tremayne asked.

"Dunno for sure. Big place. Got a big archway like a gate... only there was no walls with it. Or a gate. Just a big archway."

"Marble Arch I presume. What happened?"

"We just went round and round."

"I was sick," offered Tommy.

"Yes, I can see that," said Charles. "What do you mean round and round? Why?"

"Nobody'd let us go anywhere but round 'n round. Every time we tried to turn any this way or that there'd be tootin' and fingers waving like of which you've never seen."

"He got right stressy I'll tell you," said Masie.

"Cars everywhere, thousands—"

"The paper, Barry."

"Oh right, yes. Never seen so many cars. Couldn't go anywhere, so in the end we left it there."

"You left your car in the middle of a traffic jam in Marble Arch?"

"What else to do? This is a mad place. And we can't go back home. Jerry Richards said he was going bury us where nobody'd find us."

"So you got to arrest us," said Masie. "Can't be worse. They might even give us a family cell, do you think Mr Tremayne? After all, we aren't real criminals or such like."

Tremayne sat back in his seat and studied the three of them, each standing on their own page of The Telegraph's Sunday Supplement and surrounded by a sea of pristine white carpet. They vibrated mess. Even as the stood there, still and slightly afraid, they were making a mess. He was more interested in how he was going to keep them from ruining his carpet rather than the possibilities of a family cell. He laid out the remains of the Colour Supplement in a trail leading to the bathroom. Stepping stones.

"I need you all to go into the bathroom and don't come out until you shine." He watched as they carefully followed his trail of paper to the bathroom and closed the door. He heard the water start followed by squeals of shock and probably amusement as they tried to work out the jet system. He bent down to collect the paper from the floor.

"Breadcrumbs?" How had they done that? None of them had been eating and they all stayed on the paper, yet each sheet of paper was now surrounded by a sprinkling of breadcrumbs. He collected his hand held vacuum and cleaned up the mess.

He needed to remove these people from his sanctuary as soon as possible. The only trouble was it was too late to do anything about it tonight. Much as he dreaded the prospect, he was going to have to let them stay the night. He'd confine them to the guest room, keep the mess in one place. He could then close the door on it until Mrs Scwynsky came later tomorrow. That would solve it. He wasn't going to get stressed over this. He was a trained agent for MI6. He could withstand interrogation and torture. A little mess never *actually* hurt anybody. Did it?

He poured himself a large single malt.

The noise from the bathroom subsided, the door opened

and the three of them trailed out wrapped in large bath towels. He could throw those out in the morning. He pointed at the guest room door.

"You can stay in there tonight. There's a futon and sofa bed. I assume you have a change of clothes?"

"We brought our Sunday best, sir. He didn't want to." Masie glared at Barry. "But I told him, you never know when you're going to end up somewhere posh."

"When are you going to arrest us?" Barry asked.

"Erm... I don't think that will be necessary, Barry." Tremayne's mind raced, visions of mountains of paperwork and witness statements. Days of formalities stretched out before him. No, that would not do. "You are all valuable witnesses in a serious case. Tomorrow you'll be handed over to... the department of... erm... to somebody else."

"In that case, any chance of something to eat?" Barry cheered up. "Ain't had enough today to raise a good fart."

Despite the late hour, the streets of London were as alive as if it were midday. Paulo's Italian Trattoria was only a few blocks away. That would do them, he certainly didn't want to take them anywhere smarter than that, even if they were all done up in their Sunday best. Barry's version of 'Sunday Best' was a purple jacket and green cord trousers, while Maisie wore a pink dress that looked as though at some point it had been a bridesmaid's dress. Her more than amble bosom spilled out in all directions. Only Tommy looked relatively normal in his school uniform. Although on a closer look the badge actually said, 'Strathclyde Boarding school'. Tremayne hoped they wouldn't bump into anybody he knew.

Tremayne led the way, keeping far enough ahead that it might be seen that he didn't actually have anything to do with them.

"Just round the corner here," he said turning round.

They were gone.

He backtracked, eyes scanning all directions. No sign of

them. The smell of fish and chips caught his attention and he followed it to a small greasy cafe. He peered into the fluorescent lit interior. The Penwriths were pressed up against the counter pointing at pictures of assorted dishes, which all appeared to be just permutations of fish, burger, onion rings and chips. Tremayne sighed and sat down at a window table to wait for them. A few minutes later they joined him along with a tray full of assorted deep fried, artery clogging miscellanea.

"Help yerself," Barry said, pushing a bag of chips towards Tremayne. "More'n enough here for all and them some."

Despite himself and probably only through boredom, Charles picked at the chips. They were dripping in fat and vinegar and covered in salt. But surprisingly tasty. They reminded him of the meals he'd had at The Fishermans Plaice. Although he'd only left Takimoto's Sushi bar less than two hours ago, he suddenly felt hungry. He munched at the chips, tasting them as if they were an expensive delicacy. He even ventured a few onion rings which were actually not bad.

They returned to his flat and he made them all keep their hands away from anything until they'd been in the bathroom to scrub every trace of chip fat from them. He settled down in his recliner. His stomach was just in the early stages of mounting a protest against the sudden onslaught of unfamiliar fat. He switched on the huge plasma screen that seemed to cover most of one wall.

"Can you get X Factor on that thing?" Barry asked from behind him.

***

The following morning, three taxi changes and a half mile grumbling walk brought Tremayne and the Penwriths to the door of safe house Sierra-Whisky Five.

"You'll be safe here, but you're to stay here and not move until tomorrow. Understand," Tremayne said.

"Yes, Mr Tremayne, sir." Barry's feet made little walking movements as though he wanted to be somewhere else.

"A package will arrive tomorrow. You are to open it. You will find tickets and passports in your new identities. Clear?"

"Can I be Bernard Matthews?"

"What? No! You're to be whoever is on the passport. You're being transferred to Witness Relocation, which could be anywhere in the world. There you stay, keeping a low profile until called."

"Yes, sir. Package, new identity, witness thingy. Got it!"

"Remember. Straight on the plane. Do not talk to anybody, anywhere in the world, whoever they say they are. Nobody until you hear from me."

"Right you are, Mr Tremayne." Barry seemed almost excited. Tremayne felt a slight tinge of guilt. Slight, very slight. And only for the briefest of moments.

***

Lenny Burroughs, Bunny to his mates, was a rogue. A rogue of the old school mind, but nonetheless a rogue. If you gave him a job you knew it would be seen through and no amount of threats, violence or bribery would divert him. Tremayne had found need to draw on his services a few times in the past for those little jobs that even MI6 might think were a little too 'iffy'.

He answered the phone on the third ring. "Burroughs Print," he said.

"Bunny?"

"Ah. Charles! Long time no word. Thought you were dead in a ditch somewhere."

"Not yet, Bunny. Need a favour."

"Doubt you'd be ringing me if you didn't."

"Three passports and some airline tickets."

"Anywhere in particular?"

"Somewhere hot. Oh... and probably somewhere where

tidiness is not important. Photos are coming across now."

"No problem. Usual arrangements for the money?"

"Yes." Tremayne gave him the address for the drop-off and hung up. All being well, that should be the last he, or anyone else for that matter, would ever hear from the Penwriths.

He hoped.

***

Heathrow Airport was the usual tangle of intermingling queues. Queues for the Check Ins seemed to link up with those for the security checks and the toilets. Unwary travellers thinking they were in line to buy a Daily Telegraph in WH Smith's were likely to find themselves being frisked by a bored security official and relieved of their five quid bottle of Evian water.

He flashed his I.D. at everybody in uniform and the morass of humanity opened up in front of him like the parting of the Red Sea. There were some parts of this job he was really going to miss. The Border Police holding tank was set behind the Customs and Excise area. Not that it bore the name 'Holding Tank', it was currently labelled 'Immigration Reception Suite' but no doubt would change its name again before long.

The Border Police sergeant scrolled his forefinger down the list of names on the clip board in front of him.

"Babcock, you say?"

"Yes," Tremayne said. "Balding, pot bellied. You might remember him The Branch blew up his van yesterday."

"First name?"

"I don't know. Everybody just knows him as Babcock the Butcher. How many Babcocks have you got?"

"Currently? Let me see..." His finger continued its travels down the page. "None."

"But you were holding him here for us?"

"We were, that's true. But you lot have already collected

him. You spooks are so damned secretive it's no wonder you never know what's going on." He placed the clip board on the desk and carefully positioned the pen in the holder.

"Who collected him? MI6?"

"MI6, MI5 C.I.A. Special Branch, all the same to me. Left hand doesn't seem to know what the other left hand is doing half the time."

"C.I.A?" Tremayne queried. "They're nothing to do with us."

"Might as well be. Spend more time in here than you lot." He pulled a pile of papers from the top drawer of a large grey filing cabinet. "Give me a minute and I'll tell you who collected him."

"Why is this not all on computer?"

"It's supposed to be but some silly sod left the backup disk on a train so they've shut the system down and we're having to keep paper records until the techie guys get it all sorted. Ah... Harry Palmer, Special Branch collected him at fourteen twenty seven. There you go!" He spun the file round to show Tremayne. "See, as I said, one of your lot."

Charles studied the paper. It all seemed in order. Infernal meddlers. He thought the Branch had already thrown Babcock back to MI6 after blowing up his van and realising he was a harmless old fool. Oh well, job done.

"Thanks anyway," Tremayne said as he turned to leave. "I'll let you get on with counting your cigarettes."

This was the other part of the job he was going to miss. The XKR glided effortlessly through the early evening traffic. Puccini rolled around the leather interior, the only other sound, the gentle hiss of the air conditioning. He took the long way back in order to finish the particular movement that was currently playing. Somewhat reluctantly, he parked the car in the underground car park and gave it a last wistful look before entering the lift. That would go back tomorrow. There really was no need to hang on any longer. He'd file his report this evening. Special Branch had Babcock, goodness knows why but they could have the whole file if they wanted. The Penwriths should be safely out of the country by now and no doubt an army of search and destroy ants will descend on Little Didney as soon as his report hits Gemini's desk in the morning. Not quite the final blaze of glory he'd hoped for but he still had all four limbs and in this line of work that was a definite bonus.

He spent five minutes under the shower washing off the day's grime and then another twenty trying to scrape off thirty years of muck. He poured himself a particularly large Isle of Jura. He really ought to file his report tonight he thought as he reclined into the sofa. No hurry. He could file in the morning. He flicked the plasma screen into life and searched the myriad of channels and eventually settled on a film. It was an old spy movie from a more innocent age. Cary Grant finding himself mistaken for a spy and going on the run, pretty girl in tow. Tremayne struggled for the name, it was one of his favourites, North by Northwest. That was it. He topped up his whisky and relaxed back. He was fast asleep long before his favourite scene with the aeroplane.

***

The following morning, determined to cease prevaricating, he headed for the office with first coffee in hand and settled in front of the computer for the last time.

Elaine's number flashed up on his satphone screen.
"Hello?" he answered.
"Another alarm gone off on the Little Didney watch I'm afraid, Charles. Just what is going on down there? Gemini's keeping this one very close. Not another Royal sex scandal being hushed up is it?"
"Nothing like that, Elaine. All rather dull. What's happened now?"
"Chap called Tom Trevellick. Farmer, mostly pigs. Checked in to the Ritz, paid for three nights in cash, spent best part of a week there charging everything else and now can't pay his bill."
"Where is he now?"
"They're holding him in Bow Street police station but I

understand they're fairly keen to get rid of him."

He shut down the office for a second time. "Hell! What *is* it with these people? Why can't they leave me alone?"

He threaded his way through the traffic and parked in the visitor's bay at Bow Street police station. The desk sergeant responded rapidly and efficiently to Tremayne's I.D.

"This way, sir." He led Tremayne through to the cells and introduced him to the custody sergeant.

"Ah, yes. Thomas Trevellick. Non payment of hotel bill," the custody sergeant said reading from the screen in front of him. "Can't say we'll be sorry to see the back of this one." He pushed a form towards Tremayne. "Just sign here and here," he pointed. "And he's all yours."

Charles duly signed the transfer documents and was led to Trevellick's cell. The sergeant unlocked the door.

"Come on out now, you silly old sod." He held the door open.

Tom Trevellick shuffled nervously out of the cell. He wore slightly muddy coloured green cord trousers a check shirt and white fluffy dressing gown that bore the Ritz logo. As soon as he spotted Tremayne, he said; "Oh bugger!" He turned back to the custody officer. "I think I'd rather stay here, if it's all the same with you?"

"Come on. Sling your hook." The sergeant circled behind Tom, corralling him out through the door.

"You're that Government man they was all talking about?" Trevellick slid nervously around the edge of the whitewashed corridor, trying to keep as much distance between them as the old Victorian cell structure would allow.

"Tremayne, Charles Tremayne. And yes, I work... worked," he hesitated. "Yes, at the moment I still work for her Majesty's government."

"You gonna arrest me?"

"No, I've just arranged your release. You were already under arrest when I found you. I'd have thought you'd have noticed a minor detail like that?"

Tremayne spread a map of London out on the leather

seat and guided Trevellick into the car. As they pulled out of the police station and into the traffic he turned the air conditioning up to full. Even the Jaguar engineers had failed to anticipate this burden to which their ventilation systems would be put. Tremayne resorted to opening the windows. Traffic fumes were definitely preferable to several day old... what on earth was it? ... probably had something to with cows, he surmised.

"So, why didn't you simply pay the bill at the hotel?" Tremayne asked.

"I ran out of money," Trevellick mumbled.

"How on earth did that happen?"

"Brought a bagful with me. But that bugger on the train took a load, then him in the taxi had another handful. And then at the hotel desk when I arrived, they wanted a pile too. It's all so expensive up here. Bagful like that back home would last me a year or more."

"Credit cards?"

"Don't believe in'em. Work of the devil they is. Get you into all sorts of trouble.

Tremayne felt inclined to point out he was already in all sorts of trouble but decided not to. He felt a sudden and unfamiliar feeling of sympathy to this man. It was only fleeting and he squashed it quickly.

They drove to the Ritz and Tremayne coaxed a reluctant Trevellick in to reception. The receptionist looked up, a thin nervous looking man with greased back black hair and wire framed glasses. He looked startled.

"This is Mr Trevellick," Tremayne announced. "He's a guest of yours. Or at least he was until you decided to have him ejected."

"Well," said the receptionist. "We have this system of bill paying in operation at The Ritz Hotel. Archaic I know, but it seems to work well for most of our guests. Mr... err..." He tried to suppress a sneer and failed. "Your friend here decided not to avail himself of this system, so as we always do in these situations, we had him arrested." He looked Tremayne straight in the eye and presented his best practised obsequious smile, closing the open green folder on his desk with an air of finality.

In the time it took the folder to close, Tremayne had already calculated the distance to this nasty little man's throat and just how quickly he could tear it out. He could already feel the oily skin in his hand and see the man drop to the floor, lifeless before he hit. Tremayne's right hand twitched, as if straining to be let loose. He resisted the impulse.

He pulled his pass from his pocket and showed it to the man behind the reception desk.

"This man is a guest of Her Majesty's Government," He slid a simple business card across the desk. "If you call this number, they will confirm that all bills will be taken care of. Past and future."

The receptionist jaw had stopped working as soon as he saw the pass. He froze, hands securely planted flat on the desk.

"Is that clear?" Tremayne asked, having given up waiting for the man to respond.

Finally, "Yes, sir."

"Anything he wants, you will accept *personal* responsibility for ensuring it is provided."

The receptionist nodded.

Unable to resist grinding this objectionable little man a little more, he continued, "I can't say much, you understand. But this man is a national hero." He heard a sudden intake of breath from Trevellick's direction but ignored it. He went on, "He has just been released from an Iranian Prison where spent five years locked up for trying to save a coach load of nuns from a terrorist attack."

The noises to Tremayne's left indicated he had better remove Trevellick from here before he erupted into fits of giggles.

But just one final twist of the virtual knife. "And please see to it that there are some fresh daffodils in the room every day."

"But, sir, this is August and..." The receptionist tailed off as he caught Tremayne's look. "I'll see to it at once, sir.

Tremayne's twitching hand relaxed. Sometimes he loved

his work.

Tremayne led Trevellick back through the main doors as quickly as he could before the farmer had chance to give the game away.

They stood on the marble steps outside the hotel.

"It'll take them a while to sort your room out again." Tremayne said.

"Is Her Majesty *really* going to pay for everything?"

"Anything you desire. Food, drink, even arrange a brace of top class hookers for you if you like."

"Not too sure about that," Trevellick pondered a while. "Do you think they'd let me go see The Sound of Music?"

Tremayne froze and suppressed a shudder. The ultimate horror of a dreadful sixties musical further tortured by Andrew Lloyd Webber's own very special skills in banality.

"No, sorry, Tom. That one's strictly off limits I'm afraid. National security," he glanced at Tom to see if he was buying it. "Section seventy two of the... the Insidious Influences Act."

Tom's face fell and Tremayne felt a slight pang of guilt. Damn it! Get a grip. Then he had a sudden strange thought. That was the third of the day but what the hell. This was his last day on the job and he might as well make the most of its perks.

"Tom, have you ever been up The West End?"

***

As Tom was hardly dressed for the theatre, in fact he was hardly dressed at all, Tremayne decided a quick visit to Saville Row was in order. He chose a small tailors with a good selection of off-the-peg suits. He expected more attitude from the assistant but was pleasantly surprised. The small Italian man saw Tom Trevellick as a personal challenge, and as money was clearly no barrier, he set about kitting the farmer out with not only a black tie outfit for the evening but also several sets of casual wear. The assistant took great delight in putting together the various combinations that transformed Trevellick into a seemingly successful city type. Even Tremayne, who understood only too well the importance of image changes, was stunned.

Tom surveyed himself in the mirror. "Well I'll be buggered," he said. "Mrs Trevellick would never have recognised me... had she seen me... and not realised it was me."

Tremayne took Trevellick back to the hotel and went upstairs with him to check all was in order. The scent of daffodils was overwhelming as he opened the door. Quite remarkable. He wondered how they'd managed that at this time of year. He'd been allocated a huge double suite with private bar and reception area. Everything seemed fine.

"I'll pick you up outside at seven," he said and left the farmer to probably trash his second room at the Ritz.

**

They ambled through the crowded pavements of the early evening West End. Lights pulsed, encouraging stragglers into the brightly lit theatres. Musicals, high drama and the ubiquitous Agatha Christie all vied for their share of the theatre-goer's pound. Trevellick looked dazed as his eyes drifted between billboards, neon lights and barkers. Crowds appeared to be an anathema to the farmer as he constantly collided with pedestrians and street traders. More than once Tremayne had to head off a potential altercation with an affronted bumpee.

At one point one of the collisions appeared a little less random than the others. A tall, slim man dressed in a dark bomber jacket, jeans and trainers bumped into Trevellick then patted him on the shoulder as if to say sorry and slipped into the crowd. Tremayne moved to close in on the man. He caught up with him in seconds and pinned the man against the nearest wall, fingers locked around the man's carotid arteries. His free hand did a quick pat-down then slipped into the jacket pocket emerging with a tattered leather wallet held together with insulating tape. He held it up in front of the man's face.

"This yours?" he whispered, slowly controlled.

"Yeah. Get off me or I'll have you done."

Tremayne flipped the wallet open with one hand. Inside was a creased and faded photograph of Trevellick and a woman he assumed must be Mrs Trevellick.

"Not much of a family likeness here is there?"

"Found it I did." The man wriggled under the tightening grip.

Tremayne heard shouting behind him. He turned as he slipped the wallet in his pocket. Two doormen from a nearby theatre were heading through the crowd towards him. He pulled his pass from his jacket and held it up.

"Security Services," he shouted. "All under control." The men hesitated then caught the look in Tremayne's eyes. They melted back into the crowd.

He turned his attention back to the wriggling pickpocket under his grip.

"Your career is over." His fingers tightened. The sound of the crowds disappeared as all that existed now was this miserable life-form that preyed on the weak. He felt the pulse in the man's neck stop under the pressure. He watched as the man's eyes started to roll then flicker as consciousness left him. He became a dead weight under the grip. Stop. Not now. Something pulled Tremayne back and he let go.

The man crumpled to the floor. Simple oxygen starvation in the brain. He'd be out for a few minutes then wake with a headache from hell. Hopefully.

Tremayne turned back into the thronging street, casting around for any signs of Trevellick. Hell. Where had he got to? Heads bobbed and bodies weaved across the pavements. He pushed his way through the morass of humanity. It was like wading uphill in a mudslide. The sound of raised voices caught his attention.

He found Trevellick in a heated argument with a street vendor.

"Will you sod off, you old git!" yelled the vendor. "You

don't like me bacon rolls then don't fucking buy em." He snatched a roll from Old Tom's hand and slammed it on the metal counter. "Go on, piss off."

"'Ere, I paid for that."

"And you ain't done nothin' but bitch about it ever since." He put a two pound coin on the counter. "Take yer money and go before I call the Old Bill."

"Your sign says British Bacon, see!" Tom pointed at the menu behind the counter. "British it says. There plain as day. Nothing British about it though there ain't. That's Danish if ever I tasted it."

"Who are you? Jamie fucking Oliver? Course it's British. Straight from Tesco's this morning."

Tremayne touched Trevellick on the shoulder. "Come on, Tom," he said. "Let's go." He guided Tom away from the stall, slipping the wallet back in Tom's pocket as he did so.

"That's it," called the vendor after them. "Take yer old man back to the nursing home and keep him out of my way, I'll give 'im a smack next time."

Tremayne stopped. "Stay here, Tom. Don't move." He whirled back towards the burger bar, snatched the spatula from the man's hand and thrust it against his throat. "I'll be back in half an hour and I want to see all the 'British' signs gone." He saw the man glancing towards a chopping knife. "Really? If you think you're fast enough, go for it," Tremayne challenged, then tapped the man on the cheek with the spatula and turned back to Tom. Who had disappeared again.

He caught up with him this time in a group of people watching somebody doing Three Card Monty. More trouble looming if he didn't get the silly old fool away from here sharpish. If Trevellick stayed on the streets much longer somebody was going to end up dead. For some reason Tremayne felt his usual ice cold control slipping this evening.

"Come on, let's go." He grasped Tom's upper arm firmly and guided him across the street and into the first theatre they came across. Kylie Minogue in concert. Not quite Covent Garden but it would do. The billboards had banners pasted across them, 'Sold Out'. He approached the doorman and showed his pass. "I need to lay low with this man for a while." Doormen were useful. They always responded well to requests for help from The Service.

They were shown to a pair of seats just in front of the sound desks. Tremayne guessed these were usually kept clear to allow better line of sight for the sound crew.

"Popcorn?" Tom thrust a huge box into Tremayne's face.

"No thanks." Funny, he hadn't noticed Tom buying that. He relaxed back into his seat and debriefed himself on the past half hour. Twice he had come close to killing somebody over meaningless trivialities. Not good. He usually had much better control than that. For some reason he was taking this all way too personally.

The house lights dimmed and coloured spotlights raked across the huge stage like a Technicolor air raid. Half naked and well oiled young men cavorted through the lights to the thumping sound of heavy rock music. After a few minutes the audience erupted into applause as Kylie slid onto the stage, the grace of a panther and the magnetism of a quantum singularity.

"Oh, bugger," he heard Tom sigh to his left.

Kylie moved through the dancers, touching each one sensuously as she went. She wore what looked like nothing more than a few straps of strategically placed leather and impossibly high heels. Judging by the audience response, the song she sang was probably one of her popular hits. Tremayne had a vague thought he recognised it. The lyrics were hardly Turandot and mostly consisted of La La La La. But it had a certain basic charm. Sandy would have enjoyed this. It was her type of music. He turned to his left, almost hoping he'd find her there with him. Instead the smiling face of Trevellick turned towards him. He had popcorn in his hair.

"She knows how to move does that one." Trevillick said.

"She does seem to have a lot of energy, that's for sure." Tremayne returned.

For ninety minutes Kylie and the dancers strutted and writhed through the lights and music. Her energy amazed Tremayne. She just didn't stop. It was not only the power of the music that was hypnotic but the sexual energy she produced ran from the stage like dry ice in a ghost movie. By the time of the encore he found his feet were dancing and he actually caught himself singing along to a number he never even knew he had heard before. Finally, he stood with everybody else and applauded loudly as she took her final bow and left the stage.

They flowed out with the human river as it emerged onto the street.
"Well," he said. "That was... er... interesting. What did you think, Tom?"
"That was bloody amazing. Not seen anybody move like that since Mrs Trevellick did Oklahoma in the British Legion in seventy two."
Tremayne tried to fit together the images of the Mrs Trevellick he'd seen in the photograph with Kylie and Oklahoma. He gave up. Some things just shouldn't be imagined.

They drifted for a while along Shaftsbury Avenue before somehow finding themselves in a Fish and Chip shop. They sat at a small wobbly table with a red chequered plastic table cloth. The meal was good. Crispy batter and chunky chips. Trevellick emptied the best part of a bottle of ketchup on his chips then picked them up with his hands and planted them between two slices of bread.
"Chip butties," he said as he licked some escaping sauce from the back of his hand. "Best meal when you're really hungry." He waved the butty in Tremayne's direction. Droplets of ketchup flew like blood splatter in the shower scene of Psycho.
Only a lightning fast manoeuvre with a serviette protected Tremayne's jacket. No such fortune though for

Trevellick's suit which now looked as though it belonged to a victim of a drive-by shooting.

"Bugger it," Tom said as he dabbed at the mess. "That's one for the wash."

They caught a taxi back to The Ritz where Tremayne satisfied himself that Trevellick still had a room then he headed back to his flat.

***

It was gone midnight by the time he returned to his apartment. The evening had put him into a much more relaxed state of mind. Normality had been resumed. Tom Trevellick had actually turned out to be quite good company in the end. His tales of the various doings of the Village initially excruciatingly boring seemed to develop a certain charm over the hours.

But now he really needed to send in his report. He unlocked the console in the bookcase logged on to the MI6 servers and once more began typing.

'Money located. Split into various locations in village of Little Didney in the possession of individual residents. Local Police Constable not to be trusted. Suggest search team with assistance of Devon and Cornwall Constabulary.'
That would be gentler than the full Anti Terrorist Squad. However cussed the inhabitants of Little Didney had been, they didn't deserve that.
'Babcock in the hands of Special Branch agent Harry Palmer'
He was sure he knew that name from somewhere.
'Farmer Trevellick currently resident in the London Ritz hotel. All charges relating to his non payment have been dropped. Penwrith family appear to have fled the country, whereabouts unknown. Further, please accept this report as my formal resignation from the service from this date. Will complete all necessary documentation tomorrow.'

Once more his finger paused over the 'send' button.

Harry Palmer? Where did he know that name from?

He hit delete.

Chapter 15

The drive back to Heathrow the following morning took less than half the time it had two days previously, aided by the blue flashing lights concealed within the front light of the Jaguar.

Tremayne had contacted Heathrow security to ensure the same sergeant was made available for questioning.

"Nothing unusual struck you about the Special Branch man who collected Babcock I suppose?"Tremayne asked him.

"In what way? You're all a bit unusual if you ask me."

"How about his name? Harry Palmer? Ring any bells?"

"Not that I can say."

"Michael Caine's character in a series of spy movies in the early seventies?"

"No, more of a Great Escape man myself."

Tremayne locked himself away in a side office and set about viewing the security tapes of the afternoon. It wasn't long before he found what he was looking for. Babcock being handed over to a tall well built, dark suited man. Papers being signed, handcuffs exchanged.

"Come on, turn around," Tremayne muttered.

As if on cue the man turned to face the camera just as he led Babcock out. He smiled as though he knew Tremayne was there, watching. Mr Green. Hell! He was supposed to be securely locked up underneath Thames House. How had he got himself free and with paperwork of sufficient quality to fool HM's Border Police?

Tremayne sat in the car outside the security area at Heathrow. A sudden thought and he put a call through to The Ritz hotel.

"I need to speak to a guest, please. A Mr T. Trevellick."

"One moment, sir." He was put on hold for a short while then; "I'm sorry, sir. Mr Trevellick checked out this morning"

He called Elaine and she answered immediately.

"Charles? What on earth are you up to? We're still waiting for your report."

"Later, what's the score with Mr Green and co?"

"We had to let them go. Human rights nonsense. Liberty or the Blair Witch Woman... Possibly even Nelson Mandela, I don't know. Just know Gemini was fairly pissed about it all. Lots of noisy phone calls from what I could hear. Why do you ask?"

"He's just sprung Babcock from security at Heathrow with some fairly impressive paperwork. And I've a feeling he's got Trevellick as well."

"What are you planning on doing, Charles? Nothing stupid I hope? You're supposed to be finished with Little Didney."

"I know but somehow Little Didney doesn't seem to be quite finished with me yet" He clicked the telephone off and stared at the keypad for a good two minutes. Then "Damn it!" he yelled so loudly the car rocked briefly.

***

The road to Cornwall was beginning to feel like an old friend. The morning sunlight glared in the rear view mirror as he raced westward along the A303. He had just passed the Yeovil turn off when his phone rang. It was Sandy, she sounded panicked. He pulled the car over in a layby.

"Charles? Thank God. They're everywhere. They've got us all separated and—"

"Who? How many?"

The voice on the phone changed.

"Ah, Mr Tremayne. Different circumstances now ain't it?" Mr Green's East London voice, unmistakable down the crystal clear sat-link. We got what you want, now you get us what we want and all will be hunky, understand?"

"You'll need to clarify. What is it you have that I would want and just what would you like me to get for you?"

"That little tea-leaf Penwrith. He's had it on his toes with half the foldin' ain't he? Little shit, you bring 'im back here and you'll get this lovely lady back in one piece, clear?"

Tremayne wasn't entirely sure it was clear but he thought he understood enough. "I don't know where he is." Tremayne's mind raced as he stalled. "He's gone into witness protection, could be anywhere in the world by now... and anybody."

"We got these good folks here and we're going to start hacking bits of 'em 'til such time as you turn up with the little scroat and his ill gotten."

"Okay but I need to talk with Sandy first."

"You got one minute. Don't say I'm not generous."

"Charles?" Sandy's voice again.

"It will be alright. Trust me. How are things there?" Calculated question. Would she risk any sort of helpful answer? He wouldn't blame her if she didn't.

"There's at least eight of them. All different places with different people. They've got—" She spoke rapidly until the sound of a slap cut her short. Part of Charles regretted asking her but he'd needed that information.

"Feisty one this little thing." Mr Green's voice again. "You get us Penwrith she stays in one piece."

The phone went dead.

So, crafty little Barry Penwrith had tucked away a share for himself. Tremayne sat in the car collecting his thoughts. There were more of them than previously and they were obviously getting some inside help. Professional tactics, separating the hostages would make a successful Special Forces assault very difficult. That's if he could trust enough people to mount such an operation in the first place. Single person ingress? Not easy again due to the separation. Best option then, bring Barry back to use as a bargaining tool to get close enough to solve the problem.

A sense of tranquillity washed over Tremayne for the first time in weeks. Familiar territory now. Bring back the traitor, extract the secrets and rescue the girl.

'It's what I do. It's what I'm good at.'

***

As the car sped back towards London he dialled Bunny's number.

"Ah, Charles, your packages went off safely. But don't do that again to me though please? Bank robbers, hitmen don't even mind the odd serial killer. But that lot..."

"I promise, Bunny, but I need another favour."

"Name it."

"I need one of them back." The phone went quiet for what seemed like minutes. "Bunny? You still there?"

Finally, "You taking the piss? Is this 'Take the piss out of Bunny week'?"

"Sorry I wouldn't—"

"I know, if wasn't life or death or football or something equally important etcetera etcetera. I'm not going near that lot again. Best I can do is I'll tell you where they went, you deal with it from there."

"Thanks, I owe you one."

"Let's say five hundred then?"

Tremayne wasn't in the mood for haggling. "Deal. Where did you send them?"

As he waited for Bunny to answer his mind calculated routes to the two main airports. For South America he'd best head for Heathrow but if Bunny had sent them to Taiwan or similar then Gatwick might be better. Bunny seemed to be taking a long time replying.

"Bunny? Where did you send them?"

Another pause, and then, "Benidorm."

"Benidorm?! What on earth possessed you to send them to Benidorm?"

"You said somewhere hot and where tidiness was not necessary. I can see what you meant on that one by the way, I've never met—"

"But Benidorm? I was thinking more Paraguay or Jakarta or something. Not Benidorm."

"Give me a break, Charles. I'm not without heart you know. None of them speak any languages. They struggle with English. Put them anywhere else on the planet and they'll stick out like the proverbial. But Benidorm, nobody'll notice them there. Fit right in."

***

Driving whilst on the phone is one thing but trying to book an airline ticket on a PDA and doing ninety on a dual carriageway is a rare skill. But within five minutes he had a British Airways flight to Alicante leaving in three hours. He also noticed he'd managed to pick up a tail. A black BMW hovered just visible in the distance. At first he'd thought it an unmarked police car but they'd have pulled him by now. He accelerated and the leather seat pushed into his back. He overtook a row of traffic on the white line and for a while the BMW kept up then disappeared into the distance, stuck behind a lorry.

His MI6 pass wove its magic spell as he sped the formalities at Heathrow and soon he was high over the English Channel supping an excellent glass of Chateau le fite. He relaxed back into the comfortable seat and stretched his feet out in the complementary slippers. Just time for a quick snooze before lunch. The hostess noticed he was settling down and wordlessly slipped a pillow behind his neck.

The plane touched down exactly on time and the Hertz representative was precisely where they said they'd be. He pointed at a Mercedes SLR parked directly outside the main doors, handed Tremayne the keys and wished him Buenas Dias."

Wide uncluttered roads made the journey to Benidorm a relaxing pleasure. It also made it easier to see his latest tail. This time a motorcycle, probably a Moto Guzzi but difficult to tell at this distance. He had used his secondary, secret account for booking the tickets, standard practice when one needed to drop under the radar, yet they had still picked him up.

Bunny had handed over the final location details of the Penwriths to an old friend of his who ran a bar on the main

Avienida Castillo. Tremayne parked the Mercedes right outside the 'Dog and Duck' (Full English Breakfast with real English bacon served all day). At first sight the bright sunshine outside made the interior seem overly gloomy. At second sight he noticed the interior was gloomy. Yellowed walls proudly were draped in Union Flags and the Cross of St George. A huge plasma screen was showing what was evidently, judging by the excited crowd, some highly important football game.

He picked his way through the throng of sweaty, beer bellied, semi naked male excellence and ordered a coffee.

"Want milk and sugar with that, Luv?" asked a teak coloured woman behind the bar.

"No just coffee thank you."

She put a heaped spoonful of Nescafe in a mug and filled it from the Espresso machine.

"There you go," she said as she pushed it towards him. "Only real English coffee served here."

"Is Malcolm around?" Tremayne asked.

"Who wants to know?" she asked, suspiciously.

"Name's Charles. Friend of Bunny's."

"Mal!" she yelled toward the kitchen behind the bar. "Geezer here to see you. Another mate of Bunny's"

The bead curtains separated and a very large, shaven headed man ducked through. He wiped his leathery hands on a food spattered apron and held one of them out to Charles.

"What can I do for you? Need a place to stay? Can fix you up with a nice flat out on Calle Cadiz."

Tremayne reluctantly took the sticky hand.

"You helped Bunny find a home for a family of three a couple of days ago. I need to know where they are."

"Don't know what you're on about. Don't know no Bunny, don't do homes for folks neither." He increased the pressure on Tremayne's hand. "So you'd best be running along now. Hadn't you?"

"I can make it worth your while."

"You're not understanding me. You need to—"

The rest of the sentence disappeared into a mumble as

the man's face hit the bar. The hand that was still interlocked with Tremayne's now twisted unnaturally behind his back. Tremayne used his free hand to attack the pressure points in the man's neck. He scanned the bar looking for signs of further potential trouble. Nothing. Football had its uses.

"Where did you put them?" he asked as his fingers levered into the man's mastoid process behind the cauliflower ear.

Mal pressed his face harder into the bar in an effort to escape the excruciating pain of the nerve attack "Apartment four, Casa Bougainville on Avenida Del Mar."

"That wasn't so hard now? Thank you." He slowly released the man's hand and let him straighten up. "And I'd appreciate it if you kept our little chat quiet?"

Tremayne's eyes squinted in protest at the sudden bright light of the sun. He slipped into the Mercedes and brought up Avenida Del Mar on the Sat Nav. The car nudged its way through the logjam of humanity that filled the narrow streets. Mostly scarlet coloured tourists in gaudy hats and T-shirts interspersed with the occasional bewildered looking local. Souvenir shops and bars overflowed onto the pavements so far that pedestrians were being forced into the road.

The Casa Bougainville occupied an impressive corner plot overlooking the sea front. He parked the car and headed around the back of the building from where he could hear the whoops and splashes of excited pool activity.

The fact that Maisie had managed to find a bikini large enough to cover her ample bosom was in itself quite amazing. But the fact that such an article came in the same shade of pink that perfectly matched her husband's thong was quite horrifying. They both lay on their backs, overflowing their respective sunbeds, while Tommy did continuous dive bombs onto an inflatable dinosaur in the pool. The surrounding area was awash with burger cartons, beer bottles and empty ice cream tubs. All three were already showing signs of second degree sunburn.

"Good afternoon, Barry," Tremayne announced.

Barry jumped into a sitting position, the sunbed protesting, buckling underneath him. "Oh, bugger. Mr Tremayne sir. What're you doing here?"

"Need to take you back for a couple of days." No point in pussy-footing around.

"Look who it is, Maisie." Barry poked his near comatose wife. Her flesh rippled like waves on a pond. "It's Mr Tremayne. Come to... what'd you say?" He suddenly looked alarmed.

"Just need to pop back to Little Didney for a little while. Need your help to find something. You don't recall losing erm... ten wooden crates full of money do you, Barry?"

"No, sir, Mr Tremayne sir. Jerry and his lot took it all. Didn't they, Maisie? All of it."

Tremayne dusted a low white wall with his handkerchief before sitting on it. "I shouldn't worry about it then, Barry. They've probably gone and got themselves all confused over how many boxes there were. Ten, one hundred. Easy to miscount."

"That would be it I expect. Easy done. Remember when I had a job counting sheep for Melvyn Pikewarn. Buggers wouldn't stop moving around. Expect it's the same... sort of. Would you like some doscerveca, Mr Tremayne?

"What?"

Doscerveca. It's Spanish for beer. I'm learning the lingo. Doscerveca senior. Maisie says I speak it like a local. Makes her go all tingly she says. Don't you, Maisie?" He poked her again. "Makes you go all tingly when I do my Spanish."

Tremayne stood up. "When the others come just tell them the same, Barry. Just say it's probably a miscount."

"Right you are then... What others?"

Remember the gang that took the money in the first place?"

"You locked them all up, right? I mean they've all gone to prison now haven't they?" He was looking worried.

"Well, they did, but now they're out again. And I think

they're looking for you. In fact, I'm fairly confident at least one of them is here right now in Benidorm."

"Hmm, perhaps I'd better go with you then. You'll explain it to them, right? I mean about the sheep and how they move around makes it difficult to count?"

"I'll deal with it, Barry."

"You won't let them... you'll make sure... I mean..."

"Trust me, Barry. I'll look after you. But you are going to need to help me a little. Perhaps we might need to recount the boxes when we get back see if that helps?"

Barry looked crestfallen. "Wouldn't do any harm suppose. If it keeps them others happy I mean."

"Good. I'll sort the flight out. Tommy and Maisie can stay here alright. They'll be fine until you get back."

Tremayne sat in the Mercedes and pulled up the British Airways booking screen on his PDA. No flights for two days. He continued checking. All other scheduled airlines were fully booked for the next week. He could pull rank and get somebody bumped but that would draw way too much attention. Eventually he managed to find two seats on Econo-Air leaving Alicante at six thirty in the morning. That seemed remarkably cheap? Twenty eight pounds? He clicked on '!Book It!' Did he want seats together? Yes, another fourteen pounds. Was he carrying hand luggage? Yes, twenty pounds. Breakfast? Priority Embark? And so it went on. He felt quite drained by the time he'd completed all the hurdles.

He also felt quite annoyed that he hadn't been able to arrange flights for that day. It meant an evening and night babysitting the Penwriths. He knew he had one tail but there could be others. And if they knew the location of Barry, they no longer needed Tremayne.

He went back to tell Barry. Maisie had somehow transposed herself to the pool and was currently laying spread-eagled across the dinosaur, bobbing up and down in the waves created by Tommy's interminable dive-bombs.

"Flight goes first thing, Barry."

"As you say, Mr Tremayne, sir. We can all go out this evening for a steak and a few doscervecas. There's a great bar just down the road, they're doing an Elvis night."

"You two could do a duet," Maisie offered from the pool.

The dry heat of the day turned into the humid, sticky heat of evening. Tremayne needed a change of clothes. With Barry in tow he headed off towards the main shopping area. Over the years he had learned to blend with his surroundings, taking on the image of a local. A farmer in Azerbaijan, a telecom worker in Serbia. But here? He scanned the throngs of people creating in his mind a composite identity he could adopt. The most ubiquitous image was clearly that of the British tourist. Reluctantly he took Barry into a clothes shop, both emerging ten minutes later in jeans, sandals and England supporter's T-shirt. The purchase of some Gucci sunglasses and a couple of Rolex watches from a street vendor completed the ensemble.

***

Elvis night at the 'Queen Vic' was obviously a local highlight. The smell of beer and sweat assaulted Charles's nose before they were within fifty yards of the place. The sound of Jailhouse Rock tumbled out of the open doorway. The place was packed. Apart from the brightly lit stage the rest of the room was in semi darkness. The floor was already wet and sticky underfoot. This was not a good place to be.

"Are you sure about this place, Barry?" He held cupped hand to Barry's ear to make him hear."

"Good innit?" Barry grinned"

"If you must. Come with me, we'll find a table."

They threaded their way through the morass towards a table in the corner near the toilets and fire exit. It was currently occupied by a family of four. Tremayne whispered into the father's ear, pointed towards Barry and pressed something into the man's hand. The man immediately jumped up, eyes wide in apparent terror and dragged his family through the crowd and out of the door. Tremayne and the Penwriths settled down at the table.

Barry caught the attention of a passing waiter. "Coca Cola light," he pointed at Tommy. "Tia Maria and lemonade," towards maisie. Then "Doscerveca and another doscerveca," he said proudly pointing to himself and Charles in turn. The waiter didn't look in the slightest bit phased and slipped through the crowds with practised ease towards the bar.

A new 'Elvis' took to the stage and the karaoke machine started its distorted rendition of 'Now or Never'.
"Ooh, our favourite!" Maisie enthused. And just case Tremayne was in any doubt about it being their favourite, she and Barry set about a two part harmony seemingly in an attempt to out-volume the P.A. system.
The drinks arrived, Tia Maria for Maisie, a coke for Tommy and as expected, two beers each for Tremayne and Barry.
"See why we like this place," Barry yelled, pointing at the beers. "Always give you double measures!"

A little while later and at Barry's recommendation they were brought huge plates of steak laced with a mountain of chips and onion rings.
"I just love Spanish food," Barry said, carving into a piece of meat the size of an average Frisbee.
Expecting the worst, Charles cut open his steak, the juices ran to perfection. Just the right amount of blood. Either knife was intensely sharp or the steak was particularly tender. He hesitated briefly before risking it to his palette. Surprisingly good.

When they had finished eating Barry stood up, pecked Maisie on the cheek and headed for the toilets. Tremayne watched the crowd. Despite the seeming chaos, large numbers of people have predictable patterns. The flow is even, like muddy water circling in the road during a downpour. Once the eye is attuned, it is possible to spot anomalies instantly. The heated argument, the couple having a secret tryst or the hitman watching his target.

The big man slipped easily through the crowd towards the toilets. He was dressed in Union Flag shorts and a white T-shirt that proclaimed his love of Benidorm. He wore a leather bum-bag into which his hand slipped as he neared the toilets.

"Don't move," Tremayne instructed Maisie and Tommy. He circled to the edge of the room and slipped into the toilets after the man and Barry.

A small, terrified looking man pushed his way past Tremayne, fleeing the toilets. "Wouldn't go in there if I were you, mate." He scuttled into the crowd and was lost.

Ignoring the man's obviously sound advice, Tremayne continued in. Barry was on his knees in the centre of the room. One of the man's huge hands held the back of Barry's neck the other pressed a silenced gun into Barry's temple. He sensed rather than heard Tremayne and looked up.

"Got no problem with you," he said. "Just need some information from this little bugger here then I'll be on me way."

"Just came in for a piss," Tremayne said, moving further into the room.

"Stop there." He pressed harder with the gun causing Barry to squeal. "I know who you are. Any closer and I'll—"

The rest of his words were lost in a gurgle. The steak knife had flown through the air and embedded itself deep into the man's throat. He dropped the gun to claw at his throat. Before he dropped to the floor, Tremayne caught the man under the arms and dragged him into a cubicle. He propped him on the seat, locked the door from the inside then climbed out over the top. Barry still huddled on the floor whimpering. Tremayne pulled a handful of paper towels from the dispenser and mopped up the surprisingly small amount of blood. Flushing the towels away he grabbed Barry by the upper arm and guided him back to the table.

Tremayne gathered the for once silent Penwriths together and headed out into the busy evening street. He cursed himself for killing the man but he'd been left with no options. His original plan had been to let Barry lure him into the open and then take him somewhere quiet for a chat, find out what was going on back in Little Didney and then probably kill him. But this guy had been a professional. He obviously knew who Tremayne was and was certainly not going to let him get close enough. He probably wouldn't have killed Barry, certainly until he'd got the information he needed but there was no doubt he was about to turn the gun on Tremayne. Now, was he the only one?

Back at the apartments Tremayne reorganised the sleeping arrangements. He put them all in the same room, far away from the door then set up a bed for himself pushed tight against the only door into the room. He jammed the handle of the window with a broom and settled down for what promised to be a long night.

As it happened, the night passed without incident and Tremayne and Barry were on time for the check in desk at exactly four thirty the following morning. Did they want a window seat? Yes. A further twelve pounds. Did they want priority security clearance? Tremayne was about to flash his I.D. but thought better of it. A further eight pounds. Did they want overhead locker space?
"I've already booked hand luggage when I bought the tickets?"
"Yes sir, but that was for the allowance only. Where do you want to store the luggage for the flight?"
Another ten pounds for the overhead locker space. By the time they boarded the aircraft, he'd been separated from a further thirty two pounds.

The plane was jammed with returning holidaymakers. Mostly scarlet coloured, broke and half a stone heavier than on their outward trip. Babies whined and children complained. Tremayne pushed Barry towards the window and sat in the centre of three, flanked on the other side by a small boy whose remaining family occupied the row in front. Tremayne wedged his knees into the tiny space and searched the armrest for the recline button. There wasn't one.

They took off on time and he was soon being served with breakfast. An optimistic word for an assortment of strangely coloured blobs in a cardboard lid. Did he want coffee? Another three pounds for a cardboard mug of brown liquid that certainly owed no heritage to any coffee plantations of which Tremayne was aware.

Another small boy in the seat directly in front kept bobbing his head over the seatback to jabber with his brother. In an effort to isolate himself from the mayhem, Tremayne rented a set of headphones for six pounds and tried to lose himself by watching Shrek III on the tiny screen four rows in front. Not an entirely successful retreat as the film was stopped every twenty minutes to extol the virtues of David Beckham's latest after shave and how it could be purchased on board at ten percent off 'High Street' prices. He was going to kill Bunny next time he saw him. Slowly and in interesting ways yet to be decided, the man deserved to die a horrible death for this.

Mercifully, the flight was short and arrived ten minutes early and after a surprisingly quick transition through immigration even without the aid of his pass, they were speeding westward on the M4. Barry had not spoken a word the whole flight. The traffic was light heading west at this time in the morning and Tremayne relaxed into the comfortable seat and let the XKR have its head. Time to explain speeding tickets later.

This was not going to be an easy endeavour. At least in all his previous missions, even to some of the most remote and dangerous parts of the world, somebody always had his back. Somebody always knew roughly where he was and an exfil plan in place. Admittedly that plan was often hazy and consisted of little more than 'We send in a Special Forces squad at this point', but he always knew it was there. Somebody was watching out for him, even Elaine on the other end of the phone. But this time he was on his own. Somebody inside MI6 was involved. He had a fair idea who but until he knew for sure and how many, he was going to have to 'Run Black'. Which meant no backup and no extra resources over those he could secure for himself. He was going into a multiple hostage situation with at least eight well armed Xrays who knew he was coming. He had no support and little weaponry.

He suddenly realised he was grinning. For the first time in many years he felt truly alive. If was going to go out 'In Action' then he guessed this was more noble than most of his previous jobs. Certainly rescuing this bunch of irritating, cantankerous halfwits seemed more moral than protecting corrupt politicians or kidnapping Russian scientists. And then of course there was Sandy.

"Barry, it might be best if you can remember before we arrive where any more boxes might be." He eased the Jaguar between two lorries to join the M5 at Bristol.

Barry paused for a while before answering; "If there were anymore boxes of the sort that might have got miscounted... remember the trouble with the sheep?... wouldn't be a man's fault if he forgot to leave some of them on the van, would it?"

"No, Barry. Entirely understandable. Now these boxes you forgot to leave on the van, any idea where they went?"

"Might have got themselves mislaid in Barrow Woods, them's the ones behind my goat pen. Tolgy woods those. Lost a tractor in there once."

Chapter 16

Mr Green had rearranged the lounge bar of the Smuggler's Arms to form his headquarters. He sat in the largest of the overstuffed armchairs with his feet resting on a white lace doily on top of a small oak coffee table. He was thoughtfully scratching his head with the muzzle of a small black revolver. A satphone rested on one arm of the chair and a bone chine teacup and saucer on the other. He placed the gun in his lap and took a sip from the cup. The delicate chinaware looked incongruous in his calloused hands.

Several of the villagers were seated around a square oak dining table at the opposite end of the room. Two of Green's colleagues stood at strategic points near door and window, leaving no chance for a sudden escape attempt even if the villagers had felt so inclined.

The satphone warbled and Green stabbed the answer button.
"Hello?" He listened for several minutes, then, "Understand, Guv. Consider it done". He replaced the phone on the arm of the chair.
"They're on their way," he said to the others. "Be here in about four hours. They are to be brought here and as soon as we have that little scroat Penwrith we're to kill Tremayne. No nonsense mind, he's a tricky bastard by all accounts."
"Bullet in the back of his head and he can be as tricky as he likes," the man by the door said.
"You be careful, Mr Blue. I hear told he's already taken out Carlos in Benidorm. Doesn't do to get over confident. That's what did for Hitler you know, over confidence...." he paused thoughtfully then; "Him and that Tiger Woods."
He stood up and headed for the door, picking up a sawn off shotgun that was propped near the window. "Gonna check on the others."

Mr Green strutted down the empty main road like Gary

Cooper in High Noon. The shotgun dangled in a loose grip by his side, and every few steps Green swung it round his finger in a flourish. At one point he swung the gun up to eye level, dropped into a crouch whilst aiming the gun at a seagull on a lamppost and hissed, "Pow".

He made his way to the Police station at the back of Tiffin's Bakery and Cakes. PC Muchmore sat dolefully atop one of a number of wooden crates in the cell. Mr Purple, a tall gangly man in his twenties jumped up out of the constable's cherished swivel chair as he heard Green enter.

"Soon be here," Green said to his colleague. "Another few hours and we'll be shot of this lot and off to warmer climes."

"Not if I have anything to do with it you won't," Muchmore said assertively from his cell. "This lot belongs to Her Majesty," He tapped the packing case. "And I'm her representative here. I swore an oath."

"Then just carry on protecting it for the moment, there's a good constable."

"Why don't we just take what we've got and leg it, Boss?" the other man asked.

"'cause The Voice is a Government man. He can either help us disappear with our cut or he can make us disappear without it in other ways. Get my drift? Just one little job left to do then we're on our toes." Green circled the room like a nervous dog. He pulled at the door and the window. "You make sure nobody gets in here, right? Not nobody."

"Sure, Boss."

***

Sandy sat in the white leather recliner that faced Old Bill's huge Plasma screen. Her eyes washed over the black and white movie that was showing. Something with James Mason in but she wasn't paying much attention. Her mind instead endlessly niggled at ways to escape the houseboat within which she was currently being held. She could hear the footsteps of Mr Yellow as he paced to and fro above deck. She knew Tremayne would be coming at some point and she knew he would try to find her. How to let him know?

She banged on the roof of the cabin to attract the man's attention. He ducked his head through the hatch.
"What's up?" Mr Yellow was a young black man, probably of Jamaican background.
"Any chance of some music to listen to? These old films are driving me nuts."
"I got none. Do I look like MC Pick 'n Mix?"
She hadn't the faintest idea what he was talking about. "Any chance of picking me up some CDs from my room?"
"I ain't no gofer. Do I look like a gofer to you? 'cause if I do then you been picking up *all* the wrong signals on me, Babe." He shut the hatch again.

She waited a few minutes then banged the roof again. She had to try several times with increasing ferocity until eventually his head reappeared through the hatch.
"What is it with all this banging? You don't give a man no peace I'm gonna start some banging of my own. You read me, Babe? Go banging all the time."
"It's just that I feel so cramped just sat here. I felt... well, like having a bit of a chill, you know, loosening up a bit." She undid the top button of her blouse and waved her hand across her face as if to signify overheating.

Mr Yellow paused then; "Your one crazy mother, you know that?"
She undid another button and pushed her hand through her hair. "I just *so* like to listen to music, it always puts me in a more relaxed mood. But never mind, if it would get you into trouble. Don't want to cause problems with your boss, he's a scary man isn't he? She did the buttons up again and sat in the recliner.
"I ain't scared of Micky... err, Mr Green. I do what I like see. We're brothers we is."
"Sorry. I'll be sure to tell Micky next time I see how efficient you were."

He slammed the hatch shut. There was silence for two minutes then his head reappeared. "I didn't say Micky right? You didn't hear me say Micky. I ain't never said Micky. So don't you going telling no one I said Micky." He studied her as she sat simply smiled. "What music you want anyhow?"

"There's some CDs in a pile in my room by the stereo. Some Dire Straits would be nice?"

She heard a fizz and crackle as he switched on his walkie-talkie.

"Hey Del... Whatever... yeah I know... Mr Pink. This crazy bitch here keeps screeching on about music. Pick up a pile of CDs from her room and bring 'em down here. And make sure there's some Dire Straits."

The crackling and fizzing stopped as he switched off the walkie-talkie.

She smiled and settled back in the recliner. Men are so easy!

***

The XKR seemed to eat up the motorway and still be hungry for more. Tremayne nudged the cruise control higher. One of the good things about a 'Company' car was that it came fully equipped, there was enough weaponry in the back of this thing to overthrow the government of a small African nation. The downside of course was that it was fitted with highly sophisticated satnav tracking. The techie guys claimed this system could even tell which lane he was in.

He pulled in to Exeter Services. Barry went off in search of lunch while Tremayne set about transferring the tracking system from the Jaguar to a haulage truck whose livery claimed it was based in Truro. It wouldn't fool them for long but at least he'd be invisible from now on. He joined Barry in the restaurant.

"Do we have a plan, Mr Tremayne, sir?" Barry said finding space to talk between mouthfuls of greasy, lukewarm chips.

Tremayne did have a plan of sorts. As plans went, this one was not one of the more complicated varieties. Kill the bad guys, rescue the hostages. It didn't really get much simpler than that.

"Leave it to me, Barry." Tremayne sampled a chip with the same reticence as if it had been a delicacy from some unknown part of some endangered species presented to him at an Arab feast. Except this time, there was no temperamental sheikh to offend. He returned the chip to the plate and pushed it to one side. He found himself missing the delights of 'The Fisherman's Plaice'.

"You just go into the village where they'll probably pick you up quite quickly and take you to Mr Green."

"Take me to your leader!" Barry had brightened now his system was once more flooded with saturated fats and sugar.

"What? No. I'll tell you exactly what to say a bit later. When there's less chance of you forgetting it."

Tremayne was going to need some sort of help when he arrived at Little Didney but Barry was clearly not going to qualify for the job. He needed somebody level headed and bright. He wondered where Sandy was being held and how he would find her. His mind scanned his mental map of the village. She'd said there were at least eight of them. How would they divide up the villagers? Standard Operating Procedure would be to identify and isolate potential troublemakers, keep them separate from the rest. But would these people follow such a pattern? He had to assume they would have some sort of plan and therefore he worked through what he would do in a similar situation.

Jerry Richards, Sandy, PC Muchmore and Mrs Pomfrey would not be difficult to recognise as potential troublemakers. Keep them in separate locations but close enough so that the guards could support each other if necessary. That's four. Put the rest together somewhere confined yet large enough. That would be either the Village Hall or the Smuggler's Arms. The requirements of food and toilets made the pub the most likely option. Put two guards with them. That's six. Green probably wouldn't trust just one person with the money, so two guards there, that's eight. Plus Green himself, who would more than likely set up his base in the pub. That made nine. Put somebody on the road into the village as lookout, there's ten. Potentially ten hostiles and six possible locations to take.

All with no backup. He'd been in trickier situations.

He watched as the Truro Heavy Haulage vehicle swung out onto the motorway and headed west. He forced the rest of his coffee down.
"Wait here, Barry. I have a call to make."
He slipped outside, checked nobody was nearby to overhear then dialled a number from memory. The phone was answered quickly.
"Charles? An unusual pleasure!"
"I might have something of mutual interest," Tremayne began.

***

A few minutes later he returned to the restaurant. Barry was dipping the last of his chips into a puddle of ketchup.
"Time to go, Barry."
He turned to leave and headed for the door. Barry grabbed a final handful of chips from Tremayne's plate and scuttled out of the door after him.

Within ten minutes they'd caught up with and overtaken the truck. His satphone rang, the display showed Gemini's private number. He ignored it. A few minutes later it rang again, this time with Elaine's number. He ignored that also.

The A30 was surprisingly clear for a Saturday in late August and they made good time. The green Devon fields gave way to the open, bracken strewn moors of Bodmin. An hour later, they turned off the main road and followed the increasingly narrow lanes towards the south coast. Barry had fallen silent again and was obviously locked in deep thought. Tremayne wondered what exactly passed for deep thought in Barry's brain. It probably involved food of some sort. Then a pang of conscience made him realise that he was probably being unfair. Barry was more than likely absolutely terrified of what was about to happen. And maybe with good cause. Tremayne could only make best guesses as to Green's likely responses to his plan. It could all very easily go spectacularly wrong with quite severe consequences for Barry.

Tremayne pushed this alien display of humanitarianism back into the darkest corners of his subconscious where it belonged. He pulled the car just before the brow of the hill over which lay Jerry Richards' Used Car Emporium. He told Barry to remain in the car, checked his gun and hopped over a fence. He ran close to a hedge that led to the car forecourt and stopped at a gap fifty yards from the caravan that served as an office.

He hadn't expected any hostages to be held up here, bit too remote for backup if needed. But as this was the only road into the village, there ought to be some sort of guard or observation point. There was no sign of movement but he thought he could detect a hint of cigarette smoke in the air. Funny how the smoking ban has already become so ingrained in people's psyche that even a hired thug now pops outside for his smoke. Assuming the hostile would be watching the incoming road Tremayne skirted the building to make his approach from the village side. A man leaned against the side of Jerry Richards' caravan come office. As expected, his sole attention was on the incoming road as he peered around the corner of the caravan. He was dressed in a camouflage jacket and dark jeans. Smoke curled from the cigarette in his left hand while his right rested loosely on the barrel of a L85 rifle that hung from a strap on his shoulder. Standard Royal Marine issue weapon and certainly not the usual armoury for the average villain. Whoever was behind these guys was serious.

Although the weapon may have been of Marine calibre the owner certainly wasn't. An over confidence that the only threat would come from the main road and a lazy posture that would hinder rapid movement gave Tremayne the chance he needed. He covered the fifty metres between them within seconds in total silence. His right arm snaked around the man's throat while his right leg pressed against the rifle, preventing the man from using it. He completed the sleeper hold and waited the few seconds necessary for the panicked struggling to cease. The man slumped, a dead weight under Tremayne's grip. At this point only unconscious but if the hold was applied for another five seconds death would follow. He held the hold for ten. The man dropped in a crumpled heap slumped against the side of the caravan. Tremayne dismantled the firing mechanism of the rifle and threw the various parts into the bushes.

Back in familiar territory now, clear lines. White hats and black hats. He headed back to the car, still maintaining cover. He found Barry sat in the car exactly where he had been left.

"It's all clear up ahead, Barry," he said. "Just wanted to make sure there was nobody watching the road."

Barry nodded but stayed silent.

"Listen, Barry. I want you to stay in the car here for exactly two hours then drive into the village, go to the pub and do exactly as I told you. Do you understand?"

"Yes, sir, Mr Tremayne, sir. Two hours. Pub. Right you are."

"Let's check watches. What time do you have now?"

Barry lifted a grubby sleeve and peered closely at his watch. "Quarter past something."

"Quarter past what?" asked Tremayne, puzzled.

"Not rightly sure, sir. Only the little hand on this watch always shows seven. Don't even know if'n that's meant to be seven in the morning or seven in the evening."

Tremayne grabbed hold of Barry's wrist. The gold Rolex Oyster perpetual showed seven fifteen. "Where did you get this?"

"Bought it of a man in Benidorm. He did three for us for

the price of two. He said they were waterproof but I don't think he was right on that one. Never been the same since the bubble bath incident."

"There's a clock on the dashboard of the car. Two hours from now, Barry." Tremayne pointed to the clock. "That means four thirty. Not by your Rolex, by the clock. Okay?" This was not going to end well.

"Okay, Right you are then. Four thirty by the car clock. Do you think I'll be able to get my fifty quid back?"

Tremayne ignored him and gave a final, almost fatherly pat to the roof of the car. "Sorry about this," he said to the Jaguar. "I'll get you a full valet when this is all over. Promise."

Chapter 17

Barry's eyes never left the dashboard clock for the required two hours. Apart from the few minutes he spent watching a kestrel hunting in a nearby field. And when had to make a nature call behind the hedge and then fell into the ditch. And of course for the forty-five minutes he fell asleep.

"Oh shit!" He rubbed the vision back to his eyes and stared at his watch. Quarter past seven. That was okay then. He settled back in the comfortable leather seat. His eyes lighted on the dashboard clock. That was odd. He looked again at his watch. His disbelieving and still slightly blurry eyes darted from clock to watch.

"Oh shit!" he repeated. A moment's sleepy hesitation as to which timepiece to believe. Precision Jaguar engineering or a fifty-quid hooky Rolex. He decided to do as instructed and go with the clock, which now meant he was ten minutes late.

He slipped into the driver's seat and started the Jaguar. It purred under his grip. A few false starts with the gears and he was careering towards Little Didney, collecting the odd twig and bramble in the bodywork as he went.

***

Tremayne skirted the area of Barrow woods to which Barry had directed him. There shouldn't be any of Green's people here but this lot were unpredictable. Once satisfied he was alone he found the crates exactly where Barry had said they would be. A pile of leafy branches and brush barely disguised the wooden boxes. He set about dragging the crates deeper into the woods. He found a natural depression in the ground in which to place them then covered the area in fallen foliage before brushing away the trail he had left by dragging the crates.

He checked his watch. Four thirty. Allowing for Barry to be fifteen minutes late in his part, by the time Green had the information he wanted they should be here in around half an hour.

***

Barry arrived at the Smuggler's Arms exactly fifteen minutes late. The room froze in silence as he entered.

"Where the fuck did he come from?" Mr Blue spluttered from around a Cornish Pastie.

"Call up Mr Orange at the car place," Green shouted. "Tell 'im he's fired!"

Barry, unsure of the correct protocol in such situations, simply offered, "Sorry I'm late." He scanned the room. Mrs Wiggins and Mrs Pomfrey sat near the fire. Mr Babcock was lying on the floor. He looked asleep. He was covered in bruises and blood trickled from his nose.

Mr Green rose from the armchair and approached Barry. "You'll be the little shit Penwrith I assume?" he said. "And where's your chum? Tremayne is it?" He stopped three inches from Barry's face.

Barry stole another glance at Babcock. "The boxes are in the woods," he blurted. Tremayne had told him to hold out as long as possible. He'd done that.

"Where your pal is waiting for us no doubt?" Green tapped Barry in the sternum with a forefinger. It was surprisingly painful.

"No, sir. He's gone to Benidorm. No, not Benidorm. Switzerland. That's it. Yes he's in the woods." He hadn't realised how difficult it would be to hold out under interrogation.

Green turned to a large man near the bar nursing a shotgun. "Mr Brown, you come with me. Mr Blue you look after this lot." He stabbed the talk button on his radio. "Mr Pink, Mr Red, get your arses up to the pub now. We've got work to do."

Barry sidled along the wall as innocuously as Barry could sidle anywhere. Attempting to merge himself into the room unnoticed.

"And where do you think you're off to?" Mr Green asked.

"Just going to sit a bit. Been a long day." Barry motioned towards the fireplace where the ladies sat.

"You're coming with me." Green picked up his shotgun and waved Barry towards the door.

***

Tremayne pressed himself into his hiding place. He'd found a nest of tightly bunched conifers that afforded good cover but still allowed free movement. He heard footsteps and voices. As the group approached he adjusted his position to better observe whilst maintain cover.

"Okay, so where are they?" Mr Green poked Barry in the chest with the shotgun.

Barry's feet made little shuffling movements. "They was here, sir. Honest. All here." He waved a hand at the area recently occupied by the crates. "Or there." Hand waving over a slightly different patch of woodland.

Green gestured to the other three men. "Have a look round. Either this half-wit's telling porkies or that Tremayne's had it away."

Messrs Pink, Red and Brown poked and scuffed at the ground with little obvious enthusiasm.

"Nothing here, Guv," offered Mr Pink. A huge man with a shaven head and ears that had seen way too many rugby scrums.

"What's he done with it?" Green turned back to Barry.

"Don't know. Honest. Said he'd take it away. Wouldn't tell me so as I couldn't say nothing to no one."

Green took a deep breath, held it for a moment then swung the shotgun in a violent arc across Barry's face. Barry dropped like a demolished chimney stack. He was unconscious before he hit the ground. Green kicked him in the ribs, clearly disappointed his sport had been curtailed so quickly. He said to Mr Pink, "When he wakes up, you beat the truth out of him then make him disappear. Understand?"

"You mean..." tailed off Mr Pink

"Course I that's what I mean, you idiot." He turned to the woods. "Tremayne!" he shouted. "You hear me, you bastard? You don't bring my money back I'm going to cut bits of that woman you fancy so much."

Green called the others to heel and set off back for the village. Mr Pink poked at Barry with his foot. Barry stirred and mumbled something.

"Get up." Pink's foot pushed at Barry, turning him over on his back. Blood oozed from a cut above Barry's left eye which was already swelling closed. Dirt and debris stuck to the blood.

Mr Pink bent over and lifted Barry one handed by his shirtfront. It seemed to take him no more effort than lifting a pint of beer. Barry's good eye flickered open and he found himself staring at the toothless grin of Mr Pink.

"Wakey wakey, sunshine," said Pink. "You and me got to have a little chat." He propped Barry against a tree, carefully positioning him so he wouldn't fall. He was about to deliver a punch to the stomach when Tremayne tapped him on the shoulder.

Pink spun round just as Tremayne's roundhouse punch connected with his jaw. Pink wriggled his jaw as if clearing dust and grinned. Tremayne did a quick reassessment. This man's head had taken far more of a battering than Tremayne was going to be able to deliver quickly. A side kick to the knee and the man buckled, his head coming forward just in time to meet a knife hand strike to the side of the neck. Pink collapsed like a felled tree in a cloud of dust. Tremayne's hand poised above the throat and hesitated. The man would be unconscious for a good hour, no need to do anything further.

He half carried Barry out of the woods and left him by his goat pen. He'd be alright and it wasn't far from his cottage. But right now Sandy was the priority. How the hell was he going to find her?

Chapter 18

Mrs Pomfrey wriggled her thickly stockinged toes in front of the open fire at The Smugglers Arms. "Another muffin, dear?" She pulled the brass, long handled bed-warmer from the flames and aimed it towards Mrs Wiggins.

"Why thank you," said Mrs Wiggins, helping herself to one of the steaming muffins inside the pan. "I don't mind if I do."

"How about you, young man?" Mrs Pomfrey thrust the pan towards Mr Blue. "Would you care for one? They really are quite yummy."

"You people are all barking." Mr Blue was a small balding man of about fifty. His slightly pot belly and wire rimmed glasses hinted more at shopkeeper than villain. The rifle slung over his shoulder looked quite incongruous. He reached for a muffin and danced it from hand to hand waiting for it to cool. "What's with the fire at this time of year? It's scorching out there."

"History, my dear." Mrs Pomfrey tutted and took a large sip from her sherry glass. "Wouldn't expect you people to understand history, or good manners, do put that muffin on a proper plate and stop playing with it." Mrs Pomfrey loaded the bed warmer with fresh muffins and returned it to the flames.

Mr Blue selected a Wedgewood china dinner plate from the stack on the bar and dropped the still steaming muffin onto it. He blew on his fingers. "I know about history. I did an OU course in Strangeways."

"I'm sure you did. And I expect they taught you all about how England invented slavery, nuclear wars and rave music." She dipped into her voluminous handbag and returned with a large plastic bag. "Would you like some fudge? Goes very well with muffins."

***

Sandy turned up the volume on the hi-fi and stuffed the cotton wool deeper into her ears. Dire Straits shook the very structure of Old Bills' houseboat.

Mr Yellow poked his head down through the hatch. "Hey, crazy lady," he yelled over the music. "Why you don't listen to no real music? Bob Marley? Now that's music. He makes the groove, know what I mean? This stuff got no soul, woman."

Sandy couldn't hear a word of what he was saying. The stadium filling power of the speakers and copious amounts of cotton wool shut out all chances of communication. She took a chance and yelled, "Yes, it's great isn't it?" She started dancing to show how much she was enjoying the music.

Mr Yellow shook a puzzled head and closed the hatch. As soon as he had disappeared Sandy retired to the corner furthest away from the speakers and placed her hands over her ears. "Where are you, Charles?"

***

Mrs Pomfrey placed her empty sherry glass on the hearth and turned to Mrs Wiggins. "I think that fudge has quite gone to his head, don't you, dear?"

Mr Blue was leaning against the bar. His eyes drifted free of any focus and his jaw struggled with the last mouthful of Mrs Pomfrey's special reserve fudge. The sherry flavoured variety. "That's... that's unusual... an unusual flavour." He struggled to free his words from the cloying fudge and sherry haze.

"Would you like another muffin, young man?" Mrs Pomfrey pulled the bed-warmer from the fireplace. The brass pan glowed a dull red.

The man raised his befuddled head just as the bed-warmer was in full flight. A loud smack and a continuing ringing sound filled the room as the pan collided with the side of his head. His feet left the floor for a full second before he slammed into the corner and slid down the wall into an untidy heap. The side of his face already shining red from the impact and heat of the pan.

"Oh my!" exclaimed Mrs Wiggins. "What have you done?"

"That'll keep the little bugger quiet for a while," said Mrs Pomfrey. "Come along, dear. Time to get busy. Do keep up." She bussled to the door and peeped around, beckoning for her friend to follow.

They slid out of the pub and headed up the High Street, bobbing from doorway to doorway like a pair of mice hiding from a cat. Mrs Pomfrey had never seen the village so quiet, it was eerie. Usually a stroll to the top of the village would take a good half hour as everybody would want to stop and have a little natter. But today it was deserted and within ten minutes they were passing Top Field.

"Where are we going?" Mrs Wiggins asked.

Mrs Pomfrey stopped. She actually hadn't given that one much thought. 'Away' was as far as she had got. But upon thinking about that now as a plan it didn't really work. For a start the next village was Upper Downing and that was four miles away, and she'd come out without her bike. She also realised it wouldn't take long before the 'Rainbow People' noticed their absence and came hot foot after them.

Her eyes searched the area for inspiration. Inspiration presented itself in the form of Tom Trevellick's tractor, Old Bess. It sat just inside the entrance to Top Field, probably where Danny had parked it after dislodging it from the bookshop.

"*That's* what we need!" Mrs Pomfrey announced.

"Are you quite sure, dear?" Mrs Wiggins asked. "I mean, of all the things I'd have said we needed right now I don't think I'd have put tractor on the list."

"Don't be such a fussy wussy. If that idiot Trevellick can make it work how hard can it be? Come along now."

The ladies clambered onto the tractor and squashed themselves into the single seat.

"Now, all we need is the 'Go' button and we're singing hymns for Christmas." Mrs Pomfrey set about pressing, twisting and pulling every available lever or knob. "I'm sure it must be one of these."

Mrs Wiggins pulled her felt hat tighter down over her ears. "As you say, dear."

The tractor suddenly erupted into life.

"That's the badger!" Mrs Pomfrey shouted above the noise. "Button up, Mrs Wiggins, we're on our way."

***

Tremayne skirted round the bottom of the village below the sea wall. Loud rock music drifted across the harbour, it was coming from the direction of Old Bill's houseboat. Obviously somebody there and best avoided for now. He paused momentarily as he thought he vaguely recognised the music but couldn't quite place it and carried on.

He watched the entrance to the Fishermans Plaice from the corner of a boatshed. All was quiet so he slipped across the seawall and after a few seconds with the lock, he was inside. The restaurant was deserted and he made his way through to the back yard. Although he'd never been there, his internal satnav was working fine. He peered over the wall and saw the line of backyards and gardens belonging to the houses on the western side of the High Street. He slipped from wall to fence, lawn to patio, pausing at each one to check for signs of occupants. He counted the properties and stopped in a neatly manicured garden bordered with dwarf conifers. He listened at the final wall then peered over. Just as he'd calculated, he was next door to the yard behind Tiffin's bakery and Police Station. Of all the places in the village to secure hostages or contraband, the police station with its lockable cell must be the first choice.

He took a small telescopic mirror from his pocket and held it just above the rim of the wall. A few moments to find the correct angle and he was afforded a glimpse inside

Muchmore's office although the poor angle only allowed a very restricted view. He did however notice a pair of legs presumably belong to somebody sitting in Muchmore's chair. The legs were slender, covered in jeans and terminated in a pair of scruffy trainers. The best situational guess would be one hostile to whom the legs belonged and unknown hostages in the cell, probably no more than two. He slipped over the wall and paused. No movement inside the office. He raised his hands above his head and walked to the door.

"Alright, I'm going," Tremayne said across his shoulder. "No need to shove." He stumbled through the door arms raised.

Mr Purple jumped up and fumbled for his rifle, confusion slowing his senses. Tremayne's fingers touched the blade of his throwing knife tucked behind his neck. This was just a lad. A scared confused lad. A lad armed with an L85 rifle nonetheless and the second he'd encountered today. In the microsecond it took Tremayne draw the knife he'd adjusted his aim slightly and the blade embedded itself into Mr Purple's right shoulder instead of the throat. I must be going soft, he thought as he launched himself into the bewildered lad and took him to the ground. Within seconds Mr Purple was hogtied with a set of cable ties and a makeshift gag in his mouth.

"You could've killed him you know," PC Muchmore said from behind the cell door. "Your spy malarkey kung fu."

"What?" Tremayne asked as he unlocked the cell. "These people are armed with military issue weapons. He would have killed both of us given the chance."

The door swung open and Muchmore emerged as Tremayne dragged Purple into the cell and locked it again.

"Take this," Tremayne thrust the rifle at the constable. "Do you know how to use it?"

"I'm an officer in Her Majesty's Constabulary, of course I know how to use a firearm. We're all trained you know."

Tremayne doubted whether Muchmore had ever seen a military grade assault rifle let alone used one but there was no time to argue. "You stay here and look after the money," he said. "Here's a satphone, if things go really badly wrong call 'Elaine' on speed dial one. Oh, and shoot anybody that comes through that door that you don't recognise, clear?"

"I don't think I should do that, not without..." his words tailed off as Tremayne closed the door and slipped back over the wall.

He ticked another one off his mental tally. Three down probably another five or six to go. The odds were improving. And then he remembered where he recognised the music he'd heard. Retracing his steps across the gardens and through the restaurant he made his way towards Old Bill's houseboat moored alongside the eastern side of the harbour. As he approached the music grew louder. Dire Straits were belting out Romeo and Juliet. Clever girl, Sandy.

The approach to the boat would be difficult. The bottom of the High Street opened out to a small cobbled turning area just in front of the harbour where the boat lay. There was no cover. He pressed himself into a doorway opposite the harbour and waited. There was no movement for about fifteen minutes then a well built dark skinned man in green jacket and yellow woolly hat appeared and walked the length of the boat. He bent down and lifted the hatch.

He was shouting into the hatch as Tremayne covered the distance and leapt onto the boat behind the man. Mr Yellow was fast. He turned just as Tremayne was engaging a strangle hold. He head butted Tremayne who twisted just in time to save his nose but the impact still stunned him briefly. Yellow was on top of him and they fell to the deck exchanging short punches, knee strikes and elbows. Tremayne managed to free a hand and secured a grip on the mastoid process under Yellow's left ear. The sudden intense pain jerked Yellow back and Tremayne broke free and scrambled to his feet. Mr Yellow stumbled upright and pulled a butterfly knife from his belt.

The blade flashed in the sunlight. Tremayne launched a short kick to the man's knee and a palm heel to the base of the skull and Mr Yellow collapsed back against a bulkhead, the knife was in Tremayne's hands before Yellow hit the floor. His eyes rolled as he tried to regain focus. Tremayne kneeled into the man's chest and with his free hand twisted Yellow's head to one side to give a clear line to the carotid artery. He positioned the knife for the kill.

"Charles!" Sandy yelled from behind him. "Stop!"

He turned to see Sandy climbing out of the hatch.

"He tried to kill me," he said. "If I leave him here he'll just have another go."

"Can't you just knock him out?" Sandy looked down at the dazed Mr Yellow.

"Knock him out? These men are killers. And somebody's supplying them with high grade military weapons. You don't just knock them out! They have a tendency to wake up at the most inconvenient moments." He pressed the knife against yellow's neck. The tip broke the skin and blood trickled.

Sandy grabbed his wrist. "You're better than that, Charles. For me, please?"

He looked up at her. Two disparate instincts tore at Tremayne's conscience. The nameless one triumphed. "Find me some rope," he snapped.

Sandy scouted the deck and returned with a coil of mooring rope. He picked it up, thick heavy rope, difficult to tie.

"Find something to gag him with." He wound the heavy rope round the semi conscious man and secured it to mooring point on the bulwark. "That won't hold him for long, are you sure I can't kill him?"

Sandy gave a forced smile and handed Charles a piece of cloth. He held it up. It looked like a T shirt or vest. He glanced at Sandy, her white, thin blouse not quite buttoned.

"Just get on with it," she said.

The cloth was warm in his hands as he wrapped it around the man's head.

A noise caught Tremayne's attention just as he was tying

off the rope. A loud engine, over revving. He glanced around. "We need to get away from here." He gave the rope a testing tug then grabbed Sandy by the upper arm. "Come on, now."

As they left the boat Tremayne glanced back. Mr Yellow was sat against the bulwark in the centre of the boat. He was starting to surface and struggled against the rope. The engine noise sounded louder, it was coming from the High Street.

As they left the boat Tremayne turned back to have a final check on Mr Yellow.

"Charles." Sandy tugged his arm. "Leave him. You did the right thing."

Tremayne scanned the empty high street. What *was* that noise? "But he's dangerous. And he's surplus to requirements. Just using up the earth's resources. He needs recycling."

Sandy tried a smile. "I expect his mother loves him," she offered

"I expect he killed his mother for the rent money." He guided Sandy to the side of the street for at least some cover.

She stopped him and turned to face him, her hands cradled his face. "Charles, the whole world is not necessarily evil, you know. There's a lot of good out there." She hesitated. "A lot of love." Gently, so gently, as if trying to approach a scared rabbit she pulled his face towards hers. Tremayne felt her breath, her body pressed to his. Her eyes searched his own, he felt she could see into his soul. Just as he felt her probing his darkest corners her eyes closed and she pressed closer.

Then he recognised the noise. How could he have not remembered that? His arch nemesis with which he had already had one near fatal encounter. He grabbed Sandy and pulled her into a small doorway. Not much cover but it would have to do. "Quick, hurry."

The Money That Never Was

Old Bess thundered down the high street, glancing off buildings at each side of the narrow street. The engine revved and screamed as the smoke and smell of burning oil announced its end was near. It seemed to grow in size and noise as it hurtled towards them. They pressed themselves tighter into the doorway just as the tractor collided with the corner of the building in which they sheltered. It bounced away again and as it flew past them Tremayne noticed two figures clinging to the seat.

Old Bess cleared the last of the buildings and careered across the cobbled turning point in front of the harbour. Free now of hindrances the tractor gave what seemed like a last triumphant scream then headed over the dock edge and nose-dived into Old Bill's houseboat. Even from their doorway Tremayne could see the terrified expression on Yellow's face as the monster landed in his lap. The two figures bounced off the back of the now steaming and gurgling machine and landed in a heap on the dock.

Mrs Pomfrey pulled her companion upright then glanced from tractor to High Street. She caught sight of Tremayne and her eyes widened. She gave a funny little squeal then grabbed Mrs Wiggins and ran off along the dock at quite remarkable speed.

Tremayne ventured tentatively into the open and studied the slowly sinking mess in the dock. Old Bess still chugged and gurgled bravely as bits of boat disintegrated beneath her. The front end was buried deep into the deck and every few seconds the machine shuddered and sank further. The middle of the boat suddenly dipped and both bow and stern emerged and pointed skywards. A sound, of splintering wood, escaping steam and the still over-excited engine filled the air as the tractor slowly sank amid the remains of the boat. A final explosion just underneath water and the tractor completed its slide beneath the gentle waves.

They watched in silence as a few bits of wood bobbed around presenting the last remnants of Old Bill's home. A yellow woolly hat broke the surface and appeared to be clinging to a piece of decking.

"Well," Tremayne said slowly. "That takes care of that little problem." He turned towards Sandy just as her open hand caught him across the side of the face with a loud slap.

"You're a monster, Charles!" she shouted. "Is there nothing human left in you?"

She turned and started marching up the High Street. He caught up with quickly and grabbed her arm.

"Wait," he said, calmly deflecting a second attack as she turned towards him. "We need to be careful. Green's men are all over the place.

"I thought you'd just go marching up the street all guns blazing, like Dirty Harry with his Magnum one-point-five."

"It's a forty five."

"What?"

"He used a Magnum forty-five," Tremayne explained. "A magnum one-point-five is a type of champagne bottle.

He caught Sandy's wrist as her hand swung in again. "Will you please stop doing that?"

She snatched her hand free and turned as if to set off up the road again.

The sound of shouts snagged their attention.

"What the fuck is going on here?" The voice belonged to Mr Green and he emerged from an ally alongside the Chandlers.

Tremayne grabbed Sandy, this time she didn't resist and they pressed themselves back into the sparse cover of the doorway.

Mr Green, with companions Red and Brown stared at the still gurgling and bubbling water where the Houseboat used to be.

"Looks like it sunk, Guv," offered Brown.

"I can see that, you idiot. This'll be that Tremayne bloke. We need to find him or The Voice will crucify us." He waved his hand towards the docks. "Mr Brown, you take the west side and Mr Red you take the east."

"Sure thing, Guv," Brown said. "Er... west would be...?"

"That way, you numpty." Mr Green waved his hand in the direction of the Fishermans Plaice. "That way." He started back up the High Street.

Tremayne slipped his knife and readied his himself to leap at Green if he spotted them. But Green was too focused on his uphill march to notice the shapes pressed tightly into the alcove. They watched as he rounded the corner by the bookshop and disappeared from sight.

"He'll be going to the pub," Sandy said. "That's where the others are."

"Sandy, I want you to go hideout in Barry's cottage until this is over." He held both her shoulders forcing her to meet his gaze. "You'll be safe there. I'll come and get you later."

"And let you loose to go slaughter every last one of them?" She shrugged herself free of his grip. "I don't think so."

"Right!" Tremayne said, barely stifling his annoyance. "Just stay close and try not to get yourself killed while you're busy sharing your feelings with a murderous lunatic." He turned and started off after Mr Brown.

He felt Sandy tap him on the shoulder. "Charles?" she called, softly. He stopped and turned. This time he was too late to stop the short range right cross punch as it caught him perfectly on the jaw.

"What the...?"

"You're an arrogant, pompous, chauvinistic philistine. And you deserve to spend the rest of your life alone in that soulless, sterile supermarket of a city you keep banging on about."

He paused, trying to work out if that had actually been an insult.

"Come along," she said. "Haven't you got some people to kill?"

***

Mr Green kicked the door to The Smugglers Arms open and burst in. His eyes immediately lighted on Mr Blue sitting slumped in the overstuffed armchair. He still looked dazed and the left side of his face glowed bright red.

"Oh, joy!" Green said. "Two little old ladies too much

for you?"

"They caught me off guard, Boss." Blue pulled himself free of the chair, rubbing his face.

"Well what the hell are you hanging around here for?" Green yelled. "Get you sorry backside out there and go find 'em before I ram your head in that fire and find a use for that poker."

Blue headed for the door. "Yes, Boss. Right away."

Green stared at the chaos in the bar area and scratched the side of his head with the muzzle of his shotgun.

"Err... Boss?" Blue called from behind him.

Green turned towards the front door. "What now?"

Blue walked backwards into the room as he continued to face the open door. His arms were raised above his head. "We got a bit of a problem, Boss."

As he reversed into the bar Green saw the muzzle of a rifle following Blue in. The rifle cleared the door Green saw it was being held by PC Muchmore, The end wavered and jiggled under the policeman's unsteady grip.

"You're all under arrest," announced Muchmore as his eyes scanned the room.

"Oh, for heaven's sake!" Green exploded. "What *is* it with this place? Can't anybody keep control of a bunch of hay-chewing, half-witted inbreds?"

Muchmore ventured further into the room, his bravado failing him already. "I've called for backup. Penzance Area Car will be here directly. Then you'll know about it."

"Give that to me, you silly old sod." Mr Green walked towards Muchmore with his hand outstretched.

"Come any closer and I'll shoot!" Muchmore lifted the rifle to eye level and waggled it in Green's general direction.

"I'm sure you will. Now behave yourself and give it here." Green reached forward and calmly removed the rifle from Muchmore's failing grip.

The constable seemed almost relieved to be free of his burden of duty.

Mr Green turned to Mr Blue. "Any more little dramas? Or can we get back to the business of finding the rest of this money and getting out of this asylum?"

Blue's mouth worked silently as if trying out various replies.

"No?" continued Green. "Well fuck off then and bring those old biddies back before his little chums turn up."

Blue scuttled out of the door.

"Through there." Mr Green waved the shotgun towards a door in the back of the bar. Muchmore shuffled through with a weary, dejected walk. The door opened to the skittle alley at the rear of the bar. Slumped around on various kegs and boxes sat many of the villagers.

Mr Grey, a tall well built man in his thirties jumped up. "Alright, guv?" he greeted.

"How long you gonna keep us here?" Jerry Richards stood in the centre of the villagers. "You've got what you came for."

Green viciously jabbed Muchmore in the small of his back with the shotgun. Muchmore stumbled and Green kicked him in the back. The policeman collapsed to the floor.

"You're a monster!" Jenny Featherstone leapt to her feet, face flushed and green eyes flashing.

Mr Green fired his shotgun into the ceiling releasing clouds of dust and falling plaster. "Any more trouble from you lot and I'm going to shoot the fucking lot of you." He turned to Mr Grey. "Any aggro, shoot them. Clear?"

Grey smiled. "Sure thing, Boss. My pleasure, I'm sick of being stuck here with these carrot munchers."

Green returned to the bar just as his Satphone rang. That would be The Voice. He pressed talk. "Yes, Guv?"

"What on earth is going on down there?" The Voice asked. The was a loud background noise coming from the tiny speaker.

"What do you mean?" Green wondered how the hell he'd found out.

"I've just had to stop an armed response unit from coming down there."

"Sorry, Guv. The copper got free. It's all sorted now,"

Green lied.

"I very much doubt that. Have you dealt with Tremayne yet?"

"Working on it. He's a slippery bastard but my boys are closing in."

"You're a bunch of incompetent buffoons. This was such a simple little job." This was the closest Green had ever heard The Voice come to being angry. Somehow that made it all the more frightening. "I'm on my way down there now to sort this out myself."

So that's what the noise was. A helicopter.

"No need for that, Guv." Green panicked. "Sure we can deal with it."

"And I'm bringing a little help with me." The Voice ignored Green's pleas and the connection broke.

Mr Green slumped in the armchair. "Shit! Fucking shit!"

Chapter 19

Tremayne approached the front window of The Fishermans Plaice. He motioned Sandy to stay back as he peered through the edge of the window. He noticed movement at the back of the restaurant. It took his eyes a moment to adjust to the gloom inside.

Mr Brown was busy microwaving himself a Cornish pasty. The machine pinged and he settled down at a table facing the window. Tremayne pulled his head back quickly.
"Stay here," he said. "There's one of them in there. I want you to count to two hundred then distract him. Do you think you can you do that?"
Sandy smiled her best little-girl smile, undid the top three buttons of her white blouse and said, "What do you think?"
"Hmm, be careful."
"Yes, sir."

Tremayne slipped round the back of the restaurant and entered through the still open kitchen window. Silently he approached the main restaurant. Sandy came in through the door exactly on schedule.
"Hello," she said tugging at another button. "It's so hot. Are they serving ice-cream here today?"
Brown jumped up, half a steaming pasty still in his hand. "What? Where did you come from? Stay there." Clearly confused by Sandy's nonchalance he juggled pasty and gun eventually pointing the right one in her direction. "Don't move or I'll shoot."

Tremayne slid up behind Mr Brown and the sleeper hold was on before Brown had time to call out. A few seconds and the familiar dead weight of an unconscious thug felt comfortable in his arms. He held on.
"Stop it!" Sandy shouted. "There's no need to kill him."
Reluctantly Tremayne let the man fall to the floor.

"You'd better find something to tie him up with then. I need to find the other one before he catches up with Mrs Pomfrey and offers to take her to church."

Tremayne pulled the man over to a central pillar and propped him into a seating position. Sandy emerged from the storeroom with an industrial sized roll of cling-film.

"What the hell good is that?" Tremayne asked.

"You clearly don't frequent some of the clubs I've visited," she said. "Hold him still."

Sandy set about winding the cling-film around the man and pillar. She kept going until Mr Brown resembled a twenty-first century mummy. Only a small gap remained for his nose.

Tremayne tested the restraint. He was impressed. Brown was going nowhere.

"Very clever. Where did you learn that?"

"Better not to ask." Sandy smiled, knowingly.

"Well at least that'll keep him there until another tractor falls on his head I suppose."

They left The Fisherman Plaice and skirted the bottom of the High Street coming up around the village on the eastern side between the backs of the houses and the fields. Mrs Pomfrey must have headed this way, probably going for the woods and the multitude of hiding places offered there. If she had made it there, then there was little point in trying to find her. She'd be safe enough until this lot were dealt with. That just left Mr Red lurking around out here somewhere.

They continued heading uphill through the wooded paths that skirted the eastern edge of the village. They caught up with Mr Red just before the style that led into Top Field. He had Mrs Wiggens in front of him, poking her in the small of the back every so often to encourage her forwards.

"You've got to do something, Charles," Sandy whispered.

"Stay back," he said, closing the distance on Red and his hostage.

He swung the rifle he'd taken from Brown off his shoulder and took a line onto the back of Red's skull.

The Money That Never Was

"You can't just shoot him" Not like that, all cold without warning," Sandy exclaimed.

"What would you suggest I do? I offer him counselling?"

"Stop!" Sandy stood up and shouted. "Stop and drop your gun or he'll shoot you."

Tremayne snapped his head towards her. "What the hell are you doing?"

Red span round, his arm around the throat of Mrs Wiggins. He held her in front of his body. "Ah, brownie points for me when I take you lot in! Drop you gun or I'll blow her brains all over the primroses." He nodded towards a patch yellow flowers near his feet. "Make a nice colour contrast that would. Might do that in me front room."

"There not primroses," Sandy said. "They're buttercups."

Both Tremayne and Mr Red looked towards Sandy in amazement. For the briefest of seconds they shared a common bond.

"You're fucking mad, the lot of you." Red fired his rifle at Sandy just as Mrs Wiggins gave a struggle. A patch of ground kicked up at Sandy's feet. She gave a little yelp.

"Drop it," Tremayne said calmly, keeping the gun trained on Red's head.

Red brought the muzzle of his weapon against the side of Mrs Wiggin's head. "Won't miss this one." He pressed the rifle hard and Mrs Wiggins cried out.

"Charles," Sandy said urgently. "He's going to kill her."

A small patch of red appeared in the centre of Red's forehead at what seemed the exact moment Tremayne's gun fired. Red flew backwards and landed with a thud in amongst the buttercups.

"Job done," said Tremayne swing the rifle back onto his shoulder. "I suppose I'm going to get a lecture now about how I infringed his human rights?"

"Little shit," Sandy snarled. "His mother should have drowned him at birth."

Tremayne smiled but said nothing.

Sandy rushed over to Mrs Wiggins who knelt on the ground sobbing. She put her arm around the woman. "It's alright," she said. "It's over. He's gone."

"Where's Mrs Pomfrey?" Charles asked. His eyes constantly scanned the area.

"I don't know," Mrs Wiggins said through her tears. "She went off to find young Barry."

The sound of loud engines caught his attention and he looked upwards towards the east. A large helicopter crested the hill. It was matt black and bore no markings of any kind. He'd seen these before, many times. Usually this would be the most welcome sight you could hope for. Especially when pinned down with your defector whilst making a break for the border. But here, now, this was bad.

"Get over there, quickly," he said nodding towards a bunch of trees grouped near the back of a building. "Stay down."

"What is it, Charles?" asked Sandy.

"Trouble."

The helicopter circled the top of the village then headed towards them. Charles dived over to the woman and wrapped his arms around them, squeezing tightly.

"What...?" said Sandy

"Stay still," he hissed.

The helicopter flew over them then veered off, heading for the woods.

"They'll be using infrared to locate people before landing. Hopefully they'll think it was just one person here."

"Who are they?" Sandy insisted.

"At a guess, Special Forces. Probably S.A.S. I think somebody's growing impatient."

"S.A.S.?" Sandy queried. "But aren't they the good guys?"

"Depends which side you're on. Right now I think I'm on the wrong one."

The helicopter circled back around the bottom of the village then settled into Top Field not two hundred metres from their position. No sooner had it touched down than seven black shapes slid out of the machine and scattered across the field disappearing into the hedges. Nothing more than shadows. A few seconds later a lone figure emerged. Tall and well built. He wore a white linen suit and dark glasses. He paused and lit his cigar before heading in the direction of The Smugglers Arms.

Gemini, no surprises there then.

"What *is* going on, Charles?"
"You stay here and look after Mrs Wiggins. They'll probably pick you up but they won't hurt you. I need to lay low for a while, these guys won't hang around for long. They can't. I'll catch up with you later."

He hurried down the slope and disappeared into the tangle of small buildings at the bottom of the High Street. If Gemini has pulled in a squad of Special Forces that must mean he was running out of options. This would be a simple sweep up operation. No doubt Gemini had spun it as a hostage rescue. It's what these guys did best. Free the hostages, gather up the hostiles then hand them all over to the local commanding officer and disappear. In this case that C.O. would be Gemini.

No doubt this would be a fully deniable operation giving Gemini himself time to disappear. Tremayne wondered if the African dictator and supposed beneficiary of the money ever actually existed in the first place. He suspected not. Clever, very clever. Just a shame Gemini had picked a bunch of idiots to carry out the initial hijacking.

Once these guys have gone, Tremayne was going to need to deal very quickly with the remains of Green's chums and somehow stop Gemini before he started disposing of unnecessary witnesses. And for that he was going to need at least some help.

Chapter 20

Mr Green thought he detected a slight sound outside of the pub. He pulled himself up out of the armchair and was just about to investigate when the windows exploded inwards with a loud bang. The room instantly filled with a dark acrid smoke that tore at his eyes and throat. His ears rang and he fell to the floor not trusting his feet or senses.

He felt pressure in the small of his back. A loud, slightly muffled voice broke through the ringing. "Stay down! Stay down!" His hands were grasped and something bit into his wrists he was suddenly unable to move.

"Clear!" he heard the voice shout.

Green twisted his head from side to side. Tears streamed from his eyes. He blinked furiously and tried to wipe his eyes on his shoulders. Vision started to return, hazy and swimming but beginning to clear.

Black clad legs moved swiftly around the floor. A loud crash from the far end of the bar caused him to twist his head in that direction. The door to the skittle alley burst away and three black clad figures slid through. Two loud bangs some screaming and clouds of the foul smoke billowed out from the skittle alley and rolled across the bar floor towards him. He heard shouting. More orders to 'Stay down,' more screams and women crying.

A shot fired, loud, a rifle. It was quickly followed by two muffled 'pops'. Crashing furniture and more screaming. "Clear!"

He closed his eyes against the latest smoke invasion. A loud thud next to him as something heavy landed nearby. He forced his eyes open. Mr Grey lay next to him his eyes open and sightless. Two neat red holes in the centre of his forehead trickled blood.

New feet circled his head. White clad legs and white

The Money That Never Was

crocodile skin shoes.

"Mr Green! How nice to see you again," The Voice said. "Please do pardon the nature of my arrival but I had to make rather hasty plans, you understand."

Green twisted his head to look up past the legs. His eyes followed the whit suit upwards. He recognised the face instantly.

"*You!?*"

***

Tremayne reached the bottom of the High Street and settled into a tight alley to see if he could risk covering the open cobbled space. He heard shouts and scuffling. He pressed himself tighter into his shelter. Two black clad figures wearing hoods and gas masks were frogmarching Mr Brown up the High Street. He was still wrapped in the cling film.

Tremayne waited till they were clear then risked the dash over the open turning area. He slid into the door of The Fishermans Plaice and paused. All was quiet. He wanted to take more time scanning his surroundings. But he was no longer just dealing with a bunch of disorganised villains and he couldn't spare the time. He had to get to Muchmore before the soldiers did. The policeman wasn't going to be a huge amount of help but he was the best ally available. At least he could hold a gun.

He approached the rear of the Police Station/Bakers Shop and waited. All was quiet. He risked a peep through the rear window. The cell door was closed but the office was empty, no sign of Muchmore. Damnit!

He entered quickly and quietly, gun trained on the cell. Mr Purple looked up without stirring from his seat. "Oh, it's you back again," he said, breaking a corner off the wedding cake that sat on the little table in front of him.

"Where's Constable Muchmore?" Tremayne asked.

"He had to pop out." He munched on the cake. "This is bloody good." Crumbs flew from around his words. "Do you want some?"

"Pop out where?" Tremayne scanned the yard outside as he spoke.

"He made a phone call, I think to his boss, and then set out with the gun. Are you sure you don't want any cake?"

"No thank you." Tremayne struggled to make sense of what was happening. "What's with the cake anyway?"

"The copper gave it me. Said I was hungry like and he went next door came back with this. Feeling a bit sick now though mind." He pushed the rest of the cake away from him.

That idiot Muchmore. Tremayne's eyes searched the small room. The gun was gone but the satphone lay on the table. He picked it up and tapped in Bunny's phone number.

"Burroughs Print, flyers, leaflets and bank notes on demand."

"Hello, Bunny. I need another favour."

"I'm not bringing that lot back again. They scare me. I'm supposed to make people disappear. Not 'ave them going to an' fro every five minutes like the Tesco shuttle bus."

"Nothing like that. I need a passport and tickets for Uruguay, name of..." Tremayne paused. "Taurus. Vincent Taurus."

"When for?

"I want them dated for tomorrow."

"What's the catch, Charles? That's too easy. You could do that one on your own with one phone call. So there's got to be a catch."

"The man concerned won't be making the trip. But I need a paper trail. Oh, and a cargo manifest for one hundred wooden crates. Same destination."

"You want me to make it look likes he's actually gone? Boarding passes, argument with a Trolley-Dolly and so on?" Bunny asked. "I can fix that up for a bit more."

"Sounds good. I'll send a photo over later."

Tremayne disconnected the call and tucked the phone in his jacket.

"On the floor!" he heard a yell from outside.

He started to lift his gun then noticed two bright red dots dancing on the centre of his chest. Laser sights. Damn! He held the rifle at arm's length and dropped it to the floor then turned his back, arms outstretched. He knew the routine. He'd been on the other end of this enough times.

"On the floor!" the voice repeated.

Charles knelt down then laid himself forwards, arms still outstretched.

***

Barry heaved the wooden crate into the Jaguar's boot and slammed it shut. His eyes, wide and dilated darted all directions. So far he'd not been seen. He slid into the driver's seat, slammed and locked the door then sighed. He realised he'd probably been holding his breath since he'd left his cottage. His heart was hammering its way through his sternum as if trying to break out. Calm, Barry, calm. Big breaths. This time tomorrow he'd be back in Benidorm. Nobody tries to kill him in Benidorm. He wondered how Maisie and Tommy were getting on. He'd been worried about Maisie as she couldn't speak the lingo.

"How's she going to order pizza on a Friday if she can't speak the lingo?"

A black Porsche Carrera slid into the car park alongside the Jaguar. A cloud of dust swirled obscuring Barry's view. As it gradually cleared Barry found he was staring at the driver's side black tinted window not eighteen inches to his right. The tinting was so dark as to render it completely opaque from where he was sitting.

The Porsche sat silently for what seemed like several minutes. Barry's hands gripped the leather steering wheel, his heart rate once more on the climb. Eventually the passenger door of the Porsche opened and a tall man in a dark suit stepped out. He came over to the Jaguar and tapped on Barry's window.

"Charles Tremayne?" the man asked.

Barry shook his head. He knew his vocal system was beyond functioning at the moment so didn't even attempt speech. He pointed towards The Smugglers Arms.

The man grunted an acknowledgement then returned to the Porsche. Barry's vocal chords tested themselves by issuing a little whimper. Slowly, very slowly he started the car. The Jaguar purred into life at the first touch of the key. Barry froze waiting for the big man to return to drag him from the car.

But nothing happened. The Porsche remained as impassive as ever, a sleeping black shark waiting to flash into action. Carefully Barry eased the Jaguar out of the car park and headed up the lane. He spent more time watching the mirror than the road ahead; fortunately nothing was in his way. As he passed the 'Not Little Didney' sign at the top of the village he let out a loud whoop and relaxed back into the leather seat. Nice one, Barry! Always cool under pressure.

***

Charles Tremayne sat on the floor in the corner of the skittle alley. His hands were bound behind his back by plastic cable ties that cut into his skin. To his right sat Mr Brown, Mr Purple, Mr Red and Mr Blue, their hands tied behind them.

He'd been separated from the villagers who were congregated at the far end. As far as he could see of the villagers, only PC Muchmore, Jerry Richards and Sandy seemed to be tied. The trouble makers.

Three black clad soldiers kept close watch, Heckler & Koch guns held with a loose confidence.

He tested the strength of the ties on his wrists. They

were not going to give. He relaxed back against the wooden wall.

The door opened and Gemini stepped inside, he glanced at Tremayne but said nothing. He was accompanied by another soldier, who although dressed in the same black outfit as his colleagues, was clearly an officer.

"Well done, Captain." Gemini nodded towards Green's men. "Islamic terrorists. Deep undercover Chechnyan sleepers. You never saw them."

"Yes, sir," said the Captain, eying up Green's men. "Do you need us to take them back to the barracks for debrief?"

"Not necessary. They are scheduled for transportation to somewhere a bit more exotic, courtesy of our colonial chums over the pond. In fact," continued Gemini. "You never saw any of this."

"Understood, sir"

"How about the others?" Gemini asked

"Mostly all accounted for. Still missing a handful but the key figures you wanted are all here, with the exception of Penwrith. I have a team in the woods looking for him."

Gemini nearly managed to suppress a sharp intake. Nearly, but not quite.

"Pull them back, Captain. We haven't the time to spare chasing that one."

"As you wish, sir. This one says he works for 'Six'?" the officer said, indicating Charles. "Is he one of yours?"

"He used to be one of my best agents. But it is quite possible he's 'Gone Rogue'. Bring him through, Captain." A short thoughtful pause, and then, "And her," he said indicating Sandy.

"You heard the man," the Captain said.

"Sir!" confirmed one of the soldiers who immediately waved his gun towards Tremayne. "On your feet, sunshine."

Tremayne stood and headed for the door. He watched each soldier waiting for an opportunity, no matter how slight. But these were professionals, they gave no gaps.

Another soldier helped Sandy to her feet and guided her, hand on shoulder, to the door.

In the bar, Tremayne was nudged towards one of the big armchairs by the fire and Sandy to the other.

"Do make yourself comfortable, Charles," said Gemini. "I believe we have some catching up to do? So much has happened in the last few days."

Tremayne sat back into the chair, his arms uncomfortably trapped behind him. He scanned the room. Sandy sat stiffly in the chair, her eyes darted side to side. She wriggled trying to make herself comfortable with hands tied behind her back.

Mr Green lay on the floor of the bar. He was only semi conscious. A severe cut over his right eye ran blood down the side of his face and his jaw was swollen, probably dislocated.

"Thank you, Captain," Gemini said. "You'd better take your men back now I think. Probably best you don't clash with our American cousins."

"You going to be alright with this lot, sir?"

Gemini lifted a Heckler and Koch from the counter

"Absolutely. And please remember this was an 'Eyes Only' operation.

The captain rounded up his squad and left. A few minutes later Tremayne heard and felt the thunder of rotor blades as the helicopter banked over the pub then headed north.

Gemini strolled around the room and stopped alongside Tremayne. He placed his hand on Charles' shoulder in a companionable manner. "Such a pleasant village don't you think? Nice ambiance. Reminds me of Saint Luzarre, a little fishing village just along the coast from Biarritz. Have you ever been there, Charles? There's a little restaurant near the harbour, Antoine's I believe, they do the most wonderful bouillabaisse, exquisitely understated. You really must try it one day." He continued to circle the room.

Tremayne stretched his feet towards the fire. His foot

surreptitiously manipulated the end of a set of tongs into the flames. He glanced around. Only Sandy had noticed. She had a quizzical look on her face.

Gemini stood over Green. "Incompetence I can understand," he said as he stood on the fingers of Green's right hand. "Not forgive of course." He ground his foot hard. Bone crunched. "But at least I can understand it. We live in a world where nobody takes pride in their work anymore. But you, Charles, you're a different animal. Disloyalty is a sin beyond redemption." He turned back towards Tremayne, jabbing the gun towards him in emphasis.

The door burst open and Gemini spun around gun raised then paused briefly when he saw Mrs Pomfrey march in. She held a shotgun aimed towards his chest. She pulled the trigger and the gun barked sending lead shot into the ceiling as she herself was thrown backwards into a heap in the doorway. Powdered plaster fell from the ceiling like a Dickensian Christmas.

Gemini hardly moved. "You see! Incompetence carries its own rewards."

The brief debacle had allowed Tremayne to slip from his chair and sit in the hearth with his back to the fire. He placed his wrists over the now glowing fire tongs and pushed. A slight hiss of burning flesh and plastic then the cable ties separated. He leapt forwards just as Gemini turned with the gun, catching Tremayne across the side of his head. Tremayne stumbled to the floor just as a burst of fire from the gun splintered a neat row in the floorboards at his feet. He froze waiting for the next shot which would now surely follow.

"Sloppy, Charles," Gemini said. "Very sloppy. Pease sit down again."

Tremayne stood slowly and turned. Gemini was aiming the gun not at him but at Sandy. The message was clear and Tremayne sat back in the armchair. His wrists were beginning to smart from the burn.

"All I need from you now, Charles, is the location of the

other boxes." He pushed the muzzle of the gun into the side of Sandy's neck. She flinched away. "Then I'll be gone and you can all go back to making scarecrows, or whatever it is that passes for gainful employment in these parts."

"I don't know where they are," Tremayne said. "Somebody moved them."

"Oh, please don't try my patience, Charles. I know you too well." He fired a quick burst into the headrest of the chair in which Sandy sat. She tried to stand and he jabbed the gun into her stomach, forcing her back down. "I know your weaknesses and I won't hesitate to exploit them."

"What turned you, Gemini? You've spent your whole life fighting corruption and tyranny." Tremayne counted the steps necessary to reach Mrs Pomfrey's shotgun. Too far.

"Exactly! I've ordered hits on heads of state, overturned governments and now they won't let me smoke in my own office!

"This is all about smoking?"

"Of course not. It's also about speed cameras, injury lawyers and so-called Green Taxes. Oh, and mobile phone tariffs. Do you realise, I helped bring down the Berlin Wall and all Whitehall is interested in these days is whether their MI6 agents are on the right mobile phone tariff? Have you any idea of the time I waste on that rubbish?"

Mrs Pomfrey started to sit up, still dazed. She eyed the room.

"But you tried to have me killed?" Tremayne said.

"Just business, Charles. Why didn't you just stick to the job? Simple project really, find the money, report back to me, I send in the cleanup crew, job done. But no, you had to go off your own way. Why didn't you just report in when you'd located the money as you were supposed to then bugger off to Switzerland? Nobody would have been any the wiser. The money would have disappeared again. Why did you choose now to go getting all touchy feely about these irrelevant little people? What happened, Charles? You're the one person I thought I could rely on not to go 'Native' on me."

"They'll track you down. You can't just disappear with two hundred and fifty million and expect nobody to notice."

The Money That Never Was

"Gemini looked genuinely surprised. "What two hundred and fifty million, Charles?" He raised his arms and turned as if playing to an audience. "It doesn't exist. It never existed. Nor did the deal for the military base. All fiction. The S.A.S. are bound under the Official Secrets Act so they won't say anything. And even if they did, so what? Just another hostage rescue. Soon, I intend to retire to somewhere very hot and very remote. But even if some anally retentive clerk should notice a slight discrepancy, two hundred and fifty million is a mere banker's fart."

"All very tidy, apart from the residents here of course. What's to stop them talking?"

"Behave, Charles. You know how this is going to work, you're not stupid. This young lady is my leverage. Besides, she'll enjoy getting away from here. After all, what's her future here? Marriage to her first cousin and twenty hay-chewing sprogs? She's going to see the world, and as long as everybody here keeps quiet she'll continue to enjoy the good life. And you only have yourself to blame for that—"

Mr Green leapt up off the floor and charged at Gemini. He only managed to cover half the distance before Gemini's gun spat and he dropped to the floor with a thud that would make an airport baggage handler proud. But the momentary lapse of eye contact with his captives though gave Tremayne the chance he needed. He rolled towards Mrs Pomfrey who, as if reading his mind, pushed the shotgun towards him. Tremayne caught the gun and prayed there was still a cartridge left as he pulled the trigger. The gun barked just as Gemini brought his own to bear. The shotgun's hail of shot slammed into Gemini's left shoulder, turning him just as he fired the Heckler and Koch. The bullets ripped harmlessly across the fireplace. Tremayne dropped the shotgun and leapt towards Gemini. A swift knife hand strike on the side of his neck and Gemini toppled backwards, unconscious before he hit the floor.

Tremayne dragged the unconscious form into the armchair then turned to check on Green. He was dead. Mrs Pomfrey was dusting herself off, muttering, "Dear, dear. What a to-do."

Sandy stood over Gemini for a moment then started slapping him across the face, backwards and forwards. "A monster. An evil monster. Kill him, Charles. Shoot him."

Tremayne caught her hand. "Enough. I have a better plan for him." He pulled some cable ties from his pocket and secured Gemini's hands under his knees.

The door opened and an immaculately dressed man walked in. He was about six foot four and built like an extra from Conan the Barbarian. He scanned the room with the efficiency of sonar. He appeared satisfied.

"Cobcem rcho," he said towards the doorway.

Another man entered. Not quite as tall and nowhere near as large but he had the appearance of being infinitely more dangerous. The dark, handmaid Italian suit moved easily emphasising the taught muscular frame.

"Nice of you to turn up, Victor," Tremayne greeted. "I assume you've been waiting outside till all the rough stuff was over? Getting too old for the 'hands on'?"

"You seemed to have well under control, my good friend." Victor Tereshchenko strolled round the room, his grey, slightly hooded eyes taking in everything instantly. He stopped in front of Gemini. "He sleep like pig." He kicked Gemini's leg. "Wake up, pig!"

Gemini stirred. His head lolled from side to side. He made to move his arms and the shock of finding he couldn't jerked him into consciousness. He stared up at Tereshchenko.

"Victor Tereshchenko, as I live and breathe," he said "What on earth are you doing here?"

"My good friend Charles." He patted Tremayne's shoulder. "He tell me he has problem and interesting solution. It seems you are no longer welcome by your government, no?"

Gemini pulled at his restraints. "We have decided to go our separate ways. Irreconcilable differences you might say."

"Good, that is good. I have new opportunity for you in Russia, Mr Gemini. Many of my former comrades wish to meet with you. Talk over old times. You know how it is.

They have much to discuss with you."

For the first time that Charles could ever recall, Gemini looked scared. His eyes darted as he struggled again with the ties. "Good God, Charles. You can't allow this. This is treason for God's sake!"

"Business, Gemini," Tremayne said. "Just business. Victor's friends will pay him well for you and in return, Victor will eliminate all trace of this debacle and dispose of the rest of Green's boys."

Sandy looked shocked. "What?" she said.

"Not worry. Princess," Tereshchenko said. "They will not be hurt. We are not thugs. They will be persuaded it is in their interests to have new home in new country. They will understand. Trust me."

"Charles," Gemini's eyes widened. "We were friends. You know what they'll do to me in Moscow?"

"You betrayed me and you betrayed the people here. They didn't deserve all this. They're good people trying hard to survive in a world that has left them behind to sink and die."

"Why, Charles!" Sandy said, smiling. She touched his arm. "Almost poetic. Where did that come from?"

He turned towards her, holding her upper arms. His eyes searched hers and he saw for the first time the connection he'd been fighting. A tangible, visible thread that bridged the gap between them. He was frightened, exposed, vulnerable. His brain stopped calculating and planning. He looked from Sandy to Gemini then Tereshchenko. No words came. No thoughts came. Something had ended, something had begun.

Victor sensed the change in Tremayne and took control. "I take him now." He lifted Gemini by the arm and nodded to his minder. The big man came over and forcibly guided Gemini out of the pub.

"We meet again someday, Charles. We share a vodka and talk stories. Goodbye, my friend." He followed the other two through the door and closed it behind him.

"Sandy," Charles started. "I... I..."

"Shush." She placed her hands each side of his head,

leaned forwards and kissed him.

He felt a warmth flow between them, running along the thread. He felt alive. He felt connected. He ran his arms around her and pulled her in tight. He gazed at her as if seeing her for the first time. His eyes darted around the pub. The doilies lined up along the bar, the blazing fire and the endless knick-knacks that littered every surface. He felt he belonged. For the first time in his life, he belonged. He kissed her. He kissed her hard, frantically as if making up for lost time.

Mrs Pomfrey brushed the last of the dust from her dress. "And about time too!" she muttered as she settled herself down in her armchair by the fire.

The End